Danielle R. Graham writes both teen and adult fiction for HarperCollins. *All We Left Behind* is her first historical novel.

Danielle is also an art and play therapist in private practice and she splits her time between Vancouver and Mayne Island with her husband.

🐦@drgrahambooks
📘/drgrahambooksauthor
drgrahambooks.com

All We Left Behind

DANIELLE R. GRAHAM

One More Chapter
a division of HarperCollins*Publishers*
The News Building
1 London Bridge Street
London SE1 9GF

www.harpercollins.co.uk

HarperCollins*Publishers*
1st Floor, Watermarque Building, Ringsend Road
Dublin 4, Ireland

This paperback edition 2021

First published in Great Britain in ebook format by
HarperCollins*Publishers* 2020

Copyright © Danielle R. Graham 2020

Danielle R. Graham asserts the moral right to
be identified as the author of this work

A catalogue record for this book
is available from the British Library

PB ISBN: 9780008412418

This novel is entirely a work of fiction.
The names, characters and incidents portrayed in it are
the work of the author's imagination. Any resemblance to
actual persons, living or dead, events or localities is
entirely coincidental.

Set in Birka by Palimpsest Book Production Ltd,
Falkirk, Stirlingshire

Printed and bound in the United States of America
by LSC Communications.

All rights reserved. No part of this publication may be
reproduced, stored in a retrieval system, or transmitted,
in any form or by any means, electronic, mechanical,
photocopying, recording or otherwise, without the prior
permission of the publishers.

21 22 23 24 LSC 10 9 8 7 6 5 4 3 2

For my nephews, Parker and Declan,
and their Great Grandfather, Ted Tadayuki Kadohama

Based on true events ...

Chapter 1

The Italian Campaign, World War II, April 1944

'Hayden. Wait up.' Gordie jogged to catch up to me as I made my way from the intelligence tent to the flight strip. Our orders were to escort the bomber squadron to target a train transporting enemy supplies through Italy. 'Maybe you shouldn't fly today, pal.' Gordie matched my stride and thudded his palm against my shoulder.

I couldn't afford to miss a flight. We were only seventeen more missions from being reassigned and I was determined to do whatever it took to go home. 'I'm fine,' I mumbled, then wove against the flow of the night airmen who were headed to the mess tent for a cup of weak coffee and a breakfast of dry egg and toast.

'Are you sure?' Gordie asked. 'You weren't even paying attention back there. I don't want to get killed because your head is somewhere else.'

My jaw tightened at the reminder of the curt letter from my father folded in the lining of my breast pocket. The truth was I hadn't slept or eaten since I received the post. And

1

Gordie was right. I hadn't listened to anything our commanding officer had said during the briefing, other than noting the location of the advancement line to protect the Allied troops on the ground. I didn't need to pay attention. I knew the orders by heart. We'd done the same routine hundreds of times in the months we'd been stationed close to the Gustav Line – fly the sortie, avoid flak, and return with everyone in the squadron. 'I'm fine to fly.'

The tread of my boot gripped the metal of the wing as I climbed up onto my airplane to double-check the airscrew pitch. Gordie hung out next to the rudder and squinted through the glare of the Mediterranean sun to shoot me an uneasy glance. 'Nobody's going to question if you sit this one out. It would be safer for all of us if you take some time to grieve, maybe talk to the chaplain.'

'Time off won't help. Sitting around here without a distraction would be worse.' I checked the oxygen and pressure for the gun system, then hopped back down to the tarmac to wait for the siren. 'And talking about it doesn't change what happened. The only thing that would have made a difference is if I had been there. And I wasn't.'

As the ground crew armed his Spitfire, Gordie performed a set of jumping jacks to get the blood flowing. Between breaths and bounces he said, 'It might have ended in the same result even if you had been there. There's no way of knowing.'

Annoyed that he was probably right, I forced the buckle on my flotation vest too abruptly and it broke off in my hand. 'Hey!' I hollered over to a gangly crewman speeding by on a bicycle. 'Grab me another Mae West, would you? This one failed.' The kid thrust his thumb in the air and pedalled harder to fetch a new vest from the supply tent. Gordie transitioned his calisthenics into side bends and hamstring stretches and waited patiently to finish the conversation. A conversation I wanted nothing to do with.

'You can't blame yourself, Hayden. There isn't anything you could have done.'

That was the whole point. It was infuriating that I was powerless to change the outcome from overseas. 'If I'd had a chance to talk to her—'

Gordie shook his head to disagree and loosened his necktie an extra finger-width. 'It doesn't work that way.'

'No? How does it work then?'

He shrugged and arched to look at the sky to stretch his lower back. 'All I know is there are certain things nobody can do anything about, and this is one of them.'

More and more it felt like fighting a war was one of those futile things too. What if all my efforts were pointless? And all for nothing? I stretched my leather helmet and goggles over my ears and swallowed back the helplessness of being unable to fix anything. 'What if everything back home changes so much while we're here that we don't recognize it when we get back?'

Gordie thought about it seriously as he forced his beefy hands into his leather gloves. 'I'm more worried they'll all be the same and expect me to be the same. The war has changed me. I can't go back to my old life the way it was.'

'Yeah, well.' I exhaled as much useless tension as I could, but an entire war's worth of fury had taken up a hefty residence inside my chest. 'I enjoyed my old life. I want it back.'

Gordie cuffed the back of my head in an unsuccessful attempt to bolster my morale. 'Let's just worry about getting home alive first. We can decide what we want to do with that life later.'

I nodded in reluctant agreement. The Royal Air Force petrol refuellers linked the hose to my tank and the vapours mixed with the fumes of the freshly painted yellow, blue, white, and red rings of the side roundel of the seven-crew Lancaster heavy night bomber next to us. Gordie headed over to inspect his machine as the crewman on the bike returned with my new flotation device. I squeezed my head through, rearranged the parachute seat pack straps and climbed back up onto the wing of my Spitfire, attempting to push away all thoughts from my mind, except the mission.

High cloud, pleasant spring temperatures – a perfect day to fly.

As I waited for the signal to fire up, I slid out the photo that I kept hidden in the lining of my breast pocket. Some days it felt as if Chidori was glancing back at me with encouragement or adoration, but not this time. Her eyes pleaded with me, trying to tell me something. Unfortunately, I didn't know what, and the frustration forced tears to well up and blur my vision, so I tucked the photo away next to my father's letter. I would have given anything to forget the anguishing news from home and focus instead on better thoughts, but it felt as if all the pleasant memories of Mayne Island before the war – Chidori, my family, my Border collie, Patch, and even pleasures as simple as the sticky buns at the fall fair –

were eroding, fading farther and farther into the past with every year I was gone. I feared it wouldn't be long before all of the good memories were lost forever, replaced one by one with increasingly painful memories.

Holding position on the airstrip when the anticipation of a mission was already hammering through my system had always been aggravating. The delays were even more torturous in the irritable state I was in. The mercury rose under the cockpit shield as I was forced to wait. Every single thing that could possibly go wrong on a flight over enemy-occupied territory inched into my awareness and collided with all the other turmoil that was already holding court in my thoughts. The wool collar of my uniform scratched almost unbearably at my neck.

When the green lantern finally flashed, my engine choked, like a kid trying a cigarette for the first time. The tower signalled for the spare Spitfire but after a stutter, my machine roared to life. I should have taken the falter as an omen. Instead, I waved off the spare and taxied out onto the flare path for takeoff.

23 August 1941

Dear Diary,

A moment worthy of contemplation occurred this morning over fresh-baked buttermilk biscuits and homemade straw-berry preserves. As Obaasan basked in the sunbeam that angled through our kitchen window, she sipped her matcha tea and then uttered a phrase under her breath in Japanese.

It loosely translates into, 'every encounter happens but once in a lifetime and every meeting ends with a parting'. Concerned that it meant her health was failing, I asked her what she had meant. She seemed surprised I had heard her, as if perhaps she hadn't intended to voice her reflections aloud.

Kenji chuckled because he believes Grandmother's ramblings have become confused due to her old age. My brothers don't make as much concerted effort as I do to be attentive and patient with Grandmother. Surely they appreciate the value of learning as much from her as possible before she is gone and all of her traditional Japanese wisdom is lost on the wind forever, but perhaps they take for granted that she will always be here. I am uneasy about why she is pondering the topic of parting. She seems in good health, though, so hopefully we have nothing to fear. Nevertheless, I will take notice of each encounter I have today and be grateful for the once-in-a-lifetime opportunity that it presents.

I have to rush off now to complete my chores before the fall fair. (Chores certainly don't feel like once-in-a-lifetime opportunities to be treasured, more like never-ending, tedious monotony!) I guess I still have much to learn about unconditional acceptance.

Chi

Chapter 2

Chidori's polished black shoes poked out from beneath the crisp white bed sheets that billowed in the ocean breeze as she meticulously pegged the corners to the clothesline in front of her family's farmhouse. Full of eager anticipation, I snuck out of the forest of ancient evergreens that bordered their homestead, then crept in stealth through the long grass behind her. When I was close enough to catch a hint of the cherry blossom fragrance of her hair, I reached between the cotton sheets and tickled her waist.

She squealed in delight, unravelled us from the fabric, and slapped my chest. 'Good golly. Hayden! You startled me half to death. I expected you to be out on the boat. What are you doing here?'

My mouth opened, about to produce a jaunty answer, but the long strands of her hair shimmered in the sun like raven feathers. The loveliness of it distracted me from the dashing quip I had intended to say next.

With delicate precision, Chidori tucked the wisps behind

her ears and studied my expression with curiosity. If she knew the reason for my tongue-tied silence, she didn't acknowledge it with more than a smile before making a second attempt to encourage my participation in the conversation. 'Did you forget today is Saturday? Why aren't you out fishing with Uncle Massey and your father?'

I swiped my hand across my mouth so my wily grin wouldn't prematurely reveal my true ambition. 'I volunteered to help my ma and the committee ladies set up the craft fair.'

Chidori stepped back to put a distance more fitting for a friendship between us, then glanced over her shoulder and peeked between the sheets to check if anyone from the house had seen us standing so close. 'It was nice of you to offer to help your mother.'

'Not entirely. Truth is, I have ulterior motives.'

'Ah.' Her eyes glimmered at the admission that I was up to something rascally. 'What might those motives be?'

My long-anticipated plan was to invite her on a proper date, and if she was agreeable, begin a courtship. I had even rehearsed a heartfelt speech, but I needed to choose a more romantic moment to deliver it than during laundry chores. I stalled by teasing her. 'Is this yours?' I bent over and lifted up a silk slip from the laundry basket.

Chidori blushed, snatched the undergarment from me and then pressed her palms against my arms to playfully shove me away. 'It's my grandmother's. Don't be such a Nosey Ned.'

'Nosey Ned? Is there even such a thing?'

'Just keep your peepers and your mitts to yourself.' She transferred the undergarments to the line behind the sheets to hide them. 'You haven't answered the question. What are your ulterior motives for helping your mother at the fair?'

I pressed my index finger to my lips, then whispered, 'It's top secret.'

She shook her head at my evasiveness, but the fact I wasn't myself seemed to amuse her more than annoy her. 'You're acting peculiar, Hayden. If you and Joey are planning some sort of prank, leave me out of it.'

I shot her an impish wink, which made her chuckle.

'I want no part of whatever mischief you two are scheming to get yourself into.'

'Hopefully you'll change your mind once you hear what it is.'

'Doubtful.' She smiled to herself before she spun away to peg the corner of another sheet on the line. 'I had assumed after we graduated that you and Joey would outgrow your schoolboy shenanigans.'

'Wishful thinking.'

Chidori stopped what she was doing, mused for an extra heartbeat, and then gently shoved my arm to shoo me. 'I have chores to finish, Mr Monkey Business. And I don't want to make you late. You should get on and go help your mother. And stay out of trouble.'

'I won't be late if I hitch a ride with you and your brothers. Then, after I help my mother, I was thinking you and I could spend some time together. Maybe eat some caramel apples or enter the three-legged race or partake in some other charming country-fair pastime.'

'Oh.' She hesitated with a pause that I feared was almost

wistful, as it perhaps crossed her mind what my ulterior motive was. Fortunately, after the momentary contemplation, her mood became jovial again. 'Defending our title in the three-legged race would be fun, but I don't know if I'll be able to enjoy the fair. I have to tend to our vegetable stand at the farmers' market.'

'One of your brothers could take over for a while.'

'They can't. There's work to do back here in the greenhouses. I'll be by myself at the market until they pick me up. Besides, won't you have to help with the fish sales once the boat arrives at the dock?'

I leaned my shoulder against the clothesline post and crossed my arms, watching her peg trousers and trying to come up with a way to convince her that we could balance work and play. 'This will likely be the last fall fair until the war is over. It might be our last chance for a long time to enjoy the festivities. Maybe if you sell out of your produce quickly, we could at least hang out at the dance with Joey and Donna Mae for a spell.'

When she didn't immediately respond, I began to worry that my increasing adoration for her was not mutual and would not be reciprocated. Sweat beaded along my hairline and rolled down the side of my neck as I braced for rejection. Eventually she shot me a flicker of a grin. 'If I sell out early, I'll find you.'

'Thank you.' My fingers curled to tuck a loose wisp of her hair behind her ear.

Chidori's eyelids lowered and her brow knitted curiously as she watched me withdraw my hand. Perhaps she was taken off-guard by the affectionate gesture of me touching her hair. Or, she noticed how mesmerized I was by the way the silkiness of the strands danced across my skin. Instead of addressing the intimacy, she said, 'I should probably focus and get this done properly, Hayden.' She bent to pull a light green dress out of the laundry basket.

Since I had no intention of leaving without her, I helped with the laundry.

With adept speed, she finished hanging everything in the first basket. As I clumsily pegged a pair of trousers cockeyed to the line, her eyes narrowed in mock scorn. 'The seam of your shirt is torn. How did you manage that?'

'I caught it on a rivet when I fixed the hay baler yesterday.' I tugged at the fabric to examine the hole. 'No matter. Nobody will notice.'

'Yes, they will. I'll quickly mend it for you.' Chidori reached both her hands up to push my suspenders over my shoulders and let them drop to hang at my hip. The fingers of her left hand untucked the bottom hem of my shirt from the waist of my trousers while the fingers of her right hand unfastened the neck button. It wasn't likely her intention to cause such an effect in me, but my breath caught in my throat as she slowly made her way down, undoing one button at a time until my shirt hung open. Her hands ran over the fabric of my undershirt and then she eased the top shirt down my arms. Whether she meant for it to or not, it made my heart race and goose bumps spread across the surface of my skin.

'Stay put. I'll be right back.' With a perky spin she disap-

11

peared between the sheets, leaving me wondering if she was simply being helpful or reciprocating the affection.

I hung the rest of the laundry with a giant grin on my face, hopeful that Chidori's feelings had also deepened beyond the level of friendship, and that she might accept an invitation to accompany me on a date.

When she returned a few minutes later, she held my shirt by the shoulders so I could slip into it.

'I appreciate it.' I chuckled at the thought that she wouldn't likely be as accommodating if I asked her to mend the missing button on my grey trousers, too. Thankfully, she couldn't read my mind, but she did seem to sense that whatever I was thinking was cheeky, since she shot me a slightly maternal eyebrow-raise as she guided me by the elbow towards her father's black stake truck. It was already loaded with wood crates overflowing with a rainbow of vegetables for the farmers' market. I opened the passenger side door for her, and she climbed in as her brothers emerged from the greenhouse.

'Not fishing today, Hayden?' her brother Tosh asked.

'The fall fair is only one day a year and who knows when we'll have another one. The fish will still be there tomorrow.'

'True. Hop on.' He pointed to the back and slid into the driver's seat. Chidori's other brother Kenji and I both jumped up onto the flatbed to sit on the crates.

Toshiro was twenty-one years old and the eldest. Everyone called him Tosh. He was home for the summer after completing an undergraduate degree at the University of British Columbia. He planned to take a year off from studies and then enter law school. Tosh and Chidori were a lot alike. Kenji, on the other hand, was more like me. He was two years older than Chidori and me. He had been a good athlete and student in high school but, like me, didn't apply to university. Kenji was also an accomplished pianist, but didn't care much for music, so didn't accept the offer to play for the Vancouver Symphony Orchestra – much to his mother's chagrin. Baseball was his only real love – baseball and his sweetheart named Michiko. For the two years after he graduated high school, he lived with Tosh near the university campus in Vancouver and played two seasons with the Asahi championship baseball team. Kenji moved back home to Mayne Island at the beginning of summer when Tosh did, because he had injured his shoulder and couldn't play baseball any more. He still hadn't quite gotten over that disappointment and was extra-glum for a while because he wasn't sure what he wanted to do as his career. But his mood improved when he took a job as an accountant's assistant and he and Michiko started to go steady.

We drove out onto the dirt road that cut across the island. Chidori glanced over her shoulder and returned the smile I was already gleaming at her through the back window. If she had an inkling of what my ulterior motives were, then her amenable mood was a good sign.

A cloud of dust trailed behind us as we approached town, then billowed up to coat the two men on ladders who hoisted the 1941 Mayne Island Fall Fair banner to string it across the road. Chidori and I had both attended every fall fair since we were born. I hoped it wasn't going to be the last one ever, but the war overseas had already been progressing for two years, with no end in sight. The fall fair tradition would more than likely be suspended once more government rations on staple goods were put in place.

Tosh parked the truck next to the split rail fence that enclosed the area for the farmers' market, then hopped out of the cab. I jumped off the flatbed and strategically landed right in front of Chidori. Her palm grazed my waist delicately as she manoeuvred around me to lift a crate of tomatoes.

'Hayden,' my sister Rosalyn hollered from the porch of the Agricultural Hall. 'Ma needs your help hauling in the boxes of preserves.'

'All right. I'll be right there,' I shouted as I stacked two vegetable crates and followed Chidori and her brothers to their stand. Their wood setup was one of the bigger ones at the market, constructed like a small shed with angled display shelves along the base of the counter and a shingle shake slanted roof to shade from sun and protect from rain. It stood permanently on the fairgrounds during the growing season, so all they had to do was load up the shelves with the crates or baskets of vegetables and hang the hand-painted *Setoguchi Farm* sign from the hooks. An instant shop, and they were well known for their quality produce.

'You should go help your mother,' Chidori said quietly, not wanting to keep me from what I was supposed to be doing. 'We can manage from here.'

'You promise you'll find me later?'

'Yes, but if I don't sell out before you have to leave for the dock, you and I could maybe go for a walk. Together. This afternoon, after the fair.' She checked my reaction to the invitation briefly, but then, as if she worried she had been too forward, her cheeks blushed and she stepped around me to make another trip to the truck. Her red skirt brushed around her knees and distracted me for a few seconds before I followed after her.

'Hayden!' Ma hollered from a window in the Agricultural Hall that overlooked the farmers' market field. 'We're running short on time. I really do need your help with the jars, darling.'

Waving to let her know I was on my way, I trotted after Chidori. The air was fragrant from bushels of lavender, sun-warmed strawberries, and fresh honey that other families displayed at their stands. I dodged a carpenter who carried a chair made of woven cedar branches. I side-stepped between a booth with cinnamon-and-brown-sugar-drizzled baked goods, and a booth with wool-knit baby blankets, then snuck up behind Chidori. She surrendered a smile when I rested my left hand on her waist and leaned over her shoulder to whisper, 'I accept your invitation for a walk this afternoon, but I'm also really hoping you can find time for at least one dance.'

Her lips pressed together as she pondered. After a worry-rousing hesitation, she said, 'Maybe. Now, go on and help your mother.'

Satisfied with a maybe, I turned towards the Agricultural Hall with my hands in my pockets and whistled a tune as I swaggered with the confidence of hope and promise.

Rory Bauer and his cousin Fitz stood on the porch, arms crossed in confrontation, to block my way to the door. 'You didn't go and get sweet on that Jap girl now, did you?' Fitz jeered.

Rory chuckled as he lit a cigarette and sat down on a wood-plank bench. They both directed hostile glares at me, waiting for an answer. Not interested in an altercation, I tried to inch past them on the narrow porch. Rory stretched his legs out straight and rested his scuffed boot on the rail.

'Excuse me, Rory.'

'Excuse you for what?' Fitz laughed. 'Being sweet on a Jap?'

My composure teetered precariously. Chidori didn't approve of me getting messed up in quarrels, so I checked if she was watching – she was. Instead of confronting the Bauers, I said, 'Move your ratty feet, Rory, I need to get by.'

Rory stood and blew stale breath and cigarette smoke in my face.

Barely able to contain my temper, I used all of my self-restraint to utter through a tight jaw, 'Move. My ma's waiting on me to help her with the displays.'

'Is your ma a Jap-lover too?' Fitz asked.

My frame tensed and I inhaled to supress my irritation but fired back, 'I think you should be more concerned about who your ma's been loving, Fitz. I heard she's awful friendly with all the fellas down at the Springwater Lodge.'

'Shut your filthy mouth,' Fitz growled.

Rory shoved me in the chest, which launched me against the wood siding. My body made a loud thud and a few people, including my sister, poked their heads out the door to check what the ruckus was about. The only RCMP officer for all the Gulf Islands, Constable Stuart, stepped up onto the porch in his full Red Serge uniform that made him appear seven feet tall. 'What seems to be the problem, boys?'

'No problem,' we all said.

Rory mumbled something I couldn't quite hear, took another drag from his cigarette, and avoided making eye contact with Constable Stuart. Fitz ran a comb through his overly Brylcreemed hair and shot a greasy wink at Rosalyn, which didn't impress her in the slightest. Constable Stuart, who must have been stifling in his wool serge, used a hankie to wipe the sweat from the back of his neck and eyeballed us until Rory eventually walked away. Fitz followed. Constable Stuart directed his attention to me. I swallowed hard and focused on his bushy moustache as I waited for him to speak. 'What was that skirmish all about, Hayden?'

'Nothing I can't handle, sir.'

He frowned for a good while before nodding in a cautionary way. 'Let's hope so.' With the tip of his brown felt hat he stepped off the porch and crossed the street to give heck to a boy who wasn't paying attention to his tethered goat as it chewed up the siding on the two-cell jailhouse.

I glanced across the fairgrounds at Chidori long enough to see the apprehension in her eyes about Rory and Fitz. Then I ducked inside to help my mother.

Chapter 3

The sortie went exactly as planned. The Typhoon bombers we escorted hit all the railway targets and headed back to the airfield to rearm. Gordie and I flew another pass over the Italian foothills and farmers' fields to conduct reconnaissance. We were always on the lookout for aerodromes that had a large collection of enemy flying machines. Sending bombers in to wipe them all out on the ground was easier than fighting them in the air. Nothing much was going on, though, so we turned to head back to base.

Fifteen minutes out from our landing strip a solo Junkers flew low beneath me – a common decoy of the German Luftwaffe air force. They often sent in a solo airplane to draw us down while hiding their fighter pilots up higher. I didn't take the bait. Instead, I scanned the airspace above me. Six enemy aircraft were indeed flying above in loose formation. I called Gordie on the RT, but he didn't confirm receipt so must have had the receiver flipped to transmit. Fortunately, he noticed me tip my wings as a signal and he spotted them too. We split up and I headed for cloud cover. My Spitfire was faster than the Messerschmitts the German fighters flew, so I was confident I could outrun them. But my sureness that we could escape without a battle waned when I emerged from the cloud cover.

Gordie's airplane was being attacked by two Italian Macchi aircraft. Normally, flying machines from the Italian Regia Aeronautical would be poorly matched against us, but if the squadron of Luftwaffe above backed the Italians up, we were dangerously outnumbered. I feverishly tapped the thumb lever to flash my lights in a Morse code, hoping some friendlies were close enough to see it, then I banked and doubled back to chase behind a machine that was firing on Gordie.

My pulse pounded in my temples with all-out fear and zeal as I wound her up well over four hundred kilometres per hour and gained on them. Breathing deeply didn't help steady my hands, but there was no time to wait for them to stabilize. I increased the oxygen flow to my mask and then squeezed the ammunition trigger to fire. The tracer bullets sparked out of my wing-mounted machine guns and hit the belly of the enemy Macchi with a satisfying direct blow. My cannon shell caused black smoke to pour out of his fuselage. He went into an uncontrolled dive and I lost visual contact. Gordie rolled as the Luftwaffe enemy machines descended on us to join the fight. Overly wired from my survival instincts kicking in, I yanked and banked at the last possible second, and the burst of turbulence from the passing Messerschmitts jolted my airplane violently as I followed Gordie.

Sucking back oxygen to tame the jitters, we looped around in a tighter radius than their machines were capable of and Gordie fired a cannon, hitting the wing of one of the machines after it flew past us. It lost vertical speed rapidly, then disappeared into the clouds. Gordie gave me a triumphant thumbs up until three machines flew right up on us and opened fire.

Metal dings reverberated through the cockpit as incendiary bullets hit and sparked off my armour and wings, nearly nicking my leg and threatening to ignite my fuel. Every muscle in my body restricted, like iron cables cinching my chest to the point that my lungs couldn't expand. Gordie peeled off. It was an escape or die situation, so with the control column jammed to the dashboard, I sent my airplane into a dive. Dropping full throttle from thirty thousand feet to one thousand in seconds caused painfully intense compression in my ears, but it was my best option to shake them. I waited until the last possible moment to increase altitude and prayed not to black out from the abrupt change in air pressure as I climbed. A violent shudder and buffeting indicated a wing stall, so I thrust the control column forward again to avoid a spin. Dizzy from the exertion, I levelled the horizon and fired another cannon. It hit one Messerschmitt in the tail, which broke off. His airplane plummeted and the pilot ditched.

Frantically scanning the air space, I searched for Gordie. When I finally spotted him, I sped to saddle up next to his left wing. Before we had a chance to fly out of range, a shell hit the armour plate behind my head. The detonation blast concussed me. After a delayed reaction to recover my wits, I stomped full left rudder and sharply tipped my wings, which regretfully caused Gordie's airplane to be hit by the next round.

'Damn it.'

Smoke billowed out of Gordie's fuselage. Rapid calculations for the best way to help him, while also keeping the enemy off my tail, charged through my brain. The only option was to take down the rest of the airplanes and give Gordie a chance to limp back to the airstrip. Statistically achieving that by myself was highly improbable. But what choice did I have? I refused to abandon him. I climbed higher and looped around. Two more Macchis flew through broken cloud cover below, likely looking for me. With blind determination to save Gordie, I dropped altitude, fired my machine guns, and hit one Italian in the wing. The other one climbed. Before he disappeared into the clouds, he turned so he would be able to sneak up behind me. I slowed down and waited for him to unwittingly fly by. Once he was in front of me, I fired a direct cannon hit. Flames burst out and a projectile of shrapnel from his tail cracked the acrylic of my cockpit canopy.

Gordie glided dangerously low, just above the treetops. Smoke spewed out of every seam and rivet of his damaged rig as the last two Luftwaffe machines positioned on each of his wings. The pilots would definitely report to ground troops to pick Gordie up as a prisoner of war, so with zero sympathy, I used up the last of my ammunition to take down both airplanes. They each hit the ground with a shuddering explosion and ball of flames, which would have felt like a victory if Gordie wasn't still going down.

'Come on, Gordie. Keep her off the ground,' I pleaded under my breath. He glided on no power and slowly lost more altitude. He was going to hit terrain. 'Come on, Gordie, get out. Get out. Slide the canopy, pal.' He was too close to the ground to deploy the parachute properly, even if he did eject, but I circled and waited on edge for a glimpse of the ballooning fabric. He didn't bail. His airplane skidded on its belly across a farmer's field and erupted into flames.

'God damn it. No!' Fraught with remorse, my throat choked for air as I climbed in altitude to race back to base.

Before I could gain top speed, a cannon blew through my left wing and jolted me nearly out of the restraint, then my cockpit filled with gritty black smoke. Blinded by the toxic fumes, my fingers searched and pulled the release lever to slide the cockpit hood. The air cleared enough to see my instruments – temperature hot, oil low, petrol extremely low. My engine sputtered from the hit and then failed, so I yanked the hand pump to inject fuel, then viciously kicked the rudder bar in an attempt to keep speed. It didn't work. I was dead stick, no control of the airplane. The Sperry horizon indicator tilted sideways and the propellers spun ineffectively in the wind. Only two scenarios remained – go down with the fatally wounded machine or bail out. I didn't have much choice.

I closed my eyes, said, 'God forgive me. Have mercy on my soul,' and crawled out of the cockpit onto the slipstream. At ten thousand feet above the ground, it required complete defiance over every natural human survival instinct to balance on the edge of the wing, but I forced myself to manoeuvre into a crouch, and then jumped.

The drone of my Spitfire engine was replaced with the

intense shuddering of the air against my ears as I free-fell. The parachute released from my seat pack but, to my dismay, it suspended above me pitifully like a crumpled wad of wet paper. A strange amalgamation of utter abandonment and sheer terror waged a battle over my emotions as I plummeted through the sky towards the earth. Then, as if it had been playing a cruel joke but knew the gig needed to be up or I'd pancake, the fabric of the parachute snapped like a schooner sail catching the ocean wind. The jarring of the upward deployment nearly dislocated my shoulder joints, but the fact that my body was no longer plunging towards death was a welcome relief. The reprieve was short lived, though, as the harness straps cut across my chest and throat with crushing power. My fingers clutched desperately to fight the opposing forces of flight and gravity that strangled me as I drifted. Gasping for air was futile since I was only sucking in the suffocating black smoke of aviation carnage below. Ten metres from the ground, flames from a downed airplane ignited my parachute. It disintegrated, causing me to fall the rest of the way. I slammed into a cow pasture in the Italian countryside, hard enough to blow the seams of both my boots apart from the impact.

Sprawled out on my back, my smoke-irritated eyes blinked open. Maybe I'd been unconscious for a spell. As my head slowly cleared, I was thrilled to discover my fingers and toes responded to my mental commands to wiggle. Good news, I wasn't paralysed or shattered. Bad news, I was surrounded by flames. I sat up to remove the parachute harness, then with extreme effort rolled to my knees and stood. Stumbling blindly in socked feet, I assumed the gagging stench of burning flesh was the enemy pilots burning up, but then realized it was my own exposed skin, scorched and already peeling away. My attempt to avoid blistering-hot scraps of metal didn't go well and the pain became excruciating as my socks melted. I needed to make a run for it but didn't know which way to go, until a cross wind blew the smoke all in one direction and made my decision for me. I ran through the roaring and crackling flames to where the air was clearer. Eventually, I emerged from the wreckage scene and tumbled to the tufty grass – a meadow that was reminiscent of my acreage back home on Mayne Island, or at least I imagined it was before I passed out.

A child played in the knee-high grass of the Italian field, chasing a white butterfly. His face was Japanese like Chidori's, but his hair was blond like mine. The butterfly fluttered towards the airplane wreckage and the boy followed with his little hands raised in the air, trying to catch it. He wore a blue sweater and matching blue shoes. I yelled to warn him to stay away from the flames. He didn't hear me, though. I wanted to get up to save him, but my body couldn't move. I called to him one more time from where I lay before he disappeared into the wall of fire.

When I looked down at my body to determine why it wouldn't function, my torso wasn't actually there. Black, crusty flakes of ash were scattered where my limbs should have been. I cried out for help and a woman emerged from the flames. Her long black hair blew like raven feathers in the breeze. She was dressed all in white. Pure white. There wasn't even a smudge of soot on her. She held the boy on her hip and the butterfly rested on his finger. She smiled with sympathy, set the boy down on the grass, and whispered something into his ear. He looked over at me and said, 'Papa.'

Holding the boy's hand, Chidori walked towards me – only she wasn't really walking. More like floating.

'Am I in Heaven?' My voice was raspy and barely worked.

Chidori knelt next to me, then leaned forward to kiss my forehead.

A four-and-a-half-foot tall, grey-haired, leather-skinned Italian soldier with dirty fingernails rammed the end of his Gewehr rifle against my forehead on the same spot Chidori had kissed. I clenched my eyes shut, swallowed back the whimper that wanted to escape, and waited for the click of the trigger.

A second rifle barrel poked my ribs, prodding me to open my eyes. Rather than black, crusty flakes, I had arms. To my relief, I had legs too. They were burned, but at least I wasn't a pile of soot like in the dream. I attempted to sit up and the old soldier yelled at me in Italian. I didn't understand, so I raised my arms in surrender.

The younger soldier, whose narrow face and large eyes were proportioned like a grasshopper's, searched through what was left of my uniform, looking for my revolver. He pulled it out of my leg pocket, then yelped from the scalding metal and dropped it on the ground.

They nudged me to kneel and link my hands behind my head. Then they discussed my torn-up, bloody, and charred bare feet. The old soldier made impatient hand gestures to get me to stand. I tried, but resting weight on my feet was more agonizing than pouring vinegar on an open wound. I involuntarily moaned from the excruciating pain and fell to the ground. One of them pushed the end of his gun into my back to make me try again. I got up, but only took half a step before I stumbled to my knees. After a rest to wheeze air into my lungs, I hoisted myself up enough to crawl and hoped that wherever they planned to take me to surrender me to the Nazis was not far.

They didn't follow. They both lit cigarettes and watched me inch slowly. I travelled as far as I could, collapsed, and rolled over to stare up at the sky. High clouds, pleasant spring temperatures – a perfect day to die.

I imagined looking up at the same sky in Canada, half a world away. Maybe a bald eagle soared above, or a tree frog sang to its mate. Surrounded by the peacefulness of the island, nobody back home would have any idea I was about to be shot in the Italian countryside by fascists. I didn't want to die, and I especially dreaded facing God's ruling on people like me who took the lives of others in a war. A lot of my squadron mates celebrated every enemy they bagged, foaming at the bit to get back out and kill more. I neither celebrated nor lamented. The truth was, deep down, we all knew the other side was just a bunch of young fellows exactly like us who believed we were the evil ones. Who was to say which side was right? The only thing I knew for certain was there were a lot of us who were going to need to be granted mercy on our souls on judgement day.

Trying to accept my fate with grace, I searched the sky, looking for Heaven. All I saw were more Luftwaffe fighters, flying over in formation.

23 August 1941

Dear Diary,

Hayden gave me quite a startling and melancholy reminder that today's fall fair might be the last for many years if the war in Europe continues. I wonder if changing traditions is what Obaasan meant about parting. It would be such a shame if the fair and other lovely pastimes were to be cancelled, but there is no denying it is a possibility as we are all asked to tighten our use of nonessentials. Circumstances and attitudes have certainly changed ever since Japan signed on to join forces with Germany and Italy to fight against Great Britain and Canada. Thankfully, hostility is not yet noticeable here on Mayne Island, but I have read in the newspaper that in Vancouver and Victoria the sentiment towards Japanese Canadians has gotten increasingly prejudiced. I pray the war doesn't ruin everything festive. Or innocent. Or beautiful. But in the regrettable event that it does, I have been making an effort to observe all of the encounters occurring around me.

Speaking of one such observation: I witnessed Hayden in his undershirt this morning. Good golly that was a lovely encounter, but for the sake of propriety this is all I should write about it. Some encounters have been not so lovely, like whatever caused Hayden to get in a shoving match with Rory earlier. I have my suspicions about what caused it, but it's probably best not to speculate. I really wish he wouldn't fight, especially if it has anything to do with me.

Chi

Chapter 4

After the altercation with the Bauer boys, I vented my frustration by hauling crates of jarred plums and apricots. Ma was head of the craft fair committee and judge for the pie-baking contest, so after I finished helping her army of volunteers set up the tables, she let my sister and me both taste a few pie samples. Mrs Campbell's blueberry was by far the tastiest because she made it tart the way I liked it. But there was a tangy lemon flan that was going to give her a run for her money.

Rosalyn's mandated-by-our-mother volunteer-job had been to display the entries for the quilting category on rods suspended with wire from the rafters, but she was also entered as a contestant in the art category. One of her landscape oil paintings was on display on an easel near the stage, and she appeared nervous as I wandered around the hall to view her competition – two other oil paintings, several watercolours, an intricate wood carving of a whale, a blown-glass vase, and something that could only be described literally – a broken doll dipped in ceramic and then adorned in barnacles and gold enamelled butterflies. Oddly interesting in a circus-sideshow type of way.

'What do you think?' Rose asked me as she tugged at her lip and leaned in close to study one of the other oil paintings. 'I don't think my chances are good. This woman's brush strokes are more skilful than mine.'

I squinted, not convinced. 'Does it really matter what her brush stroke is like if her apples resemble pumpkins and her grapes are the size of watermelons?'

Rose chuckled and swatted my arm. 'Shh. Don't be cruel. Someone might hear you and I'll be disqualified for poor sportsmanship.'

'The prize for the winner is one of Ma's zucchini loaves. You can just eat one when you get home.'

Rose rolled her eyes and stuck her tongue out at me like when we were little kids. 'It's for bragging rights, not the prizes.'

'Well, you definitely have the best oil painting, but you're going to come second to that ghoulish doll thingamajig.'

'It is a curiously striking aberration, isn't it?' She laughed, then wrinkled her nose. 'Second place wins a jar of Mrs Auld's pickled beets.'

'Mmm. My favourite. Save me some.' I poked her arm playfully, stole another sample from Ma's pie-judging table, and then headed back out to the fairgrounds.

Chidori was seated on a stool at their booth, writing in one of her journals, but she put it down to assist two women who approached the counter to purchase carrots. My best mate Joey lounged on the hill beside the Agricultural Hall with his steady gal, Donna Mae. I wandered over and sat down on the prickly dry grass next to them to listen to the church musicians struggle to play a jitterbug song for the crowd.

'Hi Hayden,' Donna Mae said. 'The gang's all meeting down at the point for a bonfire tonight. Do you want to tag along with us?'

'I'll meet you down there.'

'Ooh.' She clutched the crook of my arm and shook it excitedly. 'Do you have a date?'

Not sure if I could swing it, I shrugged. 'Maybe.'

'Chidori?'

A smile crept across my face as I said, 'I hope so.'

'That's swell. It's about time the two of you finally took the plunge. You're perfect for each other.' Donna Mae sipped ginger-beer soda from a bottle and snapped her fingers along with the beat of the song. Her reddish-brown curls bounced on her shoulders as she bobbed her head from side to side.

Joey glanced over at me with concern and leaned forward to rest his elbows on his knees. 'If Chidori agrees to be your date, maybe you two should catch a ride with us. In case there's any trouble with the Bauers.'

'Thanks, but they don't concern me. And Chidori won't feel comfortable when you two spend the entire night carrying on in the back seat.'

'We won't,' Donna Mae promised. 'We'll be on our best behaviour, won't we, Joseph?'

He raised his eyebrows in a comical way. 'Maybe you should drive yourselves.'

Donna Mae slapped his thigh. 'Don't listen to him. We

won't embarrass you in front of Chidori. I don't want her to think I'm fast or something.'

'She's known you her entire life.' Joey poked Donna Mae's ribs to tease her. 'She's already heard that you're fast.'

Donna Mae shot up, brushed the dust from the seat of her wide-leg trousers, and stormed off in a huff.

'Donna! Don't be sore. I was only kidding,' Joey called after her. He laughed and reclined back on his elbows. 'In all seriousness, are you sure about Chidori? Nobody cared when you were just kids hanging out as friends. But dating? Not to mention marriage and having babies. Some people might not approve of that these days.'

'People can't tell me who to love.'

'No. But now that Japan is our enemy, some folks might make your life difficult. Is that the kind of trouble you want for her or your future kids?'

I glanced over at Chidori as she served a frail, silver-haired customer named Mrs Wagner. The woman dug through her pocketbook, searching for coins. Chidori handed her the basket full of garlic, tomatoes and potatoes, and since Mrs Wagner was recently widowed, Chidori refused to take her money. Tosh and Kenji had always teased Chidori for giving away more vegetables than she sold. Her father wasn't overly thrilled that her charitable generosity put a dent in their profits either, but it's hard to get cross with someone for having a big heart.

Joey opened his mouth to say more about my decision to pursue a formal relationship with Chidori, but he got distracted when my sister wandered up to the front of the amphitheatre stage and danced with a group of young ladies. Joey's eyes bulged and his grin widened like a hound that spotted a rabbit. 'Gosh, I love looking at your sister. Do you mind if I ask her to dance?'

'Donna Mae might mind. Besides, don't go getting your hopes up. Rosalyn's engaged.'

'Isn't her fiancé stationed in London? It can get lonely when your sweetheart is overseas. She might be in the mood for some male companionship.'

'Even if I would allow it, which I wouldn't, you haven't got a shot with her. She's moving to Vancouver in September to start a nursing job. And, by the way, she hasn't received a letter from her fiancé in a good while, so it's probably best if you don't mention him – unless you want her blubbering all over you.'

Joey's head swivelled like he was watching a tennis match as Rose moved around the dancing area. Her blue skirt spun and the waves of her white-blond hair swayed over her shoulders. He didn't break his concentration when he said, 'They brought a navy ship into dock for the fair. You want to tour it?'

'No thanks. I already know being cooped up in a ship's hull for months would be no picnic.'

'Flying a Spitfire in the air force would be a blast, though.'

'Sure, but killing a person wouldn't be.'

Joey shrugged as if that part hadn't occurred to him. 'An RAF recruiting officer was knocking door-to-door yesterday, looking to enlist boys for duty. Did he drop by your parents' place?'

'Yup.'

'Are you going to sign up on your birthday?'

'Nope. Why would I want to risk my life just because Germany was sore over how the last war ended and decided to start another one? I can't believe how many marks fall for the hype and volunteer to get killed overseas.'

'The Nazis are killing innocent people and stealing power from entire countries.' Joey tilted his Ivy cap forward to shade his eyes from the August sun that angled through the giant fir trees. 'You think we should all just sit back and let Germany take over the whole world in vengeance?'

'The countries involved should fight. I don't see why Canadians are putting their noses where they don't belong.'

'Just 'cause the enemy ain't on our soil doesn't mean they ain't aiming to be. And when they attack our allies, it's our war too. Besides, if they start conscripting for overseas service you might have no choice, pal.'

I nodded to reluctantly concede and picked at the drought-scorched grass. Conscription to fight overseas was the worst-case scenario. Fighting someone else's war over greed or pride or power – or whatever it was over, and likely dying doing it, did not appeal to me in the slightest. Especially if it meant being sent so far away from home. But maybe Joey was right. If the fight was about justness and protecting innocent lives, it had merit. And if the enemy ever set foot on our soil, I wouldn't hesitate to reconsider. But I still believed, perhaps naively, that despite the failure of the League of Nations, calmer heads would prevail. Unfortunately, the news on the radio and in the papers did make it sound as if sending more Canadian boys was inevitable, though. 'Are you going to sign up?' I asked.

Joey nearly snorted at the absurdity. 'I would but they wouldn't take me. I can barely see you from a foot away. I'd be useless with a gun. But who knows what tomorrow will bring? In case they start scraping the bottom of the barrel for skinny, nearly blind kids, I should probably seize the day while I'm still free to do so.' He slapped my back, stood, and loped over to ask Rosalyn to dance.

A gang of younger boys chased each other around the dancers in a game of soldiers. They pretended to shoot at each other with their fingers and ran through a group of schoolgirls who huddled together, planning a round of hide and seek. Donna Mae stood up against the Agricultural Hall with her arms crossed, glaring enviously at Joey and Rose as they danced. Her eyes watered and her lip quivered, so I stood and wandered over to her.

Three young ladies my age, and two my sister's age, noticed me walking over and all turned to face me, eager for an invitation to dance. 'Hi Hayden,' they all said in unison as they either flattened the fabric of their skirts or tucked flyaway hairs into bobby pins.

'Ladies,' I greeted them but extended my hand to Donna Mae. 'Would you care to dance, Donna Mae?'

Donna Mae tucked her chin down timidly and glanced at the other girls. 'You're a sweet one, Hayden, but you know I dance like a lame horse. Ask one of the other girls.'

'Just follow me. It's easy – like walking.'

'I can't walk all that well half the time either.'

'Trust me.' I pulled Donna Mae by the hand and spun her around a few times. She smiled as I ushered her across the grass in a Lindy Hop. Well, I was doing a Lindy Hop. She was doing more of a wounded Bunny Hop.

We danced for another song, then Joey cut in, which I knew he would. Donna Mae giggled as he spun her around. Chidori was watching me, but when our eyes met, she pretended to write in her journal. I shoved my hands in my pockets and casually strolled over to her stand. A customer beat me to the counter. After Chidori placed two cucumbers into the customer's basket and collected the money, I leaned in and whispered, 'Would you care to dance, Miss Setoguchi?'

Her face lit up at the invitation, but then she dropped her focus to the counter of the booth. 'I should keep working, but thank you for asking.'

'I think you should take a break. Just leave the vegetables out on the counter. You give most of them away at no charge anyway.'

'Ha ha. You are quite the comical one.' Her gaze met mine as she considered it, but then she scanned the fairgrounds and her forehead creased as something else crossed her mind. 'What was the problem between you, Rory and Fitz earlier?'

'It was nothing. I'm not here to talk about that. I'm here to convince you to take a break and have a little fun dancing with me.'

She smiled reluctantly with one corner of her mouth. 'I have to admit you are a smooth dancer.'

I chuckled. 'Thank you, but I'm still looking for the right partner.'

'I see.' Her eyebrow arched delicately.

'Maybe you could give me some pointers.'

'You seem to do just fine all on your own, Mr Pierce.' She bent over to transfer apples from a crate on the ground and restocked a basket on the counter.

'I'm surprised you noticed. I thought you were too busy to socialize, with all your customers and whatever it is you're always scribbling in that journal of yours.'

She winked and tied raffia to make bunches of beets. 'I am quite capable of doing more than one thing at a time.'

'Good to know. Let's dance one quick swing before I have to go meet my pop and your uncle Massey at the dock.'

She rolled her eyes in a subtle surrender and placed the beets on the counter. 'Fine. One dance.'

I nearly jumped out of my shoes in joy, but as she stepped out from the stand, the band announced they were going on a break.

'Wait!' I shouted and ran across the grass lot to the edge of the stage to speak to the piano player, who also happened to be the butcher. 'One more, please, Mr Cooke.'

'Sorry, kid. We played all the songs we know. Besides, we've been at it all morning and I for one need something to eat. There's a fresh-out-of-the-oven chicken pot pie over there calling my name.' He hopped off the stage and headed over to the pot-pie table with zero concern for the disappointing predicament he left me in.

As I walked back towards Chidori, I shrugged with my palms facing skyward. 'Sorry. I tried.'

She returned the gesture. 'It's okay. There will be other opportunities.'

I nodded to agree, but truthfully I was disheartened. 'The *Issei Sun* is due in a few minutes. Are we still on for a walk later this afternoon?'

'Yes.' Her excitement flickered through her eyes first before it reached her lips. 'Meet me at my house once you're finished selling the fish.'

'Dandy. I can't wait.'

Chapter 5

The oddly coupled rural Italian soldiers didn't shoot me. Instead, they arranged for a farmer to hoist me onto a primitive wood cart pulled by a scrawny, malnourished horse. They hopped a ride on the cart, too, only half-heartedly pointing their guns in my general direction since I wasn't in any condition to fight or run off.

It was a strangely emotionless purgatory to be neither safe nor in immediate danger. Possibly I was in shock from the pain of the burns, or maybe it was just such a peculiar circumstance that my body wasn't sure how to react, but I felt detached from the reality of what was happening.

An hour into the bumpy journey, the Italian farmer's cart hit a pot-sized hole on the bombed-out dirt road. The rough jolt threw me against the grasshopper soldier, who smelled like tobacco and dried sweat. He pushed me off as if I disgusted him and yelled at the farmer to instruct him to watch where he was going. I didn't understand the words but the sentiment was evident.

Dusk fell as we finally passed several stone, thatched-roof farmhouses on the approach to a German-occupied Italian village. The buildings were mostly rubble from the bombings, but laundry lines hung beside some of the structures that still had partial roofs, and I could imagine the peaceful quaintness that must have existed before the war. The farmer's cart jarringly bounced over cobblestone towards a central plaza, designed around what at one time would have been an impressive tiered marble water fountain. It was half destroyed and empty. The cart stopped in front of a town hall that had been converted by the German military into a *Kriegslazarett*, a makeshift battlefield hospital for Allied prisoners of war. Several Nazi military jeeps and an ambulance were parked outside the one-storey, wood-framed building. The Italian soldiers stood on either side of me so I could rest my weight on their shoulders as they assisted me inside to surrender me to the Nazis. A clerk took one look at my burns and directed the soldiers to haul me promptly into an office that served as a treatment and operating room. They hoisted me roughly onto a cold metal gurney and then made their leave.

A German doctor who couldn't have been much older than Tosh examined my feet and shook his head with a gravity that translated loud and clear through the language barrier. I worried it meant amputation. He pushed his spectacles up his nose and, without applying any numbing agent, began the tedious and tormenting task of cleaning the wounds with a solvent and a sharp metal utensil. I couldn't watch. And my body convulsed in an instinctual gag as the layers of charred skin fell off. My fingers gripped the cold metal table, and although I was on the verge of shouting out in agony the entire time, I cursed only twice – once when he peeled off the last fragile layer of skin, and again when he doused the raw surface with a pungent disinfectant. Holding in the pain made my heart race, the surface of my tongue dry into a paste, and sweat gush from every pore on my body.

A nurse entered the room and smiled at me with a kindness that made me momentarily forget the physical suffering. But then I ached for the comfort of home. Her dark brown hair was twisted into a bun with her white nurse's cap pinned just above it. Rose wore her nurse's cap the same way. The nurse was pretty – almost as pretty as Chidori. Almost. No woman I'd ever seen was prettier than Chidori. When we were growing up, strangers always commented on how she was as beautiful as a porcelain doll. And it was true, she did resemble the doll on my sister's shelf, with her long eyelashes, peachy-coloured cheeks, and lips that seemed always ready to kiss something. I didn't realize until I was much older how rare it was to be that striking in real life.

The doctor left and the nurse gently wrapped my feet with bandages. When she was done, she reached over to turn my hand. Her frown deepened because my palms were burned badly as well. With the antiseptic the doctor had used, she cleaned my hands, arms, and a burn that ran up my neck and jaw. I winced and bit my lip to prevent myself from cursing in front of her.

'*Entschuldigung*,' she said.

I didn't know what it meant, but it sounded apologetic. She began a full conversation with me, of which I didn't understand a word. She smiled a lot and even laughed a few times, not minding that I didn't say anything in response. And

43

when I smiled, she gently pressed her finger to the dimple on my left cheek.

'*Gutaussehender*.'

I tried to repeat the word and it made her laugh. Her friendliness was appreciated, and the only thing that made being injured, all alone in a foreign country, and in the custody of Nazis bearable. She helped me slide off the examining table into a wheelchair, then wheeled me over uneven wood-plank floors into a rectory that served as the dormitory. About thirty men reclined on iron-frame cots, playing cards or reading. Some were asleep. She placed me in front of an empty cot next to another Canadian pilot. I didn't know him, but the familiar uniform folded up on a chair next to his bed gave me a sense of comradery with the stranger. He was asleep, so I tried to be quiet and not disturb him.

The nurse tenderly helped me move from the wheelchair to the lumpy and compressed cotton mattress and then assisted me to change out of my tattered uniform. She turned her head politely so I could slip into a thin hospital gown and then under the sheet. She must have noticed me wince from the weight of the top wool blanket, because she folded up the bottom of the bed linens to leave my feet exposed.

'*Danke*,' I said. I'd heard Rory say it to his cousin before, so I knew it meant thank you in German.

She nodded to accept the gratitude before she left the dormitory.

At lights out, the guard left his post by the door to do a bed check. The heels of his boots clicked against the wood floor-

boards and echoed through the dormitory – the sound
nightmares are made of. He snaked his way through the rows
of cots. When he reached my row, the beam of his torch landed
on my face, forcing me to squint.

'*Schlafen,*' he grumbled.

I had no idea what that meant so I ignored him. I was still
rattled from the dogfight and in too much discomfort to sleep,
so I just stared at the ceiling and thought about home.

'Sleep,' he growled in English.

Truth was, I wanted to be asleep. Desperately, to make the
night pass faster. But I couldn't get the dreadful images of
Gordie's airplane going down out of my mind. The disturbing
stench of burned bodies also hadn't left me. The guard kept
the light beamed in my eyes so I glared at him. His eyebrows
angled together in contempt as he lifted his arm. The torch
slammed against my bandaged right ankle, and my entire
body contorted from a dynamite-like explosion that travelled
up my leg and halted my heart for a beat. I would have
screamed if the air had not been completely sucked out by
the blow. Instead, I writhed silently as my muscles braced
rigidly against the mattress to fight the torment.

'*Schlafen!*' he shouted.

I winced and turned my back to him.

If my mother had known I was in pain she would have sat
on the edge of my mattress and rested a nurturing hand on
my shoulder – that is, if she weren't hysterically inconsolable
over witnessing the damaged state I was in and the rudimen-
tary medical treatment I had been provided. But, of course,
she wasn't with me and I wasn't home. I was all alone in

hostile territory. And yearning for a comfort that wasn't possible only made me feel worse.

The click of his boots didn't start up again until I purposely slowed my breathing to feign sleep. Once he was gone, my body shook from the intensity of the anguish, or maybe the rage. My desperation to go home had never been worse. But that wish wasn't going to come true. At least not any time soon. I knew that. And the grim reality pained me worse than the weeping burn wounds that left me skinless and raw.

23 August 1941

Dear Diary,

I greatly admire a person who is able to remain upbeat through heartbreaking hardship. Mrs Wagner tragically lost her husband of fifty-eight years. She has no other family and she is in frail health herself, yet she finds the strength to be genuinely pleasant to everyone she meets. If the wretched hardships of war reach us here on Mayne Island, I aspire to be the type of person who can grow bolder and build strength through dreadful adversity. I pray tragedy never happens. But, if ever faced with the choice to wallow in despair or embrace love, gratitude, and appreciation, why not clutch to the contentment and awe of our fleeting life as Mrs Wagner does?

Who am I fooling? I failed to even clutch the joyous contentment spinning around right in front of my face earlier today. Hayden asked me to dance and I put it off so long that we missed our chance. That is my problem in a nutshell. I think too much. I worry too much. I hesitate too much. Hayden never hesitates. Once he knows what he wants, he bravely takes action to bring it to fruition. Admittedly, some of Hayden's actions are too impetuous and end in calamity, but I admire that he is fearless. I admire so much about him. Obaasan says if you wish to discover the most important purpose in your life, you need not look any farther than that which puts a smile on your face when you wake up in the morning. For me, that would be Hayden – without a doubt. This afternoon when Hayden and I meet, I vow to be more spontaneous and daring.

Chi

Chapter 6

Happy with Chidori's promise to accompany me on a walk after the fair, I wandered down the road towards Miner's Bay to meet my father and Chidori's uncle Massey at the wharf. The dock was located a short walk down the hill from the fairgrounds, past the general store. A lot of folks were already mingling around the benches that encircled the big old maple tree. Most of the people had come over from either the other nearby islands or Victoria to attend the fair and to eat lunch at the Springwater Lodge. The rest of the crowd were Mayne Islanders eager to get caught up on gossip from the other islands and the mainland.

When my father wasn't planting or harvesting our crops, he worked for the Setoguchis. He'd worked for both Chidori's father in his tomato and cucumber greenhouses, and for her uncle Massey on his seiner fishing boat since before I was born. I'd been helping on the boat every summer since I was ten. They were due any minute to arrive with a load of salmon to sell from the dock, so I hopped up and sat on the wood railing to wait.

Massey hadn't always been a fisherman. He had graduated

university with an architecture degree, but only people on the voting list could register to practice as an architect, and the government denied Japanese Canadians the franchise. So instead, Massey became a successful general contractor in Vancouver. He eventually invested in commercial real estate. During the Roaring Twenties he had taken a chance on the wheat stock market, which multiplied in value when Canadian wheat exports went international. Massey had a gut feeling the bubble would eventually burst, so he monitored the volatility and sold all his stocks six months before the entire stock market crashed in '29. He was one of the few investors who hadn't lost everything, and having cash on hand meant that – during the terrible economic depression that followed – he was able to buy several buildings and one entire city block at below-value bargain depression prices. But then tragedy struck him in a different way. Sadly, his wife died giving birth to their son. The baby unfortunately died too. He moved back to Mayne Island to escape the heartbreaking memories and live the simple life of a fisherman, but he still owned the real estate in the city and profited from it generously. Most local islanders didn't know how wealthy he was because he lived modestly in a small cabin near the greenhouses on Chidori's father's property, and he wasn't pretentious in any way.

A queue of folks who were keen to buy fresh sockeye formed near the Springwater Lodge. Another queue wound up the dock to be tendered out for the tour of the navy ship anchored in Miner's Bay. The *Issei Sun* appeared in the distance and chugged in from Active Pass, riding low in the water from their bountiful catch. Once they were close enough to saddle up against the floats, my father tossed the bowline to me. As I was bent over tying the knot to the cleat, a plump, dark-haired woman asked me, 'Is this your family's boat?'

'No ma'am.'

'Who owns the vessel?' Her nose wrinkled with disdain at Massey as he climbed down from the wheelhouse and tipped his straw hat.

It peeved me that she looked down her nose at him when she didn't even know him, and I had to hold my tongue. Massey wasn't bothered by rude people like that, and he usually found a way to have a little fun with them. He winked at me and replied to her, 'The vessel is privately owned by a successful businessman from Vancouver, ma'am.'

Both my father and I chuckled at his quick wit.

'What does *Issei* mean?' she addressed my father. 'It sounds foreign.'

'It means "first generation",' he answered matter-of-factly, before he tied on a rubber apron and turned away from her to open the hatch to the cold storage.

'In what language?' she pressed.

She was obviously bigoted, so I hopped on deck and pretended not to hear her. Massey and my father also busied themselves to ignore her. She asked once more to no avail, huffed, but then got in line with everyone else, because – regardless of whether it was a Japanese-owned seiner or not – they all wanted the fresh salmon.

A group of four girls who had been a year younger than Chidori and me at school huddled around each other. They stole giddy glances in my direction and giggled. One of them waved at me, which made the other ones gossip.

Massey elbowed my shoulder. 'Come on, buddy boy. Give them what they came to see.'

I shook my head to refuse.

'They've been circling around here like turkey vultures all summer, hoping you'll at least work in your undershirt.'

'Unless I slip and fall overboard, they're going to be waiting an awfully long time.'

'Showing off some muscle could be good for business.' With a chuckle he shoved me over the railing into the water.

When I surfaced and pushed my hair back from my face, both my father and Massey doubled over in laughter. The group of girls were also thoroughly amused. I pulled myself back onto the boat, but I wasn't interested in showing off for anyone other than Chidori, so I left my soaking wet shirt on out of principle. And defiance. Massey's big palm slapped my shoulder again to josh me. I ignored the goading and got to work.

The hull was filled and overflowing onto the deck with crushed ice and hundreds of salmon. I rolled my sleeves and hooked the thick and slick fish with a pike pole, then threw them to Massey one at a time. In a perfectly timed rhythm, he turned and chucked them at my father, who laid them out on a long, ice-covered wood sales plank on the dockside of the boat. Eventually the load in the hull lowered enough that I had to drop down the hatch into the marine cold storage to toss up the rest.

Even without seeing me working shirtless, customers enthusiastically scooped up the fish and passed over their fists-full of money until the hull was completely empty two hours later. About a dozen folks at the end of the line had to go home empty-handed and disappointed.

I reached up over my head and pulled myself out of the hull, smelling like salt and seaweed. And shivering from working on the ice in wet clothes. Massey removed his gloves and tossed my father a cola bottle as I stepped into the warm sunshine. He was about to toss me one too, but I waved him off. 'I can't stay.'

'You got a date?' Massey teased.

'I'm working on it,' I said.

The humour faded from his expression as he nodded and took a sip of the cola. Then he glanced at me with some sort of knowingness or cautionary tale.

'What?' I asked as my gaze shifted back and forth between him and my father.

Massey shrugged but didn't say anything. He was like that – wise with both life experience and book smarts, but he never lectured or imposed his opinions. In fact, he was unintrusive to an annoying degree. One time, when I was about fourteen years old, I had loaded up a skiff with engine parts for his boat and the whole damn thing sank. Massey knew it was too much weight but didn't stop me. He just sat there and watched the ordeal happen without saying a word. I was so hot under the collar. Partly because I'd have to buy him another engine pump. Partly because I didn't know how I was going to get the skiff and the other parts off the bottom of the ocean. But mostly I was mad because – if he had just said something – he could have saved me all the trouble. He claimed that telling me the answers didn't help me learn, making mistakes did. Then he chuckled at how fuming angry I was, which sent me into a rage. I had to walk away and didn't go back to salvage the skiff for a week. They were both thoroughly entertained that day too, but at least they helped me winch everything out of the water.

Massey's hands-off teaching philosophy didn't sit well with me then, and I still didn't agree with his methods. Probably because I was too hot-tempered for his learn-the-hard-way lessons. But admittedly I never overloaded a skiff again.

Despite obviously having an opinion about my dating endeavours with his niece, he wasn't going to tell me what he thought. I studied his expression for another few seconds to see if it would reveal any clues about what lesson he thought I should be aware of. All he did was flick his eyebrows and hand me my cash earnings for the day, so I hopped over the railing to head over to Chidori's house. 'It's been a blast. See you all later.'

Chapter 7

In the morning, the kind German nurse brought a tray with a bun and a small piece of cheese to my cot. The name written on her badge was I. Gottschalk. I didn't know what the *I* stood for, but I called her Inga and she responded. She smiled warmly, then took trays to the other fellows in the hospital dormitory. The Canadian pilot on the cot next to me was awake.

'*Bonjour,*' he said and bit into his bun.

'Hi.'

'*Est-ce que tu parles français?*'

'No, sorry.'

'Is okay. Is easier for me with the French. But I speak English. *Un peu.* You have a terror in the night I think.'

It was mildly embarrassing that everyone likely heard my nightmare startle me awake, but there was nothing I could do about that. 'Sorry if I disturbed you.'

'Is okay. We all have had the terrors.' He pointed at my feet. 'You are burned?'

'Yes. How about you?' I asked before I took a sip of water. He pulled down the shoulder of his hospital gown and revealed a chest injury covered in dressing. 'Impaled when ...' he whistled and used his hand to pantomime jumping out of an airplane.

'What's your name?'

'Michel. From Montreal. And you?' He leaned over to shake my hand.

'Hayden. I'm from Mayne Island in British Columbia. How long have you been here?'

'Three weeks.' He glanced at the door where a guard stood, then lowered his voice, 'I will be trying for staying a long time because is no good to be in the camp for prisoners I think.'

'Have you heard what to expect?'

'No, but the head nurse tries to be keeping us here for a long time. She has compassion. She must be knowing it is no good.'

I nodded and took an inventory of the other patients in the dormitory. Mostly British airmen, three American flyboys and at least fifteen other Canadians besides Michel and me. One fellow was in a coma and probably wasn't going to make it. One fellow had a broken leg and one was burned like me. His burns were worse – his eyes and nose were melted into a disfigured blob. The dormitory reeked rancid like rotting flesh. The nurses had tried to cover up the putridness with bleach, but it lingered.

'You are not eating the *petit dejeuner*?' Michel asked.

'No. You can have it.'

He wiggled his eyebrows eagerly and reached over to grab the bun and cheese off my tray.

Conversation with Michel was welcomed but I missed

Gordie already. It was strange to be in a dormitory full of soldiers and not have the big man right next to me. Gordie Calhoon, Frank Owens and I had all met on the first day of our eight weeks of Elementary Flying Training with the British Commonwealth Air Training Plan in Regina, Saskatchewan. We called our flight training The Plan for short, and it instructed us in basic aviation. Gordie was a grizzly bear of a fellow you would like to have on your side in a street fight. Frank was a hornet, who would likely get you messed up in the street fight in the first place. The three of us became instant pals and sat next to each other during classroom lessons and at meals in the mess hall.

The first week we were at The Plan, their wives sent baked goods that made me miss home something fierce.

'You want one?' Frank had asked.

'Sure,' I said, and reached to take a shortbread biscuit.

'His wife can't bake worth stink. You should probably stick to my wife's ginger snaps,' Gordie teased Frank and held out the tin to share with me.

'I'll try them both and decide which is better for myself.' I bit into each cookie and grinned. 'I think I'll need to try some more before I can make my final decision.'

'No way. One's all you're getting unless you cough up something in exchange.' Gordie leaned back on his bunk and ate another cookie.

'I only received a letter from my sister.'

Gordie stole the letter, but we were interrupted when the chief ground instructor, who was the equivalent to a headmaster at a boarding school, marched into the bunkhouse, barking commands for an inspection. We all jumped to our feet and stored the letters and cookies out of sight.

'Hayden, pal, have you seen my cap?'

'It's on your head, Frank.'

'Right.' He grinned and loped over to the end of his bunk. We all stood tall with our chests forward as the officer poked around and made us fix things that weren't up to scratch. I didn't have any corrections because I was a quick learner when it came to things like that.

'What does your sister look like?' Gordie asked me once the inspection was over and we were lounged on our bunks again. He had read her letter for a second time. 'She seems smart. I'm particularly fond of clever gals. If she's a looker, I might want to take her out on the town sometime.'

'You're married,' I reminded him.

'Yeah, yeah, do you have a photo or not?'

I handed over a picture of Rosalyn and me standing at Bennett Bay.

'Sweet Jesus! Is she single?'

'Never mind.' I threw a rolled sock at him. 'She probably wouldn't take very kindly to you being married anyway.'

'Hey everybody! Come take a look at Pierce's sister.'

The boys all gathered around and whistled. I leaned over and snatched the photo back from Gordie. 'Keep dreaming, fellas.'

'Do you have a photo of your sweetheart, too?' Frank asked me.

'I'm not showing you that. Go drool over the picture of your own wife.'

'She ain't nothing to drool at,' Gordie joked, which made Frank jump over the bunk and wrench Gordie into a headlock. Gordie was nearly twice the size of Frank, so he messed with him like he was playing with his kid brother.

We laughed a lot in those early days. Unfortunately, it didn't last.

Regina was not the biggest city, but it got pretty rowdy at night because there were so many recruits. One Saturday night, we were all excited for an evening off and a bunch of us crammed into a borrowed car to go to a local dance hall in town. The party was packed with men in uniform and a whole score of ladies drinking and dancing to a big band orchestra. We sat down at a table and Gordie ordered three beers. Frank took his bottle of O'Keefe with him and went off to ask a gal to dance.

'So, where in BC are you from, Pierce?' Gordie asked.

'Mayne Island. It's just off the coast between Vancouver and Victoria. How about you? What part of Manitoba are you from?'

'Winnipeg, but I've been living here in Regina on and off for a while because I played football professionally.'

'Oh, well, la-dee-da. I didn't know I was in the company of a celebrity.'

'I ain't no movie star, but stick with me, kid, and the ladies will treat you real nice.'

Just as he had said that, two young women in tight sweaters walked up to our table and stood with their elbows resting on either side of Gordie's broad shoulders. One was a freckled redhead, and the other had blond hair wrapped in a braided bun at the base of her neck. 'Hi there, Gordie. Who's your handsome friend?' Her hand slid over my arm.

'This, ladies, is Hayden Pierce. And word on the street is that this cat is a smooth dancer.'

I shook my head to deny it and my cheeks heated up.

'Oh, he's a sweet one,' the blond one said and held out her hand to shake mine. 'I'm Isabel. Nice to meet you.'

I nodded, then shook the other woman's hand.

'I'm Bernice.' I stared for too long because her eyes were golden-brown like a fawn's and her lashes were long enough to nearly touch her cheek when she blinked. They were both from Regina, which is why they already knew Gordie. And they were working with the Canadian Forces on electronics and instrument assembly, so they knew more about what we could expect from our training than we did. 'Would you care to dance, Hayden?' Bernice asked after we had chatted for a while.

I was thrown off by a gal so bold as to ask a fellow to dance. 'Oh, thank you, but my heart belongs to someone else.'

All three of them laughed at my naiveté.

'Honey, nearly everyone here has a fiancé, a spouse, or a sweetheart back home. It's just dancing.'

'Go ahead, kid.' Gordie pushed my shoulder to make me fall off the stool. 'Show 'em how it's done on the west coast.'

Bernice bounced over and pulled my hand to drag me out onto the dance floor. She pleaded with those big brown eyes and, since the band was playing a song I liked, I caved in and placed my hand on her waist to start to swing with her. She was a swell dancer and she smelled of soap mixed with vanilla extract, which was a welcome change from a barrack full of men. I relaxed after about three songs and Bernice said, 'Ah, there it is. A little smile. You look even more handsome when you smile.' She jitterbugged around in a circle by herself before grabbing both my hands to make me swing with her again. I was having a dandy time until she leaned in and shouted over the music, 'So, where is your sweetheart at?'

The reminder filled me with instant and aching guilt. I stopped dancing abruptly, excused myself, and walked off the dance floor, leaving Bernice behind.

Gordie was still talking to Isabel at the table, but he sent her away when I sat down, visibly downtrodden. 'What's wrong, pal?' he asked.

'Nothing.'

He slapped my shoulder. 'Don't worry, being away from home gets easier with time. Do you have a picture of the girl you're sweet on?'

I reached into the chest pocket of my serge and pulled out Chidori's picture. He frowned at it for a moment, then gave it back to me. I tucked it away, leaned my elbows on the table to hang my head, and sighed.

'You fell in love with a Jap?'

His judgemental tone, my longing to go home, and my bitter resentment over what had happened to Chidori all collided and provoked me to irrationally erupt. Without even thinking, I stood and punched Gordie in the jaw as hard as I could, which knocked him backwards off the stool. He sprawled across the floor and his lights were out for a second before he recovered. A crowd inched closer, keen to see what was going to happen next. Already committed to what I had impetuously started, I prepared my stance for him to charge at me in retaliation. He didn't, thankfully, since he was bigger and stronger than I was. He stood, righted the stool and took a swig from his ale. 'Nice shot, Pierce. Most fellas can't knock me out.'

I frowned at him, confused. 'You're not sore with me?'

He laughed and adjusted his jaw to make sure it was still connected properly. 'I didn't say that. But it was impressive.' He was clearly sore with me but chose to be the better man and walked over to ask Isabel to dance.

Ashamed that I had lost my cool with him, I left the dance hall alone. As I headed back to the base with a throbbing hand, I considered going AWOL. I missed my bed. I missed my dog. And I was worried that maybe my mother had been right. What if all I was going to accomplish by running off to war was to get myself killed? The streets of Regina were pretty much abandoned at that time of night. Hopping a train would have been easy. And it wasn't exactly deserting since I had volunteered.

I definitely would have taken off that night if I'd actually known where in the world Chidori was.

23 August 1941

Dear Diary,

Tosh and Kenji are out in the yard sawing and splitting the fir tree that was uprooted in the terrible windstorm we had in early spring. The root ball that tore out of the ground is four times taller than they are. It must have been a very old tree. Fortunately, it fell between the house and greenhouses, only crushing a small tool shed. I'm curious why after centuries of standing tall it could not endure one more storm. It was healthy and its roots were deep. The gale force must have been a direct hit that proved too powerful for even the most stoic giant of the forest. Well, the bright side I suppose is that they already have a cord of firewood that will keep us toasty warm in the winter, and they are nowhere near done yet.

I am grateful they are both home. Before Kenji moved to Vancouver to live with Tosh near the university campus, I hadn't appreciated how much I truly adored having my brothers around. It wasn't until after they were both gone and the house was deafeningly quiet that I realized I had taken their importance in my life for granted. Thankfully, I still had Hayden to make me laugh. I'm waiting for him right now. I hesitate to write down what wonderful happening I hope for on our walk because I do not want to jinx my chances. I will say that I have changed into a dress that I know is one of Hayden's favourites, and I have a flutter in my chest from the suspense.

Chi

Chapter 8

Busting with nervous excitement, I jogged all the way from Massey's boat to Chidori's house on the other side of the island, and my clothes were almost dry by the time I arrived. Her brothers were chopping up a tree in the yard, so I waved and then wandered around the side of the house. The first two pebbles I threw at Chidori's bedroom window bounced off the wooden frame. The third one hit the glass, maybe a little too hard. She opened the sash and sat on the windowsill.

'Afternoon, miss. Are you ready to go for our walk?'

'Yes. I was just writing in my journal as I waited for you.'

'Again? That has to be about the twelfth time today. Are you writing about some handsome young man you're smitten with or something?'

Her lips pressed together to hold back a discreet smile as she reached behind her back to hide the journal away somewhere. 'What a woman writes in her diary is private.'

'Ah. I see. So I'll never know?'

She shook her head and buried her face in her hand for a moment, as if the thought of me reading her private thoughts was humiliating.

'Fine. Shake a leg and hurry on down here.'

She closed the white lace curtains and disappeared into her room. Two minutes later, she stepped out the front door and met me on the porch. Instead of the red skirt she'd been wearing at the market, she wore my favourite light-blue cotton dress with a matching blue ribbon tied around her braided hair. She was quite a sight. No doubt I would be the proudest chap on the island if I had the honour of introducing her around town as my steady gal. All I needed was the right moment to ask. My palms started to sweat from the anticipation.

As we crossed the field, she glanced at me with a mischievous grin before she took off running. I chased her along the rows of glass panel greenhouses to the edge of their farm where she ducked into the forest. She disappeared for a moment but then a flash of blue cotton darted behind an arbutus tree. We used to always try to startle each other as children by popping out of unexpected places, and I was wise to her tricks, so I inched over the soft footing of pine needles without making a sound.

I lunged around the smooth cinnamon bark of the trunk she had her back pressed up against and said, 'Boo.'

She shrieked from the surprise, then wrinkled her nose. 'You smell like fish.' She giggled and ducked away.

She was used to me smelling like the farm or the sea, but since my intention was to impress her enough to convince her I was a worthy suitor, it probably would have been prudent to have washed up before coming over. I stretched my suspenders over my shoulders and let them hang at my hip to remove my smelly shirt, then tucked it into my waistband as I followed her down the dusty, tree-lined trail that led to the beach.

Determined with a plan that was unbeknownst to me, she headed straight over to where her rowboat was stowed upside down in the grass. I jogged to catch up and helped her flip it over. She lifted the bow and we dragged it together along the tiny pebbles towards the water. As I launched it she removed her black leather shoes and white ankle socks, then placed them on a log.

'Let's go, slow poke,' she said before she waded into the water and climbed over the edge of the boat.

'Where to?'

She beckoned me with the type of wave a circus ringleader might give before he pushed aside the canvas of the big top and invited you in with the promise of a spectacular extravaganza. 'It's a surprise. I want to show you something special.'

There wasn't too much about our craggy rock, forested island or the surrounding Pacific Northwest waters that I hadn't seen before, so I doubted I'd be awed, but I was happy to follow her wherever she wanted to lead. I untied my boot laces and rolled up my trousers to wade in after her.

She manoeuvred the oars with skill and turned us in the direction of the jetty, then glanced at my undershirt and pressed her lips together to hide the fact that she'd apparently admired my state of undress. I didn't mind her staring, nor did I see what the big deal was. She had seen me in only swim trunks before, but admittedly my upper body had filled out since then. She could gaze all she wanted, as far as I was concerned. But for the sake of modesty she glanced instead in the direction of the glacier-covered monolith of Mount Baker in the distance, then she offered a conversation to shift the focus, 'Do you remember the first time we ever went out in the rowboat?'

I nodded with a smile as I reminisced back to when we had been adventurous six year olds. We'd gotten it in our heads that we wanted to row to Africa to see the Saharan animals our teacher had taught us about in school. Chidori had sensibly packed sandwiches, I'd brought water in a canteen, and we'd taken turns rowing. Just before we reached Saturna Island, a fishing boat had spotted us and reeled us in.

'Whose ridiculous idea was that anyway?' she asked with a lightness to her voice that always made me feel at ease.

'Definitely yours,' I said. 'All of our misadventures were a product of a bee you got in your bonnet.'

'Oh, really?' She pointed at me accusingly. 'Whose impulsive idea was it to search the forest for the Swiss Family Robinson's tree house, which resulted in you falling into a patch of stinging nettles? And, whose idea was it to scour the rocks along the shore for pirate caves and treasures, which resulted in you breaking your arm?'

'Yeah? Well, whose idea was it to give me all her books about castaways and pirates?' I leaned over the edge of the boat and scooped a handful of water to splash at her in jest.

She chuckled and splashed me back with the oar before she leaned into her rowing. 'We might have made it to Africa if they hadn't stopped us.'

'Or if we hadn't run out of food and fresh water after the first hour.'

'True.'

As the boat glided across the gently ebbing water, I closed my eyes and let the happy memories of our youthful adventures flicker through my mind like a moving picture show. We'd undeniably had an ideal childhood – swimming in the ocean with otters, playing hide-and-seek in the twisty arbutus groves, climbing the highest peaks for a panoramic view of Active Pass and all of the Southern Gulf Islands, and lying on our backs in the sun-bathed pastures as the clouds drifted past.

Unfortunately, the threat of a broadening war reaching Canada and ruining our ideal setting was impossible to ignore. I wanted to believe we were safely hidden away and protected from the horrors of war by the isolation of our remote island paradise. I knew, though, that no place would be truly immune if the battles reached North American shores. And if I was called to duty, I'd be sent into the bowels of the fighting, regardless of whose shores the battle was on. Chidori observed the change in my mood and then gazed out at the water in a lamenting way, as if she had read my thoughts.

Once the rowboat neared the rocks of Georgeson Island, Chidori pulled the oars in and we floated serenely through shallow pools where the fish darted around beneath us. She dipped a net into the water to scoop through a flickering school of silver-sided fish. Once the net was full, she hoisted the haul into the boat.

'What are you up to?' I asked, curious about what the fish were for.

She winked as we skimmed along the southern coast of the uninhabited island until we reached the easternmost tip. Once we were ankle-deep near the shore, Chidori grabbed the net full of fish and gestured silently with her hand to invite me to join her. Then she pressed her finger to her lips to hush me.

I hopped out of the boat and dragged it up on the shore so it wouldn't float away and leave us stranded. Chidori hiked around the tip of the island and I followed. When we reached an area of tidal pools, she crouched beside a pile of boulders and dumped the fish into a collection of water that had been trapped by the receding ocean. I stepped forward on the sharp barnacles and dried seaweed to observe what she was doing.

Chidori hugged her legs into her chest and rested her cheek on her knee to watch a seal pup with its mother. The mother was injured. The right fin had been bitten by a whale or clipped by a ship. Her breathing was laboured and she didn't move when she caught our scent. The baby flopped into the tidal pool and attempted to catch the fish.

Chidori was notorious for saving injured or abandoned animals – ravens, racoons, deer, and whatever else she found in a sickly way. Once, when we were eight years old, she kidnapped the lamb her father had planned to slaughter for Easter dinner. She'd carried it all the way to our barn and made me promise to protect it with my life, which I did. That lamb grew up and lived to a ripe old age before it keeled over of natural causes in the field one day.

Knowing how much she cared about vulnerable creatures, I didn't have the heart to tell her, that even with her help, the seal pup probably wouldn't survive once the mother died. Maybe she already knew and felt compelled to do something even though it was ultimately futile. The pup barked happily and rolled around in the tidal pool for a good while before sliding back into the ocean.

'What do you think is going to happen with the war?' Chidori asked without looking at me.

I sighed and stared out over the water. 'I don't know. We're safe here, though.'

It was difficult to determine if she had heard the uncertainty in my tone, or if she had her own doubts, but she hugged her legs even tighter to her chest, as if bracing from the terrible possibilities of what could happen. The silence between us became heavy with the weight of the world's problems. I wished to travel back to a time when we were oblivious to all of the hardships and dangers in the world. A blissful naiveté. Sadly, once the innocence was gone, you couldn't get it back.

I needed the reassurance as much myself as she did, so I repeated, 'We're safe here.'

She nodded but it was obvious she wasn't entirely convinced. After another sigh she said, 'I was accepted to study at the University of British Columbia.' She glanced over to check my reaction.

After a second to let the news sink in, I said, 'That's fantastic. Congratulations.'

'Thank you,' she replied quietly, as if she still wasn't quite sure how she felt about it.

Honestly, my feelings were mixed too. I was very happy for her. But selfishly, I was also disappointed that it put a wrench in my plans for our future. It would mean her moving to Vancouver for each school year. 'When do you start?'

'I'm not going.'

'Oh? Why?'

She moved to sit on a log and smoothed her skirt over her knees. 'There's a possibility the university will be closed if all the young men are shipped away to fight in the war. The young women will be recruited to work in the factories or take over the service jobs for the absent men. And even if there are enough students left and the campus remains open, I don't know what I want to study anyway.'

'Anything you want. You were the strongest student in our graduating class. You're good at literally everything.'

'Not everything,' she protested modestly. 'But my broad interests are part of the problem. I'm intrigued by so many potential careers – medicine, teaching, music. I'm also drawn to law and astronomy and anthropology. But all of those career ideas seem lofty and trivial with a war raging.'

'They haven't shut down anything yet. Don't let what's happening in Europe stop you from living your life.'

'I would have felt reluctance even if it weren't for the war. I worry I will choose the wrong field of study and end up regretting it. I don't want to waste my time or my father's money on an education I'm not absolutely sure I want to pursue.'

'You don't have to choose a specialty right away. You could

take some general courses to start. Maybe one subject will interest you more than the others and it will become clear. At least attend long enough to give it a try and see how you take to it.'

She conceded with a shrug and then stood. 'It's too late now. The deadline to accept has expired.'

I frowned and shoved my hands in my pockets as I kicked at the dirt. 'What do your parents think of your decision?'

'My mother thought I should have accepted. My father didn't feel comfortable with me moving away to Vancouver anyway, so he's pleased that I took too long to decide.' Her eyes met mine. 'I could reapply next year. If the war has ended. What do you think?'

It was a trick question. I had learned over the years, sometimes the hard way, that when she asked what I thought she didn't actually want me to impose an opinion. She wanted validation that it was solely her choice to make. Fortunately, I knew her well enough to offer the correct answer. 'You are the smartest person I know. If you decide to attend university you will excel there. If you decide not to attend university, you will be successful in whatever you do. Do whatever makes you happy.'

She nodded with satisfaction at my reply, then walked silently back along the shore.

When we reached the spot where the rowboat teetered on the rocks, I tugged her hand to make her turn around to face me. 'Dance with me?'

Something enchanting glimmered in her expression as I slid my fingers up along the sides of her face. After a hesitation she nodded to accept the invitation and her hips pressed up against mine, which made my insides warm.

We swayed side to side in time with the rhythm of the waves and I traced my fingers along the gentle curve of her jaw.

'Would you like to know what my ulterior motives are?'

'It depends.' She tucked her chin away to hide her grin. 'How will I feel about them?'

'Well, let's find out.' I took a deep breath and simply asked, 'Would you care to be my date for the bonfire tonight?'

'Tonight? Oh, gosh.' She stepped back. 'Unfortunately, I can't tonight. Today would have been my grandfather's seventy-fifth birthday and my grandmother has planned a special dinner to honour him. I'm sorry. I didn't know you wanted to go to the bonfire.'

'I don't really want to go per se. I actually only wanted to spend time with you so I could ask you something.'

'Oh.' Her gaze rose to meet mine. 'We're together right now.'

I nodded to acknowledge that was true and danced with her some more to give myself time to rehearse the going-steady pitch that I had originally planned to deliver at the bonfire. The speech was too complicated anyway, so I just blurted out the main point. 'Would you like to go steady?'

'With whom?' she said, with the straightest expression humanly possible.

My heart flopped around in a confused panic like one of those silver-sided fish. 'Me.'

Her poker face broke and she buckled over in laughter. 'Oh my gosh. The fright in your eyes was precious. You got all nervous. It's sweet.' She gasped for air and clutched her chest before another round of merriment. 'Of course I knew that you meant you. Who else would it be? I don't know why I'm being silly. I'm nervous too. I'm sorry.' Her laughter simmered down to a chuckle. When her eyes met mine again she noticed the trepidation lingering in my expression, which is when she realized she still hadn't actually answered the question. 'Oh my goodness, Hayden. Yes, the answer is yes! Absolutely yes!' She clasped both my hands. 'I've been waiting for you to ask me that for a very long time. I'm sorry. I assumed you'd know my answer. It is yes.'

'Truly?'

'Truly. I would be honoured. Thank you for asking.'

I flung my arms around her and pulled her to my chest for a hug. 'That makes me very happy. Thank you.'

She tilted her head back so she could look into my eyes. 'It makes me happy too.'

My grin could not have been bigger if I'd tried. 'So, we're going steady?'

'Yes.' Her eyebrows rose as she stepped away from the embrace and extended her arm towards me. 'I think that means we get to hold hands wherever we go.'

I laced my fingers with hers and followed her over the rocks to step into the boat. 'I believe some people who go steady also kiss goodnight,' I said as I sat down and pulled the oars.

'Interesting.' She sat facing me and leaned back to relax as we rowed back to shore. 'How long had you been planning to ask me?'

'Gosh, a long time. I thought it best if I waited until after we graduated, though. And I was willing to wait even longer if you did decide to attend university. I didn't want to interfere with any ambitions you might have had. Why? How long have you been waiting on me to ask?'

Her cheeks blushed and she rolled her eyes slightly from the embarrassment of the truth 'A much longer time than you'd been planning, I can assure you of that.'

I chuckled. 'Well, in fairness, you have always been more advanced than me.'

'True.' She shoved my knee. 'In this case, I think I might have been about six years ahead of you.'

I shot her a jaunty wink. 'I might be slow to come around, but I guarantee I'm worth the wait.'

'Ha ha, let's hope so, Mr Modest. I guess only time will tell if you live up to that promise.' She stretched her legs out straight to extend them between my feet and under the bench I was seated on. 'I'm just grateful that when you finally did take an interest in the female persuasion it was me and not someone else who interested you.'

'You have always interested me, Chidori Setoguchi.'

She leaned forward and placed her palms on my thighs. 'And you, me, Hayden Pierce.'

The tide had changed while we were out, and the landing spot was jagged with barnacled rocks, so I hopped out and carried her like a bride to the sand. She slipped her shoes on as I pulled the boat in and turned it upside down on the logs. Neither one of us spoke but we beamed with excitement.

I held her hand to walk her home along the road. Over the crest of the hill a navy-coloured Ford four-door approached us. It was loaded down with four of the Bauer cousins. Rory sat in the back seat, smoking. Fitz slowed to a stop in the middle of the road and rolled down the window. 'Do you odd little lovebirds need a ride somewhere?'

'We're fine,' I said, and tucked Chidori close to my side.

'You know, you might be wise to be less publicly affectionate. Some folks don't think very highly of whites and Japs being amorous with each other.'

'No? Why's that, Fitzy?' I challenged.

Chidori's hand gripped mine as if she was trying to contain my temper for me.

Fitz sneered. 'Well, on account of us being at war. The Japs are helping the enemies now, ya know? British Columbia is a prime target for the Japanese Navy. It's just a matter of time before they try to move in and take over.'

'Yeah?' I said with a bite to my tone. 'Where'd ya hear that?'

'It's all over the newspapers, and people talk.'

'Interesting. Didn't you also read in the newspaper or hear people talk about how we're at war with Nazi Germany and Fascist Italy, or did you miss that part? Hitler's invading all sorts of countries and trying to take over the world. Remind me where exactly your family is from.' I tapped my chin, feigning deep thought. 'Berlin – I think I remember Rory saying that once. Geez, I never paid too much attention in geography class but isn't Berlin in Germany? You all lived there until you came here about ten years ago, isn't that right? You all still speak German, if I'm not mistaken. Golly, Chidori.' I turned to her and gasped exaggeratedly. 'What if we have Nazi spies living right here under our noses on Mayne Island?'

'Are you calling us traitors?' Fitz growled.

'Hayden, please stop,' Chidori whispered under her breath.

'I wouldn't assume you were Nazis just because you're German. The reason that I have formed a poor opinion of you has nothing to do with your nationality. It has everything to do with your personality.'

Rory flicked his cigarette out the window. He aimed it at me, but it hit Chidori in the neck. She yelped when it burned her. I turned to sock Rory in the mouth, but they sped off before I had a chance.

'Are you okay?' I brushed Chidori's braid to the side to examine the burn.

She closed her eyes, and her eyebrows cinched together tensely. Her breath became irregular, almost as if she was sobbing – only she wasn't crying. 'We can't date,' she blurted out with stunning abruptness, then hurried down the road.

I stood frozen in a speechless state for several seconds before rushing after her. 'Wait. What? Why are you saying that? Because of Rory?'

She stormed off in a tenacious silence that she had used to win arguments with me many times over the years, but this was too important to not talk about. When we reached the driveway to her family farm, I caught her elbow.

'Chi, please talk to me. You can't have a change of heart that tersely without explaining why. Not more than twenty minutes ago you said you would be honoured to go steady with me. What happened to that?'

'We got caught up in the privacy of the moment and our judgement was clouded. Maybe if we could live on a deserted island or adrift on a rowboat forever, just the two of us, everything would be fine. But the Bauers reminded me that we don't live in isolation.'

'I don't care what they think.'

'You heard Fitz. The Japanese Navy is threatening to attack us. What is the point in planning for the future if there might not be one?'

'We can't live our lives afraid. You've heard the radio announcements. They're asking everyone to keep calm and carry on – courage, cheerfulness, resolution.'

'Yes, but that's to bolster morale to defeat the Japanese. They think I'm the enemy. Do you not see that?'

'You're Canadian, Chi.'

'I look Japanese.' Her voice caught in her throat and it broke with the strain of conflicted emotion. 'What if you get called to duty and have to fight the Japanese?'

I inhaled deeply and rubbed the tension in my neck. 'I don't know.'

Her eyes cinched shut as she shook her head. 'I shouldn't have agreed to go steady. It was a mistake. I take it back.' She faced me, but her arms were still crossed protectively. 'Given the circumstances of what is going on with the war and the seriousness of our feelings for each other, I think it's best if we don't see each other any more.' Her hand flew up to cover her mouth in regret before she ran across the field towards her house.

All the air in my lungs shot out of me from the crushing weight of utter dismay.

Chapter 9

An elderly German soldier who was more civilian than military and had a fuzzy, baby-bird-like head stood guard outside the hospital ward. He asked Inga every day whether any of us was ready to be released to a prisoner-of-war camp. Usually she shook her head apologetically and we were each spared, but three weeks after I had arrived, Michel and two other RAF airmen were released to the German officers when they came by. Even though my feet were legitimately healing slowly because they were infected, Inga was regretfully not going to be able to tell the soldier I wasn't well enough to be transported to an internment camp forever. Even the fellow with the broken leg was sent away with Michel before his plaster was removed.

Inga was the only nurse who treated us with more than the basics of clinical care. The few times she wasn't that friendly were when German commanding officers came in to check on us. As soon as the officers left, she went back to being pleasant. She always removed my dressings slowly, somehow managed to act as if the wounds didn't smell worse than rotted halibut entrails, then applied the colloidal silver with gentle care. Maybe I reminded her of a brother or her sweetheart. Or she was a particularly compassionate human being. Whatever the reason, I appreciated that she always snuck me an extra roll with my dinner. And she sat on the edge of my cot until I fell back asleep after I'd had a nightmare, which was becoming a nightly occurrence.

Being confined to a hospital bed might have been good for healing the body. The boredom, however, was torturous for the mind. I had become accustomed to all types of physical hardship after I first enlisted, but none of my training had quite prepared me for mandatory bed rest.

Basic training, which I had completed at a battle drill camp in Vernon, British Columbia, was my first exposure to military combat skills like survival tips, map reading, target location and camouflage. The other recruits and I received a crash course on artillery and mortar shells, all of which we practised in the pouring rain and muck. Most fellas grumbled about the five-o'clock-in-the-morning fitness drills, but I was used to early mornings. The part I initially despised most about being in the service was being told what to do every minute of the day. I had never realized how much freedom I truly had until it was taken away by the Armed Forces. As we graduated to advanced training, fear of failure and eventually fear of dying because of a failure were also constant hardships with which we all dealt.

After I was transferred to Regina, before they let us anywhere near an airplane, Gordie, Frank and I were thrown into a mock ground cockpit, without even being told how to use the controls. I struggled to monitor the instruments at first, but I eventually got the hang of it.

A couple of recruits did wash out of Elementary Training in Regina, but Gordie, Frank and I all moved on to sixteen weeks of advanced Service Flying Training School in Saskatoon, Saskatchewan. Gordie never said anything else about me being sweet on someone who was Japanese-Canadian. In fact, because he was still sore about me socking him in the jaw at the dance, we didn't talk to each other at all unless directly related to training. The commanding officer must have sensed tension between us because he always paired us together.

Flying was a thrill, especially combat and night flying at different altitudes. I flew my first solo cross-country flight in poor weather. I couldn't see and had to nerve-rackingly rely on my instruments the entire time. After that flight, I wrote to Chidori and described the exhilarating experience of piloting an airplane. I didn't have anywhere to send the letter to, but I wanted to tell her all about the adventure anyway.

We all hated the lectures, which were dry navigational problems diagrammed on a blackboard like algebra. But we suffered through the tedium because we loved flying. Gordie's favourite part of training was formation flying. I preferred flying solo because when we practised with all twelve machines together in formation, I was always worried I was going to clip the wing of one of my buddies. Frank's favourite part of training was blowing stuff up. He was destructive in general and one time he wrecked an airplane when he overshot the landing on a short field landing exercise. He thought he was going to wash out for sure, but he just got hollered at.

Practising spins was my favourite thing to do. It made my heart pound like mad, but there was nothing better than the recovery. Harvards required specific care to fly and I did occasionally pull the stick too abruptly towards my stomach and cause a flick roll, but honestly that was a blast. Those types of mishaps helped remind me to be grateful to be alive.

Gordie was a natural with Morse code and aircraft and ship identification, so he helped Frank and me study the manual. That's what we were doing on the day of the accident.

We were seated on the grass, waiting for our training flight time, when Gordie read aloud, 'It is inadvisable to bail out above the area you just bombed.'

Frank and I burst out laughing.

'What?' Gordie asked.

'Well, no shit,' Frank said. 'That's a stupid lesson.'

The siren rang out so Gordie closed the manual, which I was glad for because talking about bailing out right before we were scheduled to practise flying in formation seemed a grim omen.

We all climbed into our yellow Harvard trainers and took off one at a time from the flare path. Once we were in formation we ran through a series of exercises, which we were getting fairly proficient at, but on the last manoeuvre I had to bank left to miss a flock of geese. My abrupt movement forced Frank out of formation. The fellow beside Frank, his name was Jed, clipped his wing. Airplane parts flew in every direction. I was ahead of the collision, but Gordie was behind them and had to pull up to avoid debris. Both Frank and Jed's damaged Harvards spewed smoke as they fell into nosedives.

Jed's canopy slid back, he climbed out of the cockpit and jumped. His parachute deployed, but Frank's canopy didn't open. To my horror, he was still in his airplane as it crashed nose first into the ground and exploded into a ball of fire in a wheat field.

It happened so fast that for a moment I wondered if it hadn't happened at all and my anxieties had imagined it, but then I saw the tower of smoke swirling up. The remaining airplanes circled around and headed back to the airstrip. My entire body trembled. 'Jesus. Jesus. Jesus,' I repeated to myself as I dropped the undercarriage and pancaked a hard landing. My hands, slick with sweat, slipped off the controls and I almost sent her into a ditch.

As soon as the airplane rolled to a stop, I slid the canopy and tumbled out of the cockpit. My legs shook so badly I slipped from the wing, then fell to my knees on the ground. My collar strangled me and I had to tear at my necktie to free up my throat enough to breathe. Gordie climbed out of his airplane right beside me. His face was as pale as if he'd powdered it with baking flour.

'Jesus,' I mumbled again and threw up.

Gordie leaned against his wing, too stunned to speak. We still hadn't moved from our shocked stupor when the prairie sky turned dusky grey and our instructor walked across the tarmac towards us. 'They want to see you boys upstairs,' he said grimly, and turned as if he expected us to follow him. I couldn't get up from my knees. My legs were blades of grass that weren't strong enough to hold my weight. Eventually, Gordie hoisted me up and made me lean on his shoulder to follow the rest of the crew from the flight to the operations office.

The room was stuffy and it started to spin as we filed in and stood in front of all the officers. Their huddled conversation was a dull drone, like insects on a warm evening, which ended in sudden synchronicity with our presence. I blinked repeatedly, but each time my eyelids closed, an image of Frank's airplane exploding into a fireball flashed through my mind like a photograph. I didn't want to relive it, so I stared up at the ceiling fan as it turned in a lazy way.

'Gentlemen, it ...' Our commanding officer spoke. His mouth moved, but my heartbeat pounding in my ears drowned out his words. The others nodded as if they could hear him. They all eventually saluted the row of officers and filed out of the room. I quickly saluted and spun around to follow them.

'Pierce.'

As I turned back, sweat ran down the side of my face and drenched my collar. 'Yes, sir.'

'It wasn't your fault, son. It was an accident.'

I glanced at him for a second, not reassured, and then left to return to the barracks.

Hours after the accident, I still sat rigid on my bunk, dazed. Gordie flipped through the pages of a pin-up magazine, without actually pausing long enough to enjoy any of the photos. 'What did they say at the meeting earlier?' I asked him.

'What do you mean? You were standing right next to me. You heard the same thing I heard.'

'I didn't hear squat.'

Gordie's forehead creased with deep wrinkles before he sat up to face me with his elbows rested on his knees.

'Jed parachuted out, right?' I asked.

'Yeah, but he hit the ground hard because we were at low altitude. He couldn't deploy the chute fully in time. He broke both his legs and probably a couple of vertebras in his back.'

'When can we see him?'

'We can't. He was transferred to the hospital in Regina.'

'And Frank?'

Gordie rubbed the back of his neck. 'Frank was killed. They said he tried to ditch, but something was wrong with the canopy. It didn't release. He couldn't get out.'

'Are you sure that's what they said?'

'Yeah. Positive.'

Frank's hat was on his cot, right where he had tossed it when we had hurried to change after breakfast. And I was agonizingly aware that inside his footlocker was a half-eaten tin of homemade cookies next to the photo of his wife and kid.

I leaned back on my pillow and stared up at the ceiling. 'It was my fault.'

'It was an accident,' Gordie said. 'They cleared you of responsibility.'

I ran my hands over my hair and would have pulled at chunks of it if it wasn't cut so damn short. 'That doesn't change my conscience. His kid is going to grow up not knowing his dad.'

'It was an accident, pal. Don't beat yourself up over it.'

Our flight instructor stepped into the barracks and gave us orders to suit up for a night flight. Gordie stood and waited for me.

'I can't fly any more,' I said, nauseous with guilt.

'You have to get back in the saddle.'

I shook my head and rolled over onto my side. Gordie ran off to follow orders. A minute later, footsteps approached my bunk. 'On your feet, Pierce!' our flight instructor barked in my ear. 'Get your ass in your aircraft before I beat it.'

'I can't.'

'Suit up or you'll be thrown in lockup.'

'No thank you, sir.'

'Get up! That's an order!'

I pulled my pillow over my ears and pressed my hands tightly against it to block out his hollering. It became quiet, as if he had left, so I opened my eyes. He was still standing over me but didn't seem as if he was going to yell. He motioned for me to take the pillow away from my ears.

'Mistakes happen, Pierce. And people die. It's a Goddamn war out there. If you let it, the war will beat you down. If you want to beat the war down, you need to get back in that airplane right now.'

Regretting all of the decisions that had brought me to that moment, I rolled over and mumbled, 'Put me in lockup. I can't fly.'

He grabbed the fabric of my shirt and jolted me to my feet. 'I know why you're really here, kid.'

I lifted my eyes to meet his gaze, wondering how he could have known.

'You think I don't notice you staring at that photo of your girl every spare chance you have? What happened to her is wrong, and you're right to fight. But if you quit now the war wins. Do you want the war to beat you?'

'No.'

'No, what?'

'No, sir. I don't want this war to beat me.'

His nose literally touched mine as he screamed, 'I can't hear you! Do you want this war to beat you?'

'No, sir!'

'I still can't hear you! Do. You. Want. This. War. To. Beat. You?'

'Sir! No, sir!'

'This war beats quitters. Are you a quitter?'

'No, sir!'

'I said, are you a Goddamn quitter?'

'Sir! No, sir! I'm not a Goddamn quitter!'

'Good.' He released the stranglehold he had on my collar and shoved my shoulder to make me walk. 'Get in your machine.'

24 August 1941

Dear Diary,

I am an utter fool. What have I done? I made a tragic mistake. Truly. I cried myself to sleep last night, dreadfully ill with guilt and remorse. I have been wishing to go steady with Hayden since I was old enough to experience romantic feelings. I waited patiently through all the years where the only things Hayden loved were baseball and his dog. Then, finally, he matured and to my luck began to see me as more than only a pal to chum around with and debate with. Then the day I had been eagerly waiting for finally arrived. And what idiocy did I commit in response to him declaring his affections? I turned him down! Actually, it's much worse than that. I giddily accepted at first and then with ridiculous fickleness I immediately changed my mind. Who does such a horridly selfish thing to another person's genuine and vulnerable heart? Oh, apparently I do.

What in the world was I thinking? Hayden must have felt as if that big old fir tree had landed on his chest and crushed his pride. The first impetuous thing I have ever done and it not surprisingly resulted in a terrible calamity. I had no idea I was capable of such a reckless betrayal, especially towards Hayden. I can't believe how poorly I overreacted to Rory and his cousins. Their opinion should not hold more weight than my own or Hayden's. How did I go from blissfully floating down the road at his side to frightfully declaring we shouldn't see each other any more? Why am I worried about something that hasn't even happened? The war hasn't reached our shores. Hayden hasn't been called to service. Our lives might never be impacted directly.

Hayden was right. I should have stayed calm and carried on. Instead, I panicked and forfeited straight away like a coward. I desperately regret that I've let anything come between Hayden and me. I need to figure out how to make amends. If I can. I don't even know where to begin to fix my rashness. If it can even be fixed. The damage to his trust might be irreparable.

But what if our worst fears do come true?

No, there is no point fretting about things that haven't happened. Stay positive. Be brave.

If Hayden is not in church today I will promptly go by his house to apologize.

Chi

Chapter 10

Sunday morning after Chidori informed me that she didn't think we should see each other any more, I was too miserable to get out of bed. Ma called me three times, but my body protested the idea of moving. My heart was broken into a hundred shards, like a stepped-on seashell.

Chidori was going to be at church. And it would be a torturous demoralization to sit through the entire service staring at her, knowing she didn't want to even give us a chance. Inconsolably dejected, I moaned and rolled over onto my side.

'Are you not well?' my mother asked from my bedroom door. She let my Border collie Patch in so he would lick my face.

I could barely muster the motivation to pull the sheet over my head. Patch jumped up on the mattress, which normally Ma wouldn't have allowed, but she knew his wiggling would force me to get up.

Ma sat on the edge of my bed and rubbed my back in the comforting way she used to when I was a young boy. 'What's wrong?'

'Nothing. I'm fine.' The truth was too painful to admit.

'Hayden, darling, I'm your mother.' She stood and pushed the drapes open to let the sunshine flood in through the window. 'I can tell something is bothering you.'

It became obvious she wasn't going to leave me be unless I told her, so I sat up with my back against the headboard. Patch rested his head on my lap and gazed up at me sympathetically with his one blue and one brown eye as I patted behind his ear. 'Chidori doesn't think we should spend time together any more.'

Mother's eyebrow twitched subtly. 'Well, surely that's for the best.'

Tension crept across my chest and up my neck as she picked my Sunday clothes out of the wardrobe. She banished Patch from my room and then laid my suit out on the foot of my bed. The idea that she was not only not bothered by the development, but in fact seemed pleased was insulting. Her insensitivity rubbed me the wrong way. 'There is nothing in the world I cherish more than my relationship with Chidori. How can not seeing each other be for the best?'

'It's just the way things are in these times of war. Japan has betrayed Canada. I know it's difficult, but it can't be helped. Get dressed, dear. We're leaving in fifteen minutes.'

'You think I shouldn't be friends with Chidori because she's Japanese-Canadian, but you don't mind that Pa works for Massey and her father. That's hypocritical, don't you think?'

She paused at the doorway, unfazed by my growing annoyance. 'You'll understand the difference when you get older.'

'I'm old enough. I know who I want to spend my time with.'

With an air of indifference, she pinned her cloche hat to her hair and said, 'You are at an age now where you should spend time with young women you could potentially have a future with. Marrying Chidori is certainly not an option.'

I swung my legs over the edge of the mattress to place my feet on the floor, then stood. 'Why not?'

'Don't play naive, Hayden. War is serious and Japan is our enemy now.'

'Only Japan? What about Germany and Italy? Joey's Italian-Canadian. Do you think it's for the best if I stop being friends with him too?'

'You're missing the point.'

'Am I? Or is everyone else missing the point?'

Ma held up her white-gloved palms to indicate she wasn't going to argue with me. 'All I'm saying is there are plenty of suitable woman for you to marry and have children with who are not Japanese.'

'Really? What makes them more suitable? Have they known me their entire lives and been right beside me for every important event that has ever happened? Will they laugh at my stupid sense of humour the way Chidori does? Did they earn awards for both music and academics like Chidori? Can they do everything from drive a tractor to bake an award-winning pie half as well as Chidori can? Are they beautiful enough to make everyone halt what they are doing when they walk into a room? Chidori is all those things and more. How could someone else possibly be more suitable simply because they aren't of Japanese heritage?'

Mother's eyelids dropped in a measured blink as she inhaled in an impatient way. 'I just want what is best for you.' She closed my door behind her when she left.

I knew what was best for me. My mother's opposition fuelled my determination to get dressed, go to church, and do whatever it took to change Chidori's mind. I wasn't going to quit.

Eating breakfast wasn't an option my stomach was comfortable with, which was fine since Ma rushed Rose and me out the door to Pop's Ford Model A. It felt as if the island had grown in diameter overnight. Although it was the longest ten-minute drive I had ever experienced, when we pulled into the parking lot of St Mary Magdalene's Church, I still wasn't sure what to say to Chidori. The Setoguchis stood near the front steps, proper and sophisticated. The sight of Chidori in a dark navy dress and beret, looking as sorrowful as if she were attending a funeral made me choke on my own spit when I tried to swallow. Before I stepped out of the car, she disappeared inside.

Not wanting to cause a scene in front of the entire congregation, I sat at the back of the church with Joey and my sister as the reverend spoke.

After the service everyone filed back outside. Chidori's family socialized near the parking lot, but she was nowhere in sight.

'Hey.' Joey stood beside me. 'Did you read this?' He handed

me the newspaper folded open to an article on page five written by a member of Parliament. 'This fella thinks Japanese Canadians should be stripped of their Canadian citizenship. He wants them sent back to Japan.'

'That makes no sense. Does he mean the ones who are Japanese nationals?'

'Nope.' Joey shook his head and talked around the tooth-pick propped in the side of his mouth. 'Everyone of Japanese race. The Canadian-born ones, too.'

'What? Why?' I scanned the strongly worded letter that incited bigotry.

Joey sat on a bench and squinted over at all the Japanese families from Mayne Island. 'The MP claims that even if they were born in Canada their loyalties could still be with their ancestral homeland. He alleges it's a threat to national security because they can spy for Japan.'

I finished the article. 'This is ridiculous. Are they really suggesting that someone like Chidori is a threat to national security? And pardon me for saying, but if anyone with family ties to an enemy country is suspect, then they should be writing about Italian families like yours too.'

His eyebrows angled together as he nodded pensively. 'They have arrested a few Italians and Germans back east for being politically involved in Fascism or Nazism or for allegedly spying.'

'Are they threatening to deport you to Italy?'

'No. You know sentiments against Japanese-Canadian industry has been brewing since long before the war. The government revoked and restricted fishing and logging licenses to the Japanese Canadians for years, just to stifle their earning potential. And it ain't no secret that white greenhouse growers around these parts would be happy to get rid of their Japanese-Canadian competitors.'

'They can't get rid of an entire group of people because they work hard and are successful at what they do.'

He shrugged, not sure what else to say.

I swore under my breath. 'Excuse me, Joey.' I walked over and handed the paper to Chidori's uncle. Because of Massey's political knowledge, business sensibility, and natural leadership qualities, he was well-respected in the Japanese-Canadian community – both on Mayne Island and in Vancouver. He'd surely have an opinion. 'Have you seen this?'

He nodded, but didn't speak. Not exactly the strong opinion I had anticipated.

'Chidori has never even set foot in Japan. The government can't make her move to Japan, can they?'

Massey made the same powerless shrug Joey had made. 'There's a war going on, Hayden. I imagine the government can do whatever it chooses.'

A panicked feeling swirled around in my stomach. 'That's not right. She's Canadian. This is her home.'

'There isn't anything we can do about it. The federal government invoked the War Measures Act.'

I shook my head, not following. 'I don't know what that means.'

Massey donned his fedora and coat, then explained, 'The War Measures Act transfers the powers of Parliament to the governor in Council. It allows them to make emergency orders in the name of national security, then pass them without consulting with or informing Parliament.'

'So a handful of politicians can do whatever they please?'

'Basically.' He scoffed. 'Also known as the Mackenzie King government's loophole to pass discriminatory policies and sell them to the masses as military strategy. Nobody will catch a clue until it's too late.'

'We have to say something.'

'If a judge can't stop them, neither can a citizen.'

'It's not right.'

He nodded to agree, but surprisingly wasn't hot under the collar about it the way I was.

'Are you coming, Hayden?' Pop called from across the parking lot as Ma and Rose climbed into the Model A.

I searched the crowd and spotted Chidori talking to Donna Mae near the garden. 'No. I'm going to walk,' I called back, distracted.

Massey took the newspaper from me and wandered over to show it to a group of the other Japanese residents. I weaved through the crowd and stood where Chidori couldn't avoid me. Her mother, who was dressed in a red suit and matching pillbox hat, bowed politely when she saw me, then gracefully walked away and slid into the front seat of their Cadillac. Her father and brothers were still talking with Massey and Mr Nagata, which gave me a moment with Chidori.

'Chidori, would it be all right if I spoke with you?'

She nodded, tears brimming in her eyes.

'Excuse us, Donna Mae.' I said before I guided Chidori by

the elbow to a spot near the roses where nobody could over-hear our conversation.

She spoke first. 'I am so incredibly sorry if I hurt you by changing my mind so abruptly. That certainly wasn't my intention.'

'Will you change it back?'

She covered her cheeks with her palms, pained by whatever multitude of thoughts were racing through her mind simultaneously. 'I'm so confused, Hayden. My opinion keeps tossing back and forth. I don't know the right thing to do. I was prepared to ... but then I ... have you read the article in the newspaper?'

'Yes, but it's only blustering. They can't treat you like the enemy. You're Canadian.'

'What if it happens? What if I am arrested and sent away to Japan? If you and I spend time together now and get even closer ...' She paused and glanced at me. 'There's no point.'

'Do you honestly believe that?'

'In my head, yes.' She tapped her temple and then placed her palm on her chest. 'In my heart, no.'

'Then listen to your heart.'

'But if I do that and we are torn apart by circumstances outside our control, it will be much worse.'

'We don't know that's going to happen. All we know for certain right now is that I want to be with you. If you want to be with me, too, then there is nothing else to worry about.'

'Gah.' She pressed the heels of her hands against the sides of her head with vice pressure. 'This is all so overwhelming. I need more time to think'

'No you don't. Listen to your heart. Either you want to be with me or you don't.'

'It's not that simple.' Her voice cracked and she obviously didn't want to start crying, so she spun to walk away. 'I need you to respect that I'm conflicted, Hayden. Please don't make this harder than it already is.'

I followed behind as she bee-lined towards the Cadillac. 'I know what I want. I'm not the one who's making it hard.'

She yanked the handle and swung the car door open. 'I'm sorry. I'm not trying to hurt you. I just need space to think. It's better to have no contact while I sort everything out,' she said in a restrained voice before she slid into the back seat and shut the door.

Her father and brothers walked up and got in the car. She glanced at me briefly through the window before they drove away. Her cheeks were streaked with tears and the sight crushed my chest.

Chapter 11

After Michel left the hospital, Inga seemed to feel sorry for me. She sat on Michel's cot and handed me some old English *Time* and *Reader's Digest* magazines.

'*Danke.*'

She nodded and held up a deck of cards. 'Rummy?'

'Sure. That would be swell.'

'Swell,' she imitated me and chuckled pleasantly as she dealt the cards.

I was about to lay an ace to meld with her run and end the round when the air-raid siren blared to indicate incoming artillery. We all glanced up at the plaster ceiling as if we could see through it to the skies above. Then, instinct took over and all of the able-bodied patients, myself included, dropped onto the floor and took cover under our cots. Two deep *whoom* sounds were followed by flashes of light and then deafening explosions shook the entire building, breaking glass and causing parts of the ceiling to fall. The nurses rushed to cover the immobile patients with sheets. Another bomb detonated with a shuddering blast and the nurses shielded the men with their own bodies to protect the most vulnerable as much as possible from falling dust and debris. The light fixtures swayed in the aftermath as the hum of flying machines faded into the distance.

The nurses deserved medals for honour and bravery. I wasn't convinced I possessed the moral fortitude and humanity required to selflessly risk harm to my own body to protect an enemy soldier who had fought against my brothers and fellow countrymen. Maybe I did have that type of compassion at one time, but if I did, I worried it had been extinguished somewhere along the way.

After the hospital personnel set everything in the dormitory right again and checked on the well-being of all the patients, Inga eventually returned to pick up our card game where we had left off. It was nice to have her company, but it made me miss Chidori so bad it smarted worse than the damn burns.

I couldn't recall the last time I had felt truly happy. Maybe on the day I graduated from flight training. They had lined us up on the tarmac in front of one of the airplanes and presented us each with the pin for our chests.

Immediately after the ceremony I had telephoned my parents to share my news.

'Hayden!' Mother shrieked when she answered the new telephone they'd just gotten installed at the house. 'Wait, why are you calling? Are you okay? What's the matter?'

'Nothing's wrong. I'm calling with good news. I received my wings today.'

'It sounds just like him, John,' she said away from the receiver.

'Yeah, that's how the telephone works,' Pop said with a

chuckle in the background. 'Talk to him. The time limit is going to run out.'

'That is wonderful news about you earning your wings. Congratulations. Can you still hear me?'

'Yes. Thanks. How's Rose?'

Ma inhaled heavily. 'Actually, she's been hospitalized again.'

'What do you mean again? This is the first I'm hearing about this.'

'Oh, yes, that's right. I forgot.' After a hesitation she reluctantly continued, 'We decided not to worry you with that news last month. It really isn't anything you should concern yourself with while you are busy training.'

I paused as I thought back to the last letter I'd received from Rose. She had seemed off somehow. Her sentences were short and the topics jumped all over the place. I assumed she wrote it in a rush. Maybe I should have sensed she was unwell. 'What's wrong with her?'

'Nothing's wrong with her. She just became too dependent on the nerve tonic the doctor had her taking for her grief. No need for you to concern yourself. They're taking fine care of her at the hospital and we are going over to Vancouver at the end of the week to stay with her when she's released. She's going to be fine.'

'Has there been any word on Earl?'

After a pause Ma said quietly, 'He's presumed dead. We haven't told Rosalyn, but she had already come to that conclusion on her own.' There was fidgeting with the telephone and then Pop came on the line.

I rubbed my face, trying to massage the tension away. 'I

have some leave time and I'd like to see everyone before they ship me overseas.'

'If we could we would make the journey to visit you in Saskatchewan, but it's not a good time to leave your sister. Would they let you take more than a week and come to Vancouver?'

All the other pilots had seen their wives or parents on leave at least once since enlisting. I was the only one who hadn't. 'I'll make a request. I don't see why it wouldn't be approved.'

'Great. Then we'll see you soon.'

The line clicked to indicate the time was about to run out. 'Kiss Rose for me, will ya?'

The call dropped and the line went dead. I looked down at the wings on my chest. I was proud of my accomplishment, but I prayed they weren't a one-way ticket overseas.

I travelled by train from Saskatoon to Vancouver for my leave. My family, Patch standing alongside, were waving fanatically from the station platform as we rolled in. If Chidori had been there with them the reunion would have been the most heart-warming moment of my life. Patch reached me first and bounded up into my arms, licking my face and squirming like a maniac. Rose, although she was pale and frail in appearance, ran to greet me too. Her spirits lifted as soon as she was able to hug me, and honestly, so did mine.

'Welcome home, brother,' she said quietly as we embraced.

I nearly reminded her it was only a temporary leave but decided against it so we could enjoy the time we had together without worrying about the inevitable future. My parents joined the family hug and both seemed very pleased and relieved to see a smile on Rose's face.

Pop carried my kit as we walked because Rose clung to my left arm as if she would never release me, and Ma had claimed my right hand to hold as we strolled. The boarding house they had rented so they could be close to Rose was very humble accommodations, bordering on rundown – a choice my mother wouldn't have accepted in the past; but money was tight and it was one of the few places that accepted the dog as well.

The lavatory was shared with the entire floor of renters, so while I washed up down the hall, my family prepared tea in the flat. Patch waited outside the bathroom door for me. Gosh, I had missed his loyalty and that goofy tongue-hanging-out face. I crouched and rested my forehead on his as I patted behind his ears. 'Sorry I had to leave you behind, pal.'

He hopped up to rest his paws on my shoulders and tilted his head to the side as if he wanted to understand. Fortunately, the past and the future were not something that occupied too much space in his thoughts. All he cared about was that in that exact moment I was home.

Rose poked her head out of the open flat door and smiled at Patch giving me a hug. 'Tea's ready.'

I stroked Patch's fur one more time and then we headed down the hall. It was a one-bedroom flat and an extra cot was set up by the window in the living room for Rose to use on the nights she stayed with them instead of going back to the nurse's dormitory – which sounded as if it might have been every night since she had taken time off from her shifts.

The couch was made up for me with a blanket and pillow. Pop was seated at the kitchen table and Ma was standing in front of the stove, pouring the tea. The radio played an upbeat big-band song in the background.

'Did you hear word about Chidori?' I asked as I sat across from my father at the table.

He shook his head and slid his glasses off. 'We haven't been home in nearly a month. I'm sure there is a letter there by now. We'll forward it to you as soon as we can.' He glanced over at Rose, who was seated in a chair and staring out the window in a daze. It was obvious why they hadn't wanted to leave her in the city alone.

'Rosalyn,' I said to catch her attention, but she didn't hear me. 'Rose,' I said louder.

The intrusion broke her from what appeared to be a disturbing daydream. 'Hmm? Yes?'

'Come sit with me, will ya? I want to know all about what's been going on around here since I've been gone.'

She nodded and forced a smile as she used tremendous effort to stand and move to sit beside me at the kitchen table. She rested her weak hand on mine. 'Why don't you tell us all about your adventures at basic training and flying school instead?'

Ma caught my gaze from across the room, pleading with me to only share stories that would cheer her up. I wouldn't have told my family about Frank's death anyway. I hadn't even mentioned it to Gordie since it happened. Luckily, I had plenty of other chummy tales that made my parents laugh. Rose even broke a genuine smile here and there. When

I heard myself share all the good times at once, it reminded me that the majority of my training had been a positive experience.

Over the course of the three days I was in Vancouver, Rose and I strolled in the park, competed head-to-head at chess in the atrium of the museum, baked an apple pie together, finished a puzzle she had left half-completed for weeks, and stayed up late into the evening sipping tea and swapping stories, as Ma played a mixture of jazz, country, and opera vinyl records on the record player that the landlady had let her borrow. I made a visit to City Hall to inquire about Chidori, but all they were able to do was give me a federal government agency address that I could write to, which I did. I had to use my Mayne Island address for the return post since I didn't actually know where I would be stationed yet. I knew the response from the government was going to be aggravatingly slow, if at all.

Rose's energy returned during my visit; she spent less time drifting away into her thoughts, and she even laughed when a Canada goose chased me unprovoked in Stanley Park and literally goosed me in the derrière. Rose's mood was so improved that Ma begged me to extend my leave. But my orders came in by telegraph and I needed to report back.

I nudged my elbow against Rose's arm as we sat next to each other on the platform bench, waiting for the train to arrive at the station. 'Please don't worry about me. Your worry doesn't make me any more or less safe. But it does make you unwell. And I worry when you are unwell.'

Tears gathered along the rims of her eyes and her thin

throat visibly gulped back the emotional heaviness she felt. 'I'm sorry.'

I extended my arm across her shoulders and pulled her closer to my side. 'Don't be sorry. Just be well.'

She nodded to promise she would try.

The train whistled its approach, so I hugged everyone, including Patch, and flung my kit over my shoulder. Ma's complexion was green-tinged, as if she was sick to her stomach. Pa smiled in a way that made it seem he was grateful to have at least gotten the time together we did. Regrettably, Rose's expression had fallen blank again.

Torn between guilt and duty, I reluctantly boarded. As the train pulled away, my parents waved. Patch barked. Rose turned and walked away, weeping. The despair of it all made me seriously question whether I was doing the right thing. I could only pray Chidori was faring better than Rosalyn. And the fearful realization that she might not be okay distressed me so much I decided to drown my worries with alcohol. Disappointingly, the strongest drink on the train's bar-cart menu was beer. According to the bartender, conversion of the distilleries to manufacture gun shell powder, synthetic rubber, aircraft de-icing fluid and disinfectant for soldiers' wounds had made alcohol for stiff drinks hard to come by. The beer wasn't strong enough to even begin to make me feel better.

The following week, Gordie and I and the rest of the green-horn pilots were put on a cross-country train. We spent two weeks in Halifax, Nova Scotia, and then shipped off over the stormy Atlantic to London, England. And just like that, a month later we found ourselves in the surreal position of flying very real Spitfires in the Mediterranean.

The soldier who had been placed in Michel's cot started to shake in a fit. Inga ran to his side and called for the doctor as white foam bubbled out of the soldier's mouth. Things like that happened so frequently, most of the other patients didn't even look up from their books or interrupt their card games.

After almost two months at the POW hospital, Inga placed a pile of second-hand civilian clothes and a pair of ratty boots on the foot of my cot. She removed my pilot wings from my tattered uniform and searched through the pockets. She found the photograph of Chidori behind the lining and gazed sympathetically at it. The letter from my father was folded in the hiding spot too. I hadn't opened it again since I read it the first time. I didn't have to. I knew the words by heart. Inga transferred the letter to the borrowed jacket, then dug a little deeper into my uniform and found the small pebble from Mayne Island. I had forgotten it was in my pocket. She handed me the wings, the stone, and the photo, then left so I could dress. The photograph of Chidori was slightly scorched, but she still gazed back as if she could see me – from wherever she was.

The guard asked Inga the question, and that day, she reluctantly nodded in my direction. The guard waved his gun to signal for me to get walking. Inga busied herself by folding sheets on a wheeled cart.

'Inga.'

She turned to face me, her eyes moist.

'*Danke.*'

She forced a smile. '*Bitte schön, Hayden.*' She glanced over at the soldier as if she expected to get in trouble. The guard didn't say anything to her, but he shoved me harder than necessary in the back with his gun to make me get moving. To where, I didn't know. I figured it wasn't going to be pleasant though.

7 September 1941

Dear Diary,

I am still very confused and my overwhelming fear continues to pile up with each radio report or newspaper article. Hayden has been very respectful about giving me space to contemplate my conflicting feelings. Although I am very certain about my devotion for him, my intense adoration almost makes it worse. The news reports on the war effort all confirm the government truly and appall-ingly is considering placing outrageous restrictions on Japanese Canadians, including notions as ludicrous as imprisonment, internment camps and deportation. How is violation of rights and forced detainment of citizens any different than the acts of Fascism or Nazism? It certainly isn't democratic. It is all very absurd and unfathomable that people born in Canada could be considered traitors. I am struggling to not take the unwarranted targeting personally.

My parents are more resolute about duty and accept that war leads to unprecedented circumstances that require everyone to make sacrifices to protect the country. They believe that if we need to prove our loyalty to Canada by enduring scrutiny, then so be it. But prison?

Although Uncle Massey diligently follows the news, he appears outwardly unaffected because he has always been the type to change the things within his power to amend and calmly accept the things outside his control. But the deep lines in his forehead as he stays up late into the night reading Tosh's law books give the impression that inwardly he is not quite as resigned.

I would prefer to simply ignore all of the politics and live in blissful denial with Hayden, but it is not realistic. Even if we pretend the war or prejudice towards Japanese Canadians does not exist, that naiveté does not make the troubles disappear. I truly do make the effort to follow the philosophy of hope for the best and plan for the worst. The problem is I'm afraid to hope for a beautiful, loving future with Hayden, knowing that it could very likely be taken from us with no warning or justification.

Hayden slipped me a letter at church today that professed his undying commitment to me. He wrote that he is willing to be patient, for as long as it takes. And he reminded me to never lose faith in him. I do admire him for his steadfast loyalty and I am saddened that he is being hurt so profoundly by something that is not his fault. I read the letter through three times during the sermon and then folded it up and slid it into my pocket, hoping that if it were out of sight I would stop mulling over the heartfelt words. I have it memorized by heart, though, so

I am preoccupied by it often, whether it is folded away or not. I dearly miss his companionship during this difficult time.

Hayden's sister is moving tomorrow to Vancouver to start her nursing job. Now that I have remembered that, I feel even worse for Hayden. The two people he confides in are his sister and me. Now he will have neither of us close by. For the very first time in my life the exercise of expressing myself in my journal feels futile.

Chi

Chapter 12

My sister was scheduled to leave Mayne Island on the *Princess Mary* steamship to start her nursing job in Vancouver. Because of gasoline restrictions, we left the truck at home and walked with the pony and cart that we had loaded up to carry her luggage to the dock. Our parents were already in town for an Active Pass Growers' Association meeting and met us at the ship. I hadn't anticipated it would be as difficult to say goodbye to Rosalyn as it turned out to be. Maybe because I was already in a rotten mood over the increasingly alarming articles in the newspapers, which Chidori would have certainly read. She was probably terrified by the talk of detainment and deportation. The farewell for Rosalyn was made even more emotional because Chidori and her brothers happened to be at the dock to deliver their shipment of tomatoes to the steamer. And to top it all off, it didn't help that my mother was nearly inconsolable.

As I hauled Rose's suitcase and a trunk of her belongings up the gangway, Chidori rushed up the dock and hugged my sister to wish her well. I stepped back off the ship onto the dock and Chidori caught my hand, squeezing it briefly to acknowledge that she knew I needed to be consoled. I wanted to hold onto her longer, but after she quickly thanked me for the letter I had given her at church, she released her grasp and rushed to go help her brothers load the last of the crates. Tosh and Kenji went about their business professionally as usual, but their demeanour was not jovial like normal. They were hurried and on edge, as if they felt unwelcome in their own home town.

Rose knew I had been taking everything hard, and when the ship's final boarding whistle blew, she cradled my face between her palms. 'I can feel it in my soul that everything between you and Chidori is going to work out just fine, dear brother. Just be patient. And don't give up hope.' She leaned in to kiss my cheek. 'I love you. And I'll only be a boat ride away.'

'I love you, too. Good luck at your new job.'

She winked and then quickly hugged my parents once more before running up the gangway. Her hair scarf blew in the wind as she waved from the deck and blew us a kiss.

After the ship had steamed out into Active Pass, I glanced over at Chidori again. She had been watching me from up by the road and seemed torn, as if it was difficult to leave when she knew I was so sad. After a steeling breath, she lifted her hand to wave goodbye, then climbed into the truck with her brothers and drove away.

The next time I saw Chidori was at a fundraiser for the Red Cross held at the Agricultural Hall. All of the farmers and artisans were set up to sell their goods and donate their profits to support the troops overseas. It was busy because folks from all the other Gulf Islands had come over on the steamship to Mayne just for the sale.

Joey and I had taken the ferry to Victoria the week before to watch a flick at the movie theatre, and while I was there, I bought Chidori a clip for her hair. I didn't know much about things like that, but the sales lady assured me the enamelled butterfly design was fashionable. She wrapped it in a small blue box and tied it with a white ribbon.

After the fundraiser I ran to catch up with Chidori as she cut across the road to walk home. I extended my arm to hand her the box, but she didn't take it from me.

'I shouldn't accept a gift. Thank you anyway, Hayden.'

'I insist.'

She sighed and stopped walking. The late fall air currents that gusted off the ocean were brisk, and she was wearing only a plaid wool skirt and cardigan sweater over her white blouse, so I removed my button-up jacket and draped it over her shoulders. She clutched the lapels and hugged the fabric around her thin frame as she watched me open the box and slide the clip into her hair. 'I miss you. So much that I can't eat or sleep.'

She clenched her eyes shut and nodded, as if perhaps she missed me just as much.

'Music doesn't make me want to dance any more. Sunshine doesn't warm my skin any more. Books can't spur my imagination any more.'

'Hayden, I—'

I held both her hands and interrupted before she could protest. 'I understand the gravity of what is being written in the newspapers, but I still have hope that the threats are nothing more than the rants of loud-mouth, bigoted bullies. I know you are worried, and we don't have to go steady if you don't want to, but can we please just go back to the way things were? I don't want to live without you. I can't.'

Her silence did not give the impression that she had nothing to say — the opposite in fact.

'You don't have to decide anything right now.' I clutched her hands to my chest. 'But would it be all right if I at least walked you home?'

'Thank you for the hair clip but it's better if you don't walk me home.' Her fingers slipped away from mine, then she dropped her gaze to the ground and picked up a pace to hurry away from me.

'Is it really that easy for you to turn off your feelings for me?' I hollered down the road after her.

'Easy?' She spun to face me and raised her voice in both volume and pitch. 'This is not easy for me. It feels like my lungs have no air, my veins have no blood, and my heart has no reason to beat.'

After a moment to absorb the impact of her words I asked, 'Then why are you still avoiding me?'

'People want us to stay apart. It's better if we do it ourselves now rather than have someone else do it to us later, don't you think?'

'No. I don't want to give up without even trying.'

She glanced up at the sky, perhaps debating whether she wanted to continue the conversation or not. After a heavy pause she said, 'If you and Kenji both applied for the same job at the lumber mill, who do you think would get the position?'

'Both of us. They're short-handed. What does that have to do with anything?'

She shook her head, frustrated that I was missing the point. 'If there was only one spot, you would get it.'

'You don't know that. We'd both have an equal shot. And if I did get it, it would be because I work hard. It's not as if things are just handed to me undeserved.'

'I didn't say you don't work hard or that you don't deserve the things you have achieved, but let's say, for example, if they had to lay off only one of you, who would be let go? If there was an opportunity to be promoted to supervisor, and all other things were equal, who would move up the ladder?'

'Depends which one of us is better at the job.'

'No, in the scenario you're both equally good at the job but one of you is Japanese-Canadian and one is not. The answer is you, Hayden. Always you. And that's not fair. Kenji works hard, too. He's talented. And he'd have to perform much better than you to even be considered. I'm not saying it's your fault that things are that way, but it will be you that has the advantage. Because you look like all of the other men in positions of power and influence.'

'Okay, maybe in some situations that's true, but what does that have to do with you and me?'

'The world sees you as an "us" and sees me as a "them". They don't see us as equals.'

'But we are equal. Don't tell me you're going to cave into believing that we aren't.'

'I don't believe it. The people in power believe it — the people who hire, make decisions, and make laws.'

'Since when have you been the type of person who walks away from an injustice without fighting for what's right? Why are you giving up before we even try?'

A frustrated flush flared across her cheeks. 'There is a difference between choosing not to fight an adversary that can't be beaten and giving up. Even if they don't specifically deport me or throw my family and me in jail. People. Won't. Accept. Us,' she articulated slowly to drive it into my thick skull. 'We can't win.'

The crease between my eyebrows deepened to hear her talk that way. 'We can. If we fight together.' I stepped in close and cradled her face in my palms. 'I don't care what other people think. It doesn't matter.'

'It does matter if the government passes a law to take me away.' Emotion rose in her voice. 'I don't want you to get hurt, and I certainly don't want to be the reason that you get hurt.'

'You shutting me out of your life hurts infinitely more than anything they could ever do to me.'

She frowned and her eyes seemed to turn an even darker brown. 'I'm sorry.'

'Don't be sorry, just let me back in. I don't want to go through even one more day without you in it.'

She stared down at her shoes. 'Why me? There are at least a half-dozen other girls on the island you could spend your time with.'

'What would even possess you to ask that question? They aren't you. They don't get out of the car to help tree frogs cross the road. They don't teach all six of the Morgan kids to play violin, even though their father can't afford to pay for lessons. Their laughs don't sound like music. And they don't know me better than anyone else on earth.'

'You could learn to have feelings for someone more like you,' she said softly, almost as if she could barely force herself to utter it.

'I don't want to.' I wrapped my hands around hers. 'But if you can honestly say that you don't share my feelings, then I will accept that. Tell me you don't care about me and I will walk away right now.'

Her eyelids lowered in a slow, tear-filled blink. 'I can't do that, Hayden. You know I care immeasurably for you.'

'Good.' I ran my finger along her cheek. 'Because if your feelings for me are as strong as my feelings for you, we can't be torn apart, no matter what happens.'

She lifted her head and met my gaze. 'How can you be so sure?'

'What did you say that time when you told me why you love going to church? Do you remember?'

Her chest rose with a deep breath before she sighed. 'I said God heals me. He forgives me for my faults and inspires me to be a better person.'

I rested my forehead on hers. 'When I'm with you, I feel

the way you feel when you're with God. That's how I'm sure.'

Her eyes brightened with a glimpse of hopefulness.

I pressed my lips to her ear and whispered, 'Give in?'

After a long hesitation, she surrendered and nodded.

My knees nearly buckled in relief. 'Thank you.'

Chapter 13

The German soldiers forced me to walk twelve hours to a train station in boots that were one size too big. Thoughts of escaping entered my mind whenever we passed a forested area, but even if I were able to slip away without getting shot, my feet were still not one hundred percent healed. They'd eventually catch me and definitely shoot me.

I couldn't say how long the train ride took because I slept. Well, I slept until I had a nightmare about Rosalyn. I was in her room trying to convince her that Earl was still alive but had been taken prisoner in a camp that didn't send out the letters and that's why she hadn't heard from him. She refused to believe me and claimed she had nothing left to live for. I tried to stop her, but I couldn't reach her. Every time I lunged closer, the bed slid farther away from me and snatched her away into darkness. I watched her become engulfed and then sucked down into the flames of hell, which startled me awake.

The soldiers who guarded me on the train gawked with odd expressions, as if I had shouted out. Obviously I had. They said something stern sounding in German to each other, then went back to playing cards. I couldn't sleep after that, so the rest of the three-train journey was torturously long. It would have been less arduous if Gordie had been there for companionship.

I had grown accustomed to going through everything with Gordie, good and bad – travelling through foreign cities, fighting in air-battle victories, and coping with the downsides of war. When he and I had first arrived in Italy we mostly patrolled over the Nile and didn't see much action until the Allies invaded Sicily. Our flying days, which had initially been peaceful, bordering on boring, switched abruptly to daily life-or-death mêlées. After a heavy dogfight one afternoon, Gordie and I sat in the shade under an olive tree near the mess hall. We were both feeling down because we'd lost one pilot when his Spitfire had collided with a Messerschmitt.

I threw stones at a tree stump. 'I'm sort of getting used to shooting down the enemy, because if I don't shoot them down they'll kill me, but I can't get used to losing one of our own.'

'Yeah.' Gordie rolled his sleeves up and rested his head back against the tree trunk. 'Thomas sat with me this morning at breakfast and told me a joke right before we went up. I can't erase his stupid laughing face outta my mind.' Gordie also threw stones at the same stump I was aiming at. 'They already cleaned out his kit from the dorm. His towel was still wet from his morning shower.'

That was one of the many disconcerting things about death. The person was gone but evidence of their existence still remained. And one thing the war had plenty of was disconcerting death. 'I hope I don't go down. That might sound selfish, but I sure as hell don't want to die.'

'Nobody does, except maybe those crazy Japs.' Gordie glanced at me as he pressed a toothpick between his lips. 'No offence to your girl. I meant those suicidal kamikaze pilots we've been hearing about.'

I nodded to acknowledge his intent and pulled up clumps of grass.

'Churchill said on the radio that we are in the presence of a crime without a name and that scores of thousands have been executed in cold blood. Do you think it's true that Hitler's army is murdering all those Jews?'

I nodded again since I had already witnessed the mistreatment of tens of thousands of innocent people by their own government. There was no doubt in my mind that a dictator could be capable of worse evils. 'I heard it's closer to a million people.'

'It can't be a million.' Gordie thought about it for a spell and then shook his head in disbelief. 'There ain't no way to logistically exterminate that many people. The reports must be false. I'll believe it when I see it.'

I tossed more stones as I thought about everything that had already happened on Canadian soil. I slipped the photo of Chidori out of the lining of my serge and stared at it.

Gordie threw an olive at my boot to get my attention. 'Look, I know we didn't exactly get off on the right foot, but we're in this mess together and I've always got your back.' He extended his arm out. 'You can count on that.'

I leaned over and shook his hand. 'Yeah. I've got your back, too.'

He nodded and we both sat quietly, comforted by the

comradery. After a good while, he said, 'You know, when you two have a kid, I bet it will look like your girl, but have hair like yours. Could you imagine a Japanese person with blond hair?'

I shrugged. 'I don't care how they look. I just want to find her and have a family with her one day.'

The post bell rang. I'd been especially homesick and longing to receive a letter, so I got to my feet and slid the photo back into my chest pocket. Gordie stood and stretched his arms above his head. 'I want a boy who looks like me and a girl who looks like my wife.'

'Let's just hope you don't get a girl who looks like you,' I joked and shuddered in mock horror.

'Yeah, let's hope.' He laughed and joined me to walk back to the barracks to read our mail.

The prisoner transport train stopped at the final destination of a whistle-stop Hungarian town. I stepped onto the platform, handcuffed and nauseously apprehensive of what came next.

As it turned out we hadn't arrived at the POW camp yet, and the guards from the train didn't speak enough English to ask them when I would be transported there or what this stop was for. They escorted me to a stone building blackened with soot. It had served as a blacksmith's shop and stable at some point in its long history. The Nazis were using it as a detention cooler for prisoners and the horse stalls, which were already fitted with iron bars, served as makeshift cells.

The commanding officer was a large, fearsome man in a button-strained uniform who tied my ankles to a chair and demanded in accented English that I divulge information about my sorties and the personnel in charge. I was trained not to say anything other than my name and rank so I just sat there.

'Something terrible happened to your sister?' he asked casually after it had turned to night outside.

That got my full attention.

I lifted my chin to meet his glare, not sure how he knew about Rosalyn. Maybe I had been talking in my sleep in front of the guards on the train, or they had rummaged through my pocket and read the letter from my father.

He methodically cracked his knuckles as he paced back and forth in front of me. 'A shame, your sister. Could have been prevented, no?'

I refused to respond, but my fingernails carved into the wood seat of the folding chair.

He smirked slightly and lit a cigarette before he continued, 'A letter of such news must make pain, yes?' He inhaled the smoke slowly, then blew it in my face. 'Your family will receive news you are my prisoner. They will feel suffering too, no?'

I scowled at him without blinking.

'You feel blame you weren't there to save your sister, yes?'

'Go to hell!' I shouted as I lunged towards him. My ankles were bound to the chair, so the best I could manage was to dig my fingers into the flesh of his neck, strangling him. The cigarette dropped out of the side of his mouth as he choked for air. His hands swiped at my arms ineffectively. I was about to rip his face off when the other two soldiers grabbed my clothes and yanked me back.

I was thrown with the still-attached chair against the wall, then they proceeded to punch me until I stopped struggling, coughed out blood, and collapsed. The CO tried again to goad me with snide remarks about Rose, but I already regretted my outburst. It was idiotic to give him a reason to kill me. He didn't deserve the satisfaction. In return for my silence, they resumed the beating until they exhausted themselves. I lay on the cobblestone of the stable ground, bleeding, while the English-speaking officer went out, probably to stuff his ugly face. Death would have been less painful and possibly preferable if it weren't for how my loved ones would receive the news.

Several hours passed as I slipped in and out of consciousness. When the officer finally returned, he righted my chair, sat down across from me, loosened his belt and asked me more questions. I didn't answer, so he got fed up and ordered them to beat me again. I was lucky they didn't shoot me, which isn't the same as being lucky to be alive. Inga would have been aghast to see my condition after all the work she had done to put me back together the first time.

Blood poured profusely from a cut above my eye, so they cut my ankles free from the chair and threw me in the horse-stall cell. I crawled onto the burlap-and-straw mattress to curl up on my side, then watched the blood from my nose create a stain that spread across the fabric. The barred window near the ceiling allowed for air but didn't lessen the smell of horse manure. It reminded me of the time I had slept in our barn back home. Rosalyn had a sick foal and refused to leave its side. Mother had asked me to convince Rose to come inside the house, but she refused to abandon the horse while it was in pain. The only thing I could do was stay by her side the whole night as the foal died. Maybe Gordie was right when he said it wouldn't have made a difference if I had been home and had a chance to talk to Rose. If she had her mind already made up, there was probably no changing it. But I sure wish I could have had the chance to try.

Ten days passed and the guards never let me out of the Hungarian horse-stall jail cell, not even to stretch my legs. And they rarely emptied the feed bucket that I had to use as a chamber pot. There were no other prisoners, only me. I was fed once a day, usually a broth that had no flavour. I wasn't given anything to read or write with, which did something terrible to my mind. And my eyebrow needed stitches. They didn't provide medical care, so the wound kept reopening.

Once the bruising along my ribs became less painful, I performed push-ups and sit-ups on the stall floor, hoping to stay strong and alert. Unfortunately, the exercise only made me feel more caged and trapped. I attempted to sing and whistle to pass the time, but with only one glass of tepid, dirty water a day, I couldn't spare the saliva. I tapped out a swing beat on the bars for hours at a time, but it got old after a while. I told jokes to myself like a mad person, and when I started to laugh hysterically at the punchlines, I knew I was in trouble.

The sun angled in the barred window near the ceiling and created different patterns on the wall throughout the day. I was somewhat comforted by the thought that the same sun shone on Mayne Island. I convinced myself the geometric designs on the cinder block were replicas of ones I'd see if I were at home with Chidori in her music solarium. If I concentrated with tremendous effort I could almost hear her play the violin. I hummed along to the tune and imagined running my finger along the contour of her face.

Two more weeks passed, according to the scratches I'd dug into the wood wall with the handle of my spoon. Then two different soldiers showed up. 'Get up,' the dark-haired one said in accented English.

I hopped up off the bed, actually excited they were there to take me away. I shouldn't have been, though, because it only got worse.

14 October 1941

Dear Diary,

Hayden was correct – spectacularly correct. Having him in my life again over this last while has been a gift that I am so grateful for, given the terrible stress that otherwise hangs heavy in our house. Hayden is the only thing that truly brings joy to my heart during these harrowing times. Whenever I need to forget about my worries, I focus on the pleasures of being close to him. Tosh and Kenji have grown quite tired of my constant sprightly singing as I tend to the poinsettia seedlings in the greenhouses. And after Hayden has visited or left a lovely note or flowers on the porch, I have to resist the urge to skip merrily as I travel to visit each of my music students at their homes. When the road is empty, I do allow myself a few jolly sashays.

Despite all of the threatening newspaper articles that loom in our minds, and the fact that I had to officially register and received an identification card to confirm that I am in their eyes an enemy alien, our lives to this point have essentially continued on business as usual. Hayden wakes well before the sun to tend to the family's horses, chickens and goats, then works at the lumber mill from six o'clock in the morning until three o'clock in the after-noon. After work, he helps his father with the other farm chores that need to be done. Although he is very busy, he still finds time to drop by my house every evening after supper and we stroll into town, sometimes meeting up with Joey and Donna Mae or sometimes just the two of us share a milkshake at the Springwater Lodge. Last weekend the four of us got together at Donna Mae's to play The Landlord's Game. Joey bought up all the properties and railroads, so we each ended up giving him all our play money by the end, but still it was an entertaining way to pass a rainy afternoon. This Friday night we all took the ship to watch a film in Victoria. What a hoot that was. Joey and Donna Mae have a predictable habit of sparking a theatrical quarrel with each other over the smallest thing, one of them storms off in a huff, they eventually make up, and then they spend the rest of the evening steaming up the windows in the back seat of Joey's father's Buick Century.

Hayden and I do not quarrel or spend time in the back seat of a car. We haven't even shared a goodnight kiss yet. I know it is not because Hayden doesn't want to; I see the desire cross his expression every time we part. I have surmised that he reluctantly pulls himself away because nothing has changed in the war news reports and our future is still anxiously uncertain, so he is afraid to spook me. But since there are so very few bright spots in my life besides Hayden, I have decided to stop holding back and instead jump in with both feet to make the most of whatever time together we are granted. I plan to initiate a romantic gesture that will leave no doubt in his mind how a goodnight kiss would be received. But first, I need to learn how to kiss. There must be a book for that.

Truthfully, my moods waver back and forth indecisively. Sometimes when we are surrounded by other young people who are laughing and carrying on in rambunctious youthfulness I almost forget about the war, but then I turn on the radio, or open a newspaper, or hear my father and Uncle Massey talk in hushed voices in the parlour. I can't make out everything they say but the tone is always grave, and when Tosh joins them, his frustration and urgency is audible.

Mother can sense the tension too. Although she never speaks of her worries, she sews when her mind is heavy with concerns. Needless to say, we all have lovely new outfits fashioned from repurposed fabric for church on Sunday. If circumstances don't improve soon she will have to open a rationed fabric and notions tailor shop as an outlet for all of her nervous energy.

Grandmother has always been emotionally stoic and enduring by nature. Obaasan assumes that seemingly unbearable injustice will unavoidably occur as a natural part of any person's life. Rather than fear the turbulent times she believes we need simply remind ourselves that we are far more resilient than we think and powerful enough to survive the worst imaginable evils with dignity. I can appreciate that type of strength, but I am not sure how to conjure it.

Kenji is more like Hayden, in terms of optimism. Kenji is not like Hayden in terms of quick temper. I'm not sure Kenji has a temper at all. The most annoyed I have ever seen him be is when his teammates were not putting forward their best effort in a baseball game. He is genuinely not concerned about any of the news that is only a rumour at this point. He says he will cope with whatever happens when and if it happens. His motto is that worrying before-hand only robs you of today's pleasures. However, examples of prejudice and bigotry are becoming increasingly more commonplace in Vancouver and Victoria. Some are quite disturbing, even Kenji cannot deny that.

I aspire to one day be as calm in the face of adversity as Kenji, but until such time I will at least adopt the optimistic attitude that he and Hayden share. None of the threatening rumours have come true. I pray they never do. But even in the event things change in the future, there is nothing we can do to stop the war, so why not *enjoy the here and now? Speaking of which, I have to go. I'm about to surprise Hayden with a romantic gesture that is designed with no other purpose than to bring a smile to his face.*

Chi

Chapter 14

Patch bounded with excitement across the freshly tilled soil to let me know I had a welcome visitor. Chidori walked across the potato field towards me, wearing her yellow wool coat that I had always been fond of. The other girls at our school had worn brown, grey, or navy overcoats. Chidori always stood out in the crowd like a ray of sunshine. Her steps were buoyant and a basket swung from the bend in her elbow as if she could hear music in her head. I turned the tractor engine off and hopped off the seat. 'Afternoon, Miss.' I tipped my Ivy cap.

'Good afternoon, Mr Pierce.' She patted Patch's head and then folded over the linen cloth in her basket to offer me a cookie. 'I baked these and thought you might be interested in a snack. Oatmeal raisin.'

'Mmm.' They were still warm from the oven and especially appreciated since my mother hadn't made any baked treats for quite some time due to rations on baking supplies. Chidori's family had an entire storage barn of staple dry goods, so they weren't as low on essentials as the rest of us. 'Thank you.' I reached for a second one before I'd even bitten into the first. 'It's a nice surprise to see you. I thought you tutored that bratty little Osborne kid on Tuesdays.'

'He came down with the mumps, so I had some extra time.'

'Is it wrong of me to be grateful for his misfortune?' I stole a third cookie.

'Yes, it is wrong. And he's not a brat.'

I shrugged to disagree. 'He's always running wild in town, being sassy to his elders. Seems to me he could use a good scolding to teach him some manners.'

'Well, his mother died from tuberculosis, and his father works out of province on the railroad. His grandmother, who is in frail health, cares for him by herself. I don't believe he needs scolding. He responds very well when someone with patience simply takes the time to supervise and guide him.'

'Oh.' I finished chewing. 'I didn't know about his family situation. But I'm still glad he got stricken with the mumps. These cookies are delicious.' I reached to take a fourth, but she slapped my hand and swung her body around to pull the basket away from me. I tickled behind her ear, making her giggle.

'Quit it. You're going to ruin your dinner.' She whirled around again in an attempt to keep the basket away from me, but I lunged from behind and bear-hugged her so she couldn't move.

'Why'd you bring a whole basket full if you didn't want me to eat all of them?'

'They were supposed to be for your entire family.' She stopped squirming and her body relaxed into my hug with her back nestled against my chest.

Not wanting to ruin the moment of closeness she was allowing me, I aborted the mission to swipe another cookie and cinched my arms more snugly around her. 'Is baking cookies and hand-delivering them a gesture a friend would make, or is that something more reserved for someone you're enamoured with?'

She placed her palm on my forearm and then ran her hand across my coat sleeve in a tender touch. 'Both.'

'Hmm.'

She stretched to place the cookie basket on the tractor seat and slid her hand into the pocket of her overcoat. 'This came for me in the post.' She passed me an opened envelope from the University of British Columbia. 'It's from the dean.'

I unfolded the paper and read the letter. He had written to express his disappointment that she had not responded to the offer for admission. She was the top student who had applied and he was eager to have such a strong scholar study with them. He asked her to reconsider for the following fall term, and he offered a scholarship to pay her tuition for every year of her entire degree. 'Holy smokes. Congratulations. This is something to be very proud of.'

'Thank you.'

'Are you going to take the offer?'

She hesitated before she said, 'We will have to wait and see what happens with the war first.'

'I'm sure it will be over by next year. The scholarship is a once-in-a-lifetime opportunity.'

'If I accept, won't you miss me while school is in session?'

'I could find a job and move to Vancouver too.'

'I wouldn't want you to uproot everything for me.'

'Why not? Mayne Island will always be here to come back to.'

She kicked at the dirt with her toe as she considered it. 'I don't want to tear you away from home. Maybe we could visit each other on weekends. And I'll be home for holidays and the summer break.'

'I am happy to do whatever works. We'll figure it out.' I pointed over her shoulder at the portion of my family's property that overlooked the valley. 'You see that ridge?'

She nodded.

'My father plans to give me the property my grandfather's old homestead cabin is on for my birthday. I've been saving all my pay-cheques from the mill to build a house that has at least five bedrooms. It will probably take me three or four years to finish it, same amount of time it would take you to finish your university degree.'

'That's a large house for one person.'

'Well, yes, but I'm hoping I'll be married by then to a fine, intelligent woman who has a career as a teacher or a lawyer or an astronomer or something. Then maybe she and I will fill all those rooms with little ones. She'll teach them all about music and literature. I'll teach them about sports – that's all I'll teach them because my wife will be better than me at everything else.'

Chidori laughed. 'I guarantee your wife will be better at sports than you too.'

'Ha ha. You're comical. You know I'm an ace on the baseball diamond.' I moved to whisper in her ear, 'I have a dream that this fine woman and I – and Patch – will live in that house happily ever after. What do you think of my dreams for the future?'

She snorted, amused. 'Five bedrooms? Your future wife would be pregnant for years!'

Her tone made me chuckle. 'How many children do you want to have?'

'Two. One boy and one girl.' She turned to face me, clutching my coat pockets to draw me closer. 'Would the house you're building have a crystal chandelier in the dining room perchance?'

'If that's what my love wants.'

'And a music solarium?'

'Of course.'

She sighed peacefully as she took a moment to enjoy the vision of my dream home in her imagination. 'That sounds wonderful.'

The late afternoon sun glowed on her skin and the splendour of it took my breath away.

She studied my love-struck expression and then her eyes lit up from a thought that crossed her mind. 'Do you remember when you asked me if I write about a handsome young man in my diary?'

I nodded.

'Well, the truth is, I do. I've been writing about him in my diary ever since I learned how to print. At first he was just a sweet little boy who made me laugh and went on adventures with me. But then I became quite smitten with him when we were about twelve years old. At that time he was mainly interested in me because I pitched well enough to help him practise his batting, and I had memorized our science text-books and could help him identify all of the different species of reptiles he had dug out of a ditch somewhere. But then one day we grew up and it became clear that he felt as lovingly towards me as I did towards him. Unfortunately, I did something very foolish. I was terrified of losing him, and I told him I didn't want to write about him in my diary any more. It was the worst mistake I had ever made in my entire life. Fortunately, he gave me the chance to take that decision back. Well, to be more accurate, he was relentless in his mission to convince me to take it back.'

I laughed.

She tucked her hair behind her ears. 'Anyway, I thought you might be interested to know how happy I am that, even though we are living against the distressing backdrop of a war, the young man is still creating special moments for me to write about in my diary every day, sometimes several times a day. And although our future is frighteningly uncertain, as I listen to him talk about his vision of a life together, my affections for him grow even deeper, which I honestly wouldn't have guessed was possible.' She paused to take a breath and wrung her hands in anticipation of my response. 'What do you think of that?'

'I think …' I removed my cap and stuffed it in my pocket, then laced my fingers with hers. 'Would it be all right if I kissed you, Miss Setoguchi?'

'Oh.' Her cheeks blushed and she reached up to hide it with the palm of her hand.

She hesitated for an awkwardly long time, which made me nervous. 'Was that too forward?'

'No, it's not that. It's just that I don't know how to kiss.'

I laughed, which made her entire face turn pink.

'It's not kind to laugh, Hayden.'

'I'm not laughing at you. It's just funny because kissing's not something you need to know how to do. You just do it.'

'How do you know? Have you kissed many girls?'

'Well, no. I haven't kissed anyone, but if Joey and Donna Mae figured it out, I'm sure we'll be able to muddle our way through.'

Chidori laughed and then bounced back and forth between the heels and toes of her saddle shoes – partly keen, partly anxious. 'Okay.'

She tilted her chin up to look into my eyes. I leaned forward and pressed my lips against hers. After a slight hesitation, she moved her mouth to kiss me back. It was tender and sweet at first but intensified when I rested my hand on her hip and drew her closer to my body. I slid my other hand to rest my palm beneath her ear and then caressed her cheek with my thumb. Her fingers clutched at the fabric of my coat lapels and she rose onto her tiptoes to kiss me more ardently. My breath became rapid, along with my heart rate, as she ran her hand under my coat and across my chest. Kissing her was the most pleasant sensation I'd ever felt. I could have done it all afternoon, but she eventually leaned back to catch her breath.

She clutched her chest in exhilaration and said, 'Golly. No wonder Joey and Donna Mae spend all their time doing that.'

I chuckled with a sliver of pride for impressing her as I

grabbed the cookie basket, then stretched my arm across her shoulder. 'Is it all right if I walk you home and sneak another kiss before we say goodbye?'

She snuggled in next to my side as we started to walk. 'That would be fine with me. Very fine indeed.'

Chapter 15

I was transferred from the horse stable lockup to Budapest and thrown on a boxcar train with hundreds of other POWs from all over. It was strangely reassuring – despite the terrible circumstance – to be among other men like me, but the boxcar was so crowded we couldn't even lie down. We sat back to back, with our knees tucked into our chests, just so there would be enough room for everyone to sit down. The stench from all the sweaty bodies mixed with the soaked-in urine of the livestock normally transported in the car was almost more than I could bear. I tried to recall Chidori's blossom scent to block out the putridness, but I couldn't remember it. I could somewhat remember Inga's talcum-powder scent, so I used that to get me through as the cramped train bumped and rolled along the countryside.

The train stopped twice a day to let us out to relieve our bladders. We were only given something to eat once a day, usually a bun with a slice of mouldy cheese. My throat was parched because we drank from a stream only once during the entire four-day trip. That's all the guards got too. I almost felt sorry for them.

One British pilot fell ill during the journey and was so weak that he went into convulsions during one of the train stops. He vomited uncontrollably and soiled himself, so the guards shot him. We rolled away with him still lying next to the railroad tracks, and oddly, the thought that crossed my mind was that he was lucky to be out free in the fresh air and sunshine.

As night fell outside on the third night, I sat with my back up against an American pilot. The French-Canadian fellow next to me slumped over in his sleep and leaned against my shoulder while I nodded off to the rhythm of the rocking train. Out of the darkness of the boxcar, the dead British soldier appeared and stood in front of me. His eyes were missing and when he opened his mouth vomit spewed out. Then he collapsed in a heap onto my shoulder. I violently pushed his disgusting soiled and bloody weight off me.

Then the body punched me back, waking me up.

'Sorry.' I held up my hands in surrender once I was fully alert to the fact that I had acted out my nightmare on the poor airman beside me. I repeated, 'Sorry, I was dreaming. I had a nightmare. Sorry.'

He did not appreciate the assault, nor accept the apology.

The entire boxcar woke from the ruckus, and the French-Canadian continued to shove me until someone said, '*Cauchemar*,' to translate. His demeanour softened slightly once he understood, but he elbowed me once more for good measure.

'Sorry,' I mumbled.

Although still furious with me, he stood down. Everyone else settled and propped their backs against each other. Fortunately for me, nobody had a lot of extra energy to waste on fighting. It quieted quickly and snoring filled the thick air a short time later. I struggled to keep myself awake so it wouldn't happen again, but the sway of the train made it hard to stay alert. I drifted off and my head bobbed.

The wheels screeched to a halt at the break of day. My morale was so low I could barely drag myself off the train to get our one meal. The airman standing next to me could tell I was struggling, so he snatched my piece of bread from my hand and stuffed it in his mouth. I swung my arm and landed a weak slap across his jaw that made him spit it out onto the ground. Three other prisoners scrambled on their hands and knees to pick it up. They tore it apart in the frenzy like a pack of wild dogs, each ending up with only a few crumbs.

While the guards were distracted by the scrum, I scanned our surroundings for an escape. A densely forested area, not too steep terrain. My foot edged back. The other one followed. I inched away from the group, waiting for the opportunity to turn and make a run for it. One of the guards shot his Gewehr rifle in the air to get the attention of the prisoners squabbling over the food and then shoved them one at a time to load them back on the train. Nobody noticed me. It was my chance.

My inching widened into full steps backwards. As I

reached the perimeter of the forest, bushes rustled and a voice behind me said in accented English. 'You make run. I make dead.'

My eyes clenched shut, waiting for the crack of his gun and the blast to my back. The branches swished as he stepped out and approached me. The barrel of his gun stabbed into my back, but to my mixed relief he didn't pull the trigger. He prodded me back into the train, then slammed the door closed.

We arrived at our destination in German-occupied Poland that afternoon and marched for two hours to a POW Stalag Luft camp.

Hell.

30 October 1941

Dear Diary,

There is such astounding beauty in the world – the sound of a wren calling to its mate, the aroma of cedar logs in the fire, and the geometric pattern the autumn chill paints on the metal of the tractor. Admittedly, I am particularly enchanted with descriptions of the minute exquisiteness of the world right now because I have just completed a collection of Robert Frost poems that I signed out of the library. I have always loved words but Mr Frost's poetry has made me even more infatuated. He captures all of the wonderment and innocence in very simple elements of rural life, along with the isolation and desperation of grander universal sentiments. Wisdom and naivety in equal

measures. Nature kissed with golden hues, roads not travelled, fences mended, being acquainted with the night, the
brief overcast moment on an otherwise sunny day, and
what to make of a diminished thing. I am entirely beguiled
and aspire to write that well one day. More importantly,
training myself to observe both the simple and extraordi-
nary splendours around me helps bolster my hope and
faith in God and the good in humanity, despite the evils
that continue to occur.

Why would anyone would want to destroy the living
artistry of nature? Why do men fight in wars? Why do
they willingly commit murder of innocent people? Why do
they revel in atrocities that reduce once-glorious places to
rubble? I don't understand the hunger for power that drives
war. I could never hate something so much as to want it
killed, especially not something pure of virtue.

To my absolute dismay, Tosh volunteered to join the
Canadian Forces to prove his patriotism to the country. To
my great relief, he was turned away with no explanation.
I imagine, although Japanese Canadians fought for Canada
in the last war, the Canadian military is no longer overly
keen to train young men of Japanese descent to be soldiers.
I am extremely grateful for that particular prejudice. Tosh
is only angrier now because his loyalties have been
prejudged and the government refuses to give him a chance
to prove himself.

I should go now. Hayden is coming over for a visit later
this afternoon and I have a few finishing touches to complete
on the surprise I made for him. Well, truthfully, the surprise

is more for me. He will likely not be as amused by it as I am, but he will be a good sport, especially now that it has become so very important to carry on with our lives with as much normalcy as possible.

For the record, I should note that a kiss from Hayden is worthy of a Robert Frost poem.

Chi

Chapter 16

Halloween fell on a Friday night and the Mayne Island school had planned a community dance at the old Miller barn to lift war-weary spirits. It was slated to be fun for all ages with apple bobbing, a Jack-O-Lantern carving competition, a costume contest and dancing. Chidori was keen on attending and invited me over to her house on Thursday after my shift at the sawmill to show me the costume she had made. Unfortunately, I was running late because I had to stay at the mill to finish an order. There wasn't as much construction going on in general, with so many men overseas and less pocket money to go around. And rumour in the company was that the mill might need to shut down if the war didn't end soon and production didn't return to normal, so when an order did come in we hopped to it to get it filled and sent off on the barge. I hadn't stacked the hay bales into our barn for my pop yet but, as luck would have it, Donna Mae's kid brother had the good timing to ride down the road past my house on his dandy Schwinn bike, whistling and dragging a stick behind him in the dirt. I paid him a quarter to finish my chores for me so I could clock out early. My father wouldn't

Danielle R. Graham

have approved of my priorities, but he was out fishing with Massey anyway so was none the wiser.

Chidori sat on the steps of their porch, bursting with excitement as I jogged up their driveway in my work coveralls. I dropped down breathless on the step beside her and kissed her cheek. 'All right, let's see this costume you can't wait to show me.'

She reached into a canvas duffel bag and gleefully pulled out a tangle of red yarn.

'You're going as a mop head?'

'It's not a mop head. It's a Raggedy Ann wig.' She stretched it over her own hair. 'See.' After a pause to wait for my reaction she said, 'You would be well advised to gush over how much you love it since it took me hours to make it.' She rummaged through the duffel again and pulled out a blue dress, white apron with red bows, and red and white striped stockings. 'I repurposed some of my childhood dresses and a tablecloth for the fabric. What do you think?'

'I think you're probably going to win the contest.'

'Wait.' She clapped excitedly. 'You haven't even seen the best part yet.' She bit her lip with nervous anticipation as she dug into the duffel and pulled out another, shorter, red yarn wig, a red and white chequered man's shirt, blue short pants, and another pair of red and white stockings. 'Would you like to be my Andy?'

'Good Lord, no. I'm not wearing that.'

Her lower lip pouted out. 'Why not?'

'It's humiliating. I'll be the laughing stock of all my friends and probably most of the island too.'

150

'Pleeeeease. It will be so delightful if we go as Raggedy Ann and Raggedy Andy. We would surely win first prize.' She shook the yarn of the wig in an attempt to entice me. 'You wouldn't want to make me sad, would you? I worked really hard on it.'

'Why couldn't you have worked really hard on a Babe Ruth costume, or something swell like that?'

She laughed. 'I'm sorry. But I promise I'll dance with you as many times as you like if you go as Andy.'

'That's bribery.'

'It certainly is. Try the wig on. I want to see how it looks.'

'Fine. But the only reason I'm agreeing is because a six-foot Andy doing a Lindy Hop will be a sight to behold and not soon forgotten.'

She giggled when I tugged the wig on, but her hands flew up to quickly hide her expression so I wouldn't change my mind based on the mockery. 'It looks wonderful.'

'You realize Rory and Fitz are going to harass me worse about this than they do about me being sweet on someone who is Japanese-Canadian.' I took it off and tossed it in the bag.

The cheerfulness dropped off her face and she removed her wig too. 'You're right. I'm sorry. It was a silly idea. We won't go.'

Feeling regretful for bursting her bubble I stretched the wig back on. 'I was only teasing you. I don't care if people laugh at me. We're definitely going, and we're a shoo-in for best costume.'

She sighed and stared down at her clasped hands. 'You have the wrong idea about Rory, by the way.'

'Wrong how?'

'Well, Fitz might have an issue with me being Japanese, but Rory doesn't.' She glanced over at my expression as I tried to figure out what would have made her believe that. My eyes narrowed as the reason sunk in.

'Is he sweet on you?'

'I don't know if I would call it that exactly. But he used to write me poems.'

'Poems? Rory?'

She chuckled at my shocked tone as she hopped up and walked over to sit on the porch swing. 'Which part is giving you that perplexed look, the fact that Rory writes poetry or the fact that he was sweet on me?'

'Both.' I stood to join her on the swing and we swayed casually. 'I mean, I understand why he would have been sweet on you. I'm just shocked I never noticed. And I'm flabbergasted that he can spell, let alone compose poetry.'

'Well, admittedly, he's no Robert Frost. But his imagery and tone are quite sentimental.'

'When was the last time he wrote to you?'

'Just before the fall fair.'

My mouth dropped open at how recently it had been carrying on. I was astonished that I'd had no idea.

'You have nothing to worry about, Hayden. I was clear with him that the feelings weren't reciprocated. He asked if it was because I had feelings for you. When I told him yes, he was very hurt. Perhaps I should have told you, but out of respect to Rory, I felt it would be unkind to gossip. Please don't humiliate him by sharing it with anyone else. I'm only mentioning it to you now so you don't get in a quarrel with him over something that isn't true.'

'How does that tidbit of information make things better? Now, I'm going to get in a quarrel with him over something that is true.'

'No. I forbid you to lose your temper.'

'That's going to be tricky, since I still owe him at least one bop to the eye for throwing that cigarette and burning you.'

'He apologized for that.' She glanced sideways at me before continuing, 'He meant to hit you and regretted that he burned me. He came by the house the day after it happened with flowers. I accepted the apology but not the flowers.'

I laughed with some satisfaction at the image of Rory having to walk away dejected with the flowers still in hand. 'Rebuffing him a second time means he's probably extra sore now. If he starts something, what do you expect me to do?'

'You'll do nothing,' she said with the authority of a schoolteacher.

'What makes you so sure?'

A calculated grin stretched across her lips. 'Because I said so. And if you do fight with him, no kissing with me.'

'Oh really? Is that so?' I slid my hand under her open coat and tickled her ribs, which made her squeal and kick her legs. 'You're full of all sorts of sassy bribes and threats today, aren't you, missy? Don't you care that he tried to burn me with the cigarette? That warrants a quarrel, I think.'

'Nope.' As she giggled and squirmed away from me, her mother opened the front door. I still had the Raggedy Andy wig on and Chidori was basically lying on the porch swing fighting me off from the tickle attack. It must have been quite an improper sight. I quickly stood and removed the wig. Chidori sat up and straightened her coat.

Mrs Setoguchi's expression hung halfway between disapproval and amusement. 'Hayden, would you care to join us for tea?'

'Yes, ma'am. Thank you.'

She nodded and retreated back into the house. Once the door shut, Chidori pointed at me with utter delight. 'You should have seen your face.'

'I thought your mother was going to scold me.'

'She would have, but,' Chidori sprung to her feet and shoved my shoulder to make me turn and face the greenhouses. Her father and brothers were crossing the yard, approaching the house. 'Whenever my brothers misbehaved exceptionally badly, my mother left the discipline to my father.' She winked. 'You're in big trouble now, mister.'

I glanced back at her brothers and father, wondering how much they had witnessed of us carrying on. I knew she was joshing me, but since I held her father's opinion in high regard, I couldn't help but feel the nerves of a little boy who'd just been caught red-handed in an act of mischief.

Chapter 17

The POW Stalag Luft guards lined up all the new arrivals and filed us into a hall to be deloused with powder, which was fine with me since the boxcar was probably infested, and I preferred to be rid of creepy crawlers. I was still coughing from the chemical residue when they escorted me, along with fifteen other fellows, through the yard that was overlooked by guard towers in each corner of the compound. We were assigned to Barrack III, which was one of five wood-framed bunkhouses and already half full with inmates. The prisoners who had been there for months or years called themselves *Kriegies*, short for *Kriegsgefangen*, which was German for POW.

'Welcome to your new home,' a fellow named James announced as we each filed in and placed our threadbare blankets on a bunk. 'Let me give you the tour,' James joked, since there was nothing to tour in the one large room. 'We eat here.' He pointed to the long table with benches next to the pot-bellied wood-burning stove, which was also the only source of heat. 'We play cards here.' He pointed to the table again. 'And we do everything else here.' He pointed to the table once again and chuckled. 'Those dandy jugs in the corner are the urinals. Get used to it. The guards only escort prisoners once a day to use the toilets.' The smell of urine had already coated my nostrils before I even knew they were there.

Ivan took over the orientation and pointed out the dirt-caked window. 'Normally all the barracks are permitted in the yard at the same time, but because most of the yard is currently covered in mud, the goons just made a rule that each barrack has different allotted exercise times. We're locked in here until it's our turn.' Ivan moved to the middle of the room next to the stove and opened the drawers of a free-standing cupboard to show us the contents. 'We're supposed to get rations for cooking, but it's been a good while since we received even the basics. The guards promised more is on the way, but the trains keep getting bombed to hell, so I'll believe it when I see it.' He held up a curved piece of tin can. 'This is your spoon and fork and knife until the Red Cross care package arrives. And don't touch any of my proper utensils or I'll slash you with your tin-can spoon.'

A fellow named Conrad leapt from his bunk to swing from the rafter beam and landed next to me. 'I hope you're hungry, boys. Breakfast will consist of one lavishly thick cup of black coffee. Your lunch will be an enticing slice of hard black bread with a chunk of always dry, sometimes mouldy cheese. And dinner will be a decadent sauerkraut or broth soup that has a robust aroma reminiscent of goat piss. Mmm.' He closed his eyes and kissed his fingertips to emphasize the delicious-ness of the menu. The other new arrivals laughed, but I didn't find it particularly funny.

The wooden slat bedframe and scratchy straw-filled burlap sack mattress was similar to the one in the stall in the Hungarian detention cooler. I hopped up and sat on mine to attempt to make myself at home. Unfortunately, the warmth of the stove didn't actually reach the bunks along the perimeter of the walls. And wrapping the thin blanket around my shoulders to fend off the cold draught that blew in through the cracks in the siding planks did little good either. Not exactly cosy like home. It would be barely better than sleeping outdoors, but at least I finally had a bunch of mates to keep me company.

F/O Pierce Duration as POW: 92 days.

It's been three months since I arrived at the Stalag Luft. *The first week I was here I wrote to my parents to inform them of my location at the camp, and I asked them to let Chidori know too, if they could, but I haven't received any letters back. The fellas who have been here longer say they haven't received a post delivery in four months. Writing my flight log to myself will have to do for now.*

We were told the guards would read our journals, but I don't think they can read English. My breath is making frost clouds as I lay on my cot writing this. I should move closer to the stove where the other fellas are seated around the table, talking about food – food is the only thing they talk about more than female companionship. The conversations about ladies and food go pretty much the same.

They talk about the best they ever had in detail, then about everything they want to try once we're free.

Sometimes the guards crawl under the bunkhouse to eavesdrop on our conversations. We know when they're down there because we can hear their German shepherd dogs panting under the floorboards. If they understand English they probably enjoy the exaggerated stories about Montreal smoked meat and prostitutes as much as we do. As far as I can tell, the goons eat the same food as we do and rarely get leave to see their families or sweethearts. I think it's fair to say we're all starving in more ways than one.

I've read every English book in the camp twice. I read one French book cover to cover too, not that I understood it but sounding out the words gave me something to do. I thought about writing my own book, but I don't want to waste all my writing paper. Some of the other men sketch because they aren't much for writing. Jack created a portrait of me. He's talented – perhaps too talented since I look exactly like a hungry, sleep-deprived, and melancholy prisoner. I asked him to sketch the house I want to build back on Mayne Island. He's only half-done, but it's a beauty, with a music solarium for Chidori. The memory of it makes me want to cry, both happy and sad tears at the same time.

Chapter 18

My legs were antsy in anticipation of catching heck from her father for tickling Chidori on the porch swing. I stepped into the foyer of the Setoguchi house and Chidori took my coat to hang it in the closet, then she tossed the duffel with the Raggedy Ann and Andy costumes onto the shelf. Her father and brothers entered through the back door, laughing about something, so that eased my worries somewhat. Unfortunately, I was terribly underdressed in coveralls. I removed my boots and ran my hand through my hair to tidy it up, then took a few quick inhalations to calm my nerves. Mrs Setoguchi wore a tailored royal blue dress which had red birds printed on the fabric, and her hair was curled perfectly in place. Chidori inherited her smooth, glowing skin and rose petal lips from her mother.

'Welcome Hayden. Please come in.' Mrs Setoguchi swept her arm to invite me from the foyer to the reception room. She treated me in the manner of a formal guest, even though they all knew me – literally since birth because their grandmother was the midwife who had helped deliver me.

The Setoguchi house was one of the biggest on the island.

They each had their own bedrooms and they had two flush toilets, which I had always thought was quite something since we only had an outhouse. Her mother changed the custom-made drapes four times a year with the seasons. And the living-room walls were covered in floral wallpaper from Paris that shone at certain angles. My favourite part of the house was the solarium at the back. They used it as their music room and, on warm summer evenings, I sometimes sat at the edge of the forest to listen to Chidori play the violin.

Massey's truck rolled up the driveway and he parked out back. He entered through the back door and washed his hands at the kitchen sink before joining us in the living room. He had come straight from the dock, also wearing his coveralls, which made me feel not quite so out of place. We all knelt on the floor around a low, black lacquered table from Japan. Chidori's petite grandmother shuffled into the room quietly from the kitchen and poured nine cups of tea. The teapot was a flattened angular shape, made of iron, with a bamboo handle. The cups were a slate colour on the outside and bright red on the inside. There were no handles on the cups, so their grandmother carefully held them nestled in the palm of her hands and passed one to each of us with a slight bow. Tea etiquette was very particular, so I copied exactly the way everyone else held the cups and sipped. Chidori watched me intently. It was difficult to know if she was impressed I was doing it correctly, or if she was amused because I was doing it wrong.

'Hayden-san,' her grandmother said and passed a plate of biscuits to me. 'Try.'

I took one biscuit and bowed, but I was reluctant to eat it in case I made crumbs on their expensive rug. '*Arigato*,' I said.

Chidori placed her hand on my knee briefly to acknowledge that I had pleased her grandmother with my manners.

Mr Setoguchi glanced at how she had touched me but didn't say anything. He was Massey's younger brother and had been born on Mayne Island after the family immigrated to Canada when Massey was two years old. Mr Setoguchi's first name was Hiro, but since he employed upwards of twenty men in the busy season, everyone, including my father, called him Mr Setoguchi or Boss. Chidori's grandfather had been an agricultural expert and taught Chidori's father everything he knew about growing tomatoes, cucumbers and plums. The grandfather died suddenly from a heart attack when Chidori and I were nine years old, and after his death, Mr Setoguchi expanded the greenhouse business exports beyond Mayne Island to both Victoria and Vancouver and then eventually to the rest of the province. He was more formal and serious than Massey by nature, so I had always felt both admiration and intimidation when I was in Mr Setoguchi's presence; the pressure was made more intense by the fact that my relationship with Chidori had become serious.

After tea service was finished, Chidori's grandmother retired to the kitchen. Massey and the boys relaxed and moved to stretch out on the elegant European furniture. Chidori and her mother cleared the dishes and disappeared into the kitchen as well. Her father sat on a wingback chair and lit his pipe. I debated whether I should stay kneeling on the floor or move to the chesterfield. My knees answered the question for me when they started to lock up painfully. I nearly fell over as I tried to stand and move.

'So, what exactly are your intentions with our sister, Hayden?' Tosh asked to tease me.

Massey glanced at me and then over at his brother. Mr Setoguchi's expression didn't change.

Even though Tosh was only saying it to be funny, I cleared my throat and rubbed my palms on my trousers. My forehead started to sweat and the perspiration dripped down the side of my face. My mouth became so dry I worried I wouldn't be able to speak. 'Well, we have been going steady. And I, eventually I, would be honoured to become engaged. To be married one day. If she is agreeable.' My heart revved out of control as I spoke.

Kenji threw a pillow at me, and both he and Tosh laughed. 'Look at him. He's going to faint.'

Mr Setoguchi stood. He wasn't very tall, but he was imposing with his broad shoulders and heavy brow. He cleared his throat and spoke in a gruff way, 'I like you, Hayden, but I'm going to save you the trouble of asking my permission. The answer is no. I'm sorry, but I don't think it's best for either of you.'

Tosh and Kenji's joshing came to an abrupt halt. Massey looked at me with a sentiment that could best be expressed as, *you just overloaded the skiff, dummy*.

Tension clamped down on my throat, but I was able to choke out, 'With all due respect, Mr Setoguchi, why?'

'We need to accept the culture we currently live in, not fight against it.'

My ears burned hot and my heart pounded in preparation for the worst of my temper to unleash, which I didn't want to happen in front of her entire family. I took a deep breath and unclenched my fist, then spoke slowly to contain my frustration. 'Again, with all due respect, I would be good to her – you know that, and it has nothing to do with my blue eyes and blond hair.'

He shook his head, steadfast. 'Sorry, Hayden. You will more than likely go off to war after your birthday. And there is a very good chance we will be forced to evacuate to an internment camp, or worse, if the rumoured government sanctions on Japanese Canadians are imposed. It is my wish that you and Chidori not court now. I forbid it.' He bowed his head slightly before crossing the living room to the foyer. We all watched, frozen, as he stepped out the front door.

Chidori stood motionless in the doorway that led to the kitchen. Tears filled her eyes, then once the the shock wore off, she ran in her stocking feet out the front door and across the grass towards the forest.

I started to go after her, but when I stepped out onto the porch to put my boots on, her father, who was sitting on a rocking chair smoking his pipe, said, 'Let her be, Hayden. You go on home now.'

I paced, debating whether I should express what was on my mind. He raised the pipe to his lips as he rocked slowly and stared out at the cornfield, infuriatingly silent. An urge to shove him against the wall and shake him until he said something built in my muscles, so I left before I did something rash.

Chidori had taken the path towards the road. She had no shoes on and only a pullover knit top over her blouse, so she wouldn't have gone too far. But I didn't know which direction she'd gone in. It was probably better to give her time to calm down anyway, so I headed home.

In the middle of the night, my father and Patch woke me. 'Get up, son,' Pa whispered. His tone was unusual.

'What's wrong?'

'Get dressed and come downstairs quickly.'

Patch growled and ran ahead of my father. Anxiety pounded through my heart as I pulled on trousers and a shirt. I bounded down the steps two at a time to the landing as I stretched my suspenders over my shoulders. The front door to the house was open. Mr Setoguchi, Tosh and Kenji all stood on the porch with lanterns and grim expressions.

'What's wrong?' I asked frantically as I searched for my left boot, then hopped on one leg to pull it on.

'Chidori didn't return home,' Tosh said. His voice was composed but his eyebrows creased together with acute concern for her well-being, and the implication made my body flinch, as if a bomb had dropped in front of me.

'They want to know if she came here,' my father said with a stern glare directed at me.

'No. I haven't seen her.' Terror flooded through my veins. No matter how angry she had been with her father, she wouldn't have stayed out past nightfall. The possibilities of what could have befallen her sent a chill across my skin. I didn't even want to consider what might have kept her from making it home safely. 'Did you check if her rowboat is gone?' I asked Tosh.

He shook his head. 'Not yet. Massey drove into town to search and we came here first after we realized she wasn't in her bed.'

'Send someone to check if she's at Donna Mae's.' Without waiting for any deliberation, I took off running towards Bennett Bay. It was the most likely place she had gone. It was also the most likely setting for a catastrophic accident. Kenji and Patch were the only ones fast enough to keep up with me. Kenji ran with me to the beach with his lantern still in hand. I stumbled a few times in the dark as we scrambled across the rocks and climbed down to the spot where she kept her rowboat. It was gone. Huffing for air, we both stared at the empty spot on the beach, then gazed out along the inky water. My breath passed through the light of the lantern and the sliver of moonlight that peeked out from behind a cloud. Kenji had a coat on, but I didn't. My teeth started to chatter from the cold and the dread.

'What's that?' Kenji pointed out over the ocean to our right.

Something white floated offshore. I tugged someone else's rowboat into the water to get a closer look. Patch hopped up on the bow to stand watch and Kenji held the lantern up over the ocean as I rowed. We approached the bobbing object – an empty rowboat. When the lantern illuminated the *Chi Chi* painted on the bow, the sight made my insides drop to my boots.

The water around us was black like oil. Even if I could see well enough to dive in and search, if she had gone overboard sometime in the afternoon, we were much too late to save her. Kenji called her name, then tracked the light of the lantern across the water, looking for something. Anything.

We floated, staring at the darkness, listening for a sign that by some miracle Chidori was alive and maybe treading water. The waves lapped against the bow and a mast bell rattled in the distance from a sailboat anchored in the next bay over. A gasp of breath broke the silence and Patch barked in the direction the sound had come from. Kenji spun around to angle the light towards what turned out to be only an otter popping his head up, curious as to what we were doing. Several golden orbs from lanterns gathered on the beach. The hairs stood up on my arms when someone from shore called her name. The eerie desperation in the voice floated through the chilled night air, then faded into nothingness.

My chest heaved to fight back the pain of the grief as I stared at her boat drifting next to us. The fishing net was missing. I snatched the oars and rowed feverishly. Shocked by my abruptness, Patch stumbled and leaned against Kenji's leg for support as the boat lurched through the water. The wind worked against us and I struggled to make ground. Finally, I caught a current that pulled us up alongside Georgeson Island. I jumped out with the lantern and left a confused Kenji in the boat as Patch and I scrambled over the rocks towards where the seal pup had been weeks earlier. The stench hit my face and caused acid to rise in the back of my throat. An eagle or some other predator had pecked at the mother seal's carcass and large chunks of rotted flesh hung off the exposed bones.

The baby was gone, but Chidori's fishing net lay on a rock nearby.

'Chidori!' I called, and the sound echoed across the water. 'Chi!'

My voice bounced off the surrounding islands, rebounding back to me. Patch barked and the sound reverberated in the same way. I swung the lantern from left to right in case she had slipped on the rocks and hurt herself. Something made a sound in the forest behind me. The muscles in my spine tightened as I spun around and held the light up.

Shoeless and hugging herself, Chidori stepped out onto a boulder.

Relief swamped me like a tsunami and I nearly collapsed as Patch barked and wiggled excitedly. 'Thank the Lord,' I said as I scrambled over the rocks and up the embankment. I flung my arms around her and squeezed so tightly she could likely feel my heart throb. Choked up, I leaned back to hold her face and stared into her eyes with immense gratitude until I found my words. 'When I saw the empty rowboat I thought the worst.'

She realized how shaken I truly was and her expression became more serious. 'I'm sorry I gave you a fright. I'm fine. Only cold.'

I exhaled all the stress that had built up in my chest, then kissed her forehead. I couldn't even bear the thought of what would have happened to me if she hadn't been found alive. 'How many times have I told you to secure the boat properly so you won't get stranded?'

'One million times, at least.' She grinned and tapped my

lips with her finger. 'Does my father know you're off searching for me?'

'Yes. He came by my house with your brothers and woke me. Kenji is just on the other side of those rocks. I'm sure he's eager to see you. He almost cried when we found your rowboat adrift in the bay.'

'Truthfully?' She kissed the tip of my nose. 'Kenji never cries. Did you almost cry when you found my boat adrift in the bay?'

I pulled her tighter against my body and whispered into her ear, 'The thought of you drowned at the bottom of the ocean tore a hole in my chest, ripped out my still-beating heart, and threw it into the salty water. I have never felt such pain. If I hadn't noticed your fishing net was missing, I probably would have jumped in and let myself sink to a watery grave next to you forever.'

'Gosh, I'm relieved that you didn't do something so rash. That would have been a tragedy of Shakespearean proportion given that I'm safe and sound.'

'Don't joke, Chi. It was a terrifying thought. I don't ever want to know what it would feel like to lose you.'

She nodded to agree and then dropped her gaze to the ground. 'As much as I hate to admit this, we might lose each other because of the war. What if my father is right?'

'We might be separated temporarily, but for as long as I live, you won't lose me. And we don't need your father's permission to enjoy the time God grants us together.'

She sighed and leaned in to rest her head on my chest. 'I want his approval.'

'Then I'll figure out a way to convince him. It might take some time, but he'll eventually warm to the idea. I'm sure of it.'

She was quiet as my words sunk in. I could tell by the way she let her weight sink against mine that my speech had an impact and that she was considering the possibility that, with time, her father would agree. But she and I both knew there were outside forces much more concerning than her father's approval.

'We just can't quit. Okay?'

Chidori stepped back from our embrace and nodded. I reached over to lace my fingers with hers and led the way back to where Kenji was searching on the other side of the island. He didn't normally outwardly express emotions, so when he rushed over and embraced her with a quiet intensity, it choked me up again. He gave her his coat before we loaded into the boat. Patch took his post on the bow. Chidori slid closely beside me and her hand skimmed across my thigh as I wrapped my arms around her to keep her warm.

Kenji rowed us over to her boat and towed it in behind us. When we got close to the beach, men shouted, desperate to know if we'd found her. Kenji shouted back and jumped out of the rowboat once the water was knee deep. While he was pulling us up onto the shore, I bent my head down and whispered in Chidori's ear, 'I love you.'

Light from the lantern illuminated only the contours of her face, not her expression. My breathing stopped as I waited for her to respond. She was completely silent, then sat forward to break our embrace. She paused and inhaled deeply as she threw her legs over the edge of the boat, then finally she said, 'I love you too, Hayden – with all my heart. Thank you for coming to find me. And for your promise to never quit.' She glanced over her shoulder, blew me a kiss, and then turned to jump into the ankle-deep water with Patch leading the way.

She waded to her mother who stood on the shore with a blanket ready to wrap around her shoulders. Other women who had joined the search escorted her away towards the house. I leapt onto the beach. My father and Tosh helped Kenji pull the boats up onto the sand and Mr Setoguchi walked over to me. His solid, wide-stance frame was silhouetted by the glow from the lanterns of the men behind him. His breath rose in a silvery cloud around his head as he met my gaze with his chin held high.

'Thank you for rescuing her, Hayden.' He shook my hand and bowed his head subtly before turning to follow the crowd of people huddled around Chidori.

Chapter 19

'Goon up,' Harold hollered as the barrack door swung open. The guard stepped in and gestured with the barrel of his Gewehr to make us fall in line. He led us across the compound to the latrine and motioned for us to disrobe. The outfit Inga had given me hung off my frame like I was a boy dressed in my father's clothes. I had no way to know how much weight I had lost because there was no scale or mirror, but I was definitely faring more poorly than the others. My bunkmates didn't seem to mind the conditions all that much. They behaved as if it was no different than being at Boy Scout camp with a gang of friends. Most of them even preferred being a POW to fighting, and at first I did too, but the novelty wore off quickly for me because I had no purpose to wake up to in the morning. Laundry day was one thing I did look forward to, so I eagerly dropped my trousers and removed my shirt. Although they allowed us a short communal shower once a week, they only permitted us to wash our clothes once every month, and I detested being filthy like a beggar.

The guard shouted at us to hurry up, so I scrubbed my trousers, shirt and undergarments clean and wrung them out.

Then I ran back through the foggy mist in the buff to hang them to dry from the rafter in the barrack.

It's possible that another reason I struggled as a prisoner more than the other POWs was because, although I had made efforts to outgrow my adolescent petulance and stubbornness, I still hated being ordered around and told what I could and could not do by someone I didn't respect. I hated not being in control of my own life. And not knowing anything was the worst. Would I ever see Chidori or my family again? There was a possibility they weren't even aware I was alive. How was the war going? Would I suffer through all the hardships only to die of starvation or be killed by the Third Reich?

Not that anyone was, but I really wasn't cut out for incarceration. I had to constantly remind myself that the conditions could have certainly been worse. I was alive, which meant one day I would be free to go home to Chidori. That's all that mattered.

'Come on, Hayden. Shake a leg! The Red Cross packages and the post finally arrived,' Arnold hollered from outside.

My clothes were still damp so, naked except for my boots, I wrapped my blanket around my shoulders and followed him to an area in the yard where a bunch of fellows tore open wooden crates filled with milk powder, corned beef, sardines, prunes, salt, tea, clothing items for the cold weather, medical supplies and toiletries. The YMCA also sent packages that arrived at the same time. I flipped through a couple of new books. One was a book of poetry by Robert Frost. Chidori had raved on once about how much she loved his poems, so

I placed that one to the side with an Agatha Christie Hercule Poirot mystery and *Of Mice and Men* by John Steinbeck. Hank blew on a trumpet and Roger joined him with a tambourine to play a Louis Armstrong song. It was like Christmas. Another crate, packed full with a phonograph, records and sports equipment, had also been delivered.

'Pierce!' Jacob shouted. He extended his arm towards me with an envelope clutched in his fist as he dug more letters out of the postbag with his other hand. The envelope had my name scrawled across the front. What a sight for sore eyes that was. I hustled over to snatch it from him and tore the seal open. My mother had written it, which I was glad for because she tended to go on and on – a welcome trait when starved for news from home. Pop wasn't much for words, so his letters had always left me longing for more – or brutally shocked by his abruptness in at least one case. I could not have been more grateful to read about the mundane goings-on of Mayne Island. I sat on a stump and flipped open the box of a harmonica that I'd picked from the crate. The metal sunk into my palm in a familiar way as I unfolded the letter and started to read.

True to form, Ma wrote ten pages, double-sided, about everything that had been going on since we had last corresponded. She avoided the topic of my sister. There was also no mention of Chidori or the Setoguchis. I reread the entire thing again to check that I hadn't skipped a page or a paragraph. Ma spent several pages talking about her relief that I was alive and despair that I had been taken prisoner. The church congregation was apparently praying for me. She discussed things she had been reading in the newspaper about the war – most of which had been blacked out by the censors. Then she went on a less serious tangent about how one of our goats had gotten into our neighbour's house and chewed its way through the kitchen cupboards. She also felt it was important to update me on the news that her friend from bingo had come down with a dreadful cough but recovered. How could she forget to mention Chidori? I had specifically asked them to update me on her. It made me worry that her avoidance meant the news was bleak and that Ma had purposely omitted the topic because she knew I was in no state to receive more miserable news. No, I refused to believe that. I had to convince myself that Chidori was well and my parents simply had no new information to share with me. Chidori had to be well. She was fine. And happy. Safe. I needed that to be true or I'd have nothing to keep me hopeful, so I pretended that Ma had written all sorts of encouraging and inspiring things about Chidori in the letter.

'Isn't all this Red Cross equipment terrific?' Luke asked me as he bounced a basketball on the frozen dirt.

I walked over to the crate and picked up a baseball, rotating it to feel the familiar texture of the leather and stitching against my fingertips. 'I would be happier if it were an announcement that the war is over, but it's definitely better than nothing.'

'Damn right. Go long.' Luke cocked his arm to throw a football, so I tossed my blanket, letter and harmonica on the picnic table next to the baseball and took off in my birthday suit to run a route. My legs wobbled and my breath almost instantly became raspy. I only made it halfway across the yard and turned to look for the pass. It hit me in the face and made my nose bleed.

Huffing for air, I walked back and tossed the football to him. 'Looks like I'm going to need to work on my fitness.'

'Spring training. We'll make teams and play real games once the weather gets better.'

To recover from being winded, I propped my hands on my knees. 'I was hoping we'd be going home before spring.'

He nodded and said with unconvincing conviction, 'Sure. We'll be going home before then. Now go put some clothes on before they shoot you for being crackers.'

I chuckled and shrugged. Running around in the buff was liberating at least.

F/O Pierce Duration as POW: 115 days.

A fellow named Billy lit his farts on fire today to entertain us. The gas turned the flame blue. We laughed off our chairs to watch him bend over, spread his cheeks, and hold a match up to his arse. It made us laugh even harder when he accidentally set his trousers on fire. I haven't laughed that hard since I was still on Mayne Island and chumming around with my childhood friends. I wonder if Joey and Donna Mae got married. Ma never mentioned them either. Next time I write, I'll send it to Joey. Maybe he'll tell me the truth about Chidori. Unless I don't want to know the truth.

28 November 1941

Dear Diary,

Hayden and I have secretly seen each other almost every day since the night of the rowboat incident. Although I will eventually confront my father with the truth, we have tried to hide each rendezvous so my father won't be cross. In mid-November, Kenji and Michiko happened to drive by us while Hayden was walking me home along the road, hand in hand. And Tosh caught us kissing behind the greenhouses one afternoon. They either haven't mentioned it to Father or he knows and is choosing to accept it. I am not sure which. In case it is the first option, I think it is best for now if we continue to be discreet. It is my greatest wish that the war will simply end one day out of the blue and nobody will care any more whether Hayden and I are together. I realize that is magical thinking and I will need to come up with a more practical solution sooner rather than later, but I need more time to think about the right course of action.

It is my sense that Hayden's mother has not warmed to the idea of us going steady either. Truthfully, she has never been overly genial towards me. Once, when Hayden and I were children, we were playing Tarzan on a rope strung from the rafters in their barn, and I fell from the ladder. I scraped my knee, elbow and chin very badly. Hayden rushed me into the house as blood dripped, shouting for his mother. Instead of cleaning my wound and applying bandages, she shooed me home. Hayden walked hurriedly with me to my house and stayed with me as my mother administered first aid. I'm not sure he ever realized how oddly cold his own mother's reaction had been. I would venture to say that she is not a nurturing person by nature, but I have witnessed her be very gentle and caring towards Hayden and Rosalyn, so she is capable of it.

Hayden insisted on inviting me to his birthday dinner. Initially, his mother made excuses for why it would be better if it were only a family affair, since his sister was coming home from Vancouver for the weekend. He informed his mother if I wasn't there they wouldn't be celebrating his birthday at all. She finally conceded and made a roasted turkey and birthday cake. We all enjoyed a few rounds of cards after dinner and then Hayden played the harmonica that I had given him as a gift, while Rose and I danced. We had a very pleasant evening, even his mother could not deny that.

We don't need our parents' approval, but it would certainly be nice. I am not comfortable with going against the wishes of people whom I admire. Hopefully there is some way we can convince them to accept our affection for one another. But we might have much more dire problems to contend with now that Hayden is old enough to enlist.

Chi

Chapter 20

On 8 December 1941, Chidori ran across the frost-covered horse pasture towards the barn where I was changing the oil in my father's truck. She wore a charcoal-coloured coat, and against the backdrop of the bare maple and birch trees, the grey sky and the snowflakes that fell, the scene was reminiscent of a photograph – as if all colour had drained from the world. Her hair was blowing wild. I hadn't seen her look that frantic since the time she ran to get me after my father had had an accident on Massey's boat. He'd gotten caught up in the rigging and had been thrown overboard. Neither Massey nor my father knew how to swim, so he would have definitely drowned if Chidori hadn't been at the dock the day it happened. The way my father told the story was that she dove in, dragged him to safety, and then took off running to get me before he even had a chance to thank her.

I wiped the grease from my hands with a rag and met her at the barn door. 'What's wrong?'

She bent over with her palms propped on her thighs to catch her breath. 'Japan bombed Pearl Harbor in Hawaii yesterday. Canada is officially declaring war with Japan. And the United States is finally going to join the war now too.'

'I know. I heard on the radio. Don't worry, the Japanese fighters can't reach us here. It's too far for the airplanes to fly. And it will be a big help to the effort once all the American troops show up.'

'You don't understand.' She shook her head and sucked back another deep breath. 'They took Uncle Massey.'

'Took him? What are you talking about? Who took him? Where?'

Hearing her distress, my father, who had been up in the loft fixing a hole in the barn roof, climbed down the rungs of the ladder as she continued, 'Constable Stuart showed up at our house in the middle of the night with three men who he deputized on the spot – men who have all worked for my father at some point. My father was out in the greenhouses, stoking the wood stove, when he heard the raucous. The men kicked down the door of Massey's cabin, dragged him out of bed and shoved him into the back of a car. They arrested him.' Her gaze flitted back and forth between us, hoping at least one of us would know what to do.

'Arrested him for what?' my father asked.

'We assume for being born in Japan. My father and Tosh asked repeatedly why he was being detained, but nobody would answer them. Maybe it's because Massey knows so much about politics and they fear he is a dissident. Or the government has started repatriating anyone born in Japan.'

Pop removed his beat-up felt fedora and leaned against the truck. 'Massey has lived in Canada for over forty years. That can't be the reason.'

Chidori clutched my father's arm in desperation. 'Mr Pierce, you could ask Constable Stuart what the reason is. He'll talk to you.'

'He's not going to tell me anything he hasn't already told your father.'

'Yes, he will.' She clasped her hands together in a prayer position to plead for his assistance. 'Please. They'll listen to you because you're like them.'

Both my father and I were taken back by her comment. Pop ran his hand through his hair and frowned as he considered the situation. My father was a kind, decent, patient and hardworking man, but he didn't have the wealth, education or social standing of Chidori's father or Massey. The idea that my father's skin colour would somehow make him more influential with the officials than her father was preposterous. But, admittedly, probably true.

Chidori started to cry. 'They took Michiko and her family too. Kenji is beside himself. I don't know what to do.'

My father and I exchanged a concerned glance as I stretched my arm across her shoulder to pull her safely to my side.

'They're going to take the rest of us soon.' She pressed her hands to her mouth as if she couldn't bear the words she spoke.

'Everything will be fine.' I kissed the top of her head. 'It's going to be okay. I promise.' I hoped my reassurance sounded convincing because the truth was, I really wasn't sure.

Massey's arrest was the initial blow to the chin that left us all staggering in confusion. The wallops that followed – like a set

181

of waves – battered, bloodied and bruised us while we were still reeling. On 15 December, eight days after the bombing of Pearl Harbor, representatives from the Canadian government showed up on Mayne Island to seize Massey's boat. I was at the dock when the officers arrived. A skinny man in uniform approached the *Issei Sun*, so I hopped on board and stood with my hands on my hips. 'May I help you?' I asked him.

'We have the authority to seize the seiner owned by Masaru Setoguchi.'

'It belongs to me. Massey sold it to me.'

The officer held out his hand. 'Show me the bill of sale, please.'

'I don't have one. It was a verbal agreement.'

'That won't do.'

'Well, it's going to have to. Fishing is my family's livelihood. You can't take something that belongs to someone else.'

'Actually, I can.' He held up a poster with the orders that granted him the authority. 'Vacate the vessel or be arrested.'

I sat down on the cold storage hatch and shrugged defiantly. 'Arrest me.'

He sighed and pushed his cap back on his head. He obviously wasn't in the mood to get into an altercation – especially not with someone twenty pounds heavier than he was. Instead, he called Constable Stuart over.

Constable Stuart rested his hands on the railing. 'Come on, Hayden. They don't want any trouble. They have to confiscate the vessel by official orders from the government. You can plead your case at the courthouse in Vancouver and maybe buy it back.'

'Stealing something and selling it back to the rightful owner is bull, and you know it. You're going to have to arrest me. I'm not leaving.'

Chidori ran up the dock as Constable Stuart and the skinny officer boarded the *Issei Sun*. They grabbed one of my elbows each. I struggled to free myself and it turned into a wrestling match as they tried to clamp handcuffs around my wrists. Once they triggered my temper, I became impossible to hold down without aggressive force. A knee crushed against my chest. A palm slammed against my throat and locked my head down on the deck. Both officers breathed heavily as I continued to thrash.

'Hayden, stop resisting,' Chidori gasped. She boarded the boat and dropped to her knees next to my face. 'Stop fighting. It's not worth it. I don't want you to go to prison. Control your temper. Please. Let it go.'

Her eyes filled with tears, so I stopped struggling and let Constable Stuart lift me to my feet. He torqued my right arm behind my back. 'I don't want to arrest you, Hayden, but sure as heck I will if you don't leave quietly.'

It wasn't fair that they were stealing Massey's property, but I wasn't prepared to abandon Chidori over it. Her hand slid around mine and I let her pull me away from the officers. We climbed off the vessel and she tugged me up the dock towards the Springwater Lodge.

The navy officials roped the entire fleet of Japanese-Canadian-owned fishing boats from all the Gulf Islands together, then towed them in a pontoon towards the mainland. All of the Mayne Island fishermen stood on the dock, watching. Their expressions were flat and didn't change as the fleet disappeared. I couldn't muster the same stoicism.

'Maybe I'll be able to buy her back.'

Chidori sighed, heavy with doubt, then walked away.

Ten days later, I returned from a trip to Vancouver and ran straight to Chidori's house from the boat dock. I could see her through the glass in the back greenhouse, stoking the stove to protect the plants from the chill. I paused in front of Massey's cabin and held up my lantern to the window. Everything was exactly as it had been the day he had been pulled from his bed. The blanket was still strewn on the floor and the desk chair was toppled. I didn't understand why they had left it that way. Maybe they simply hadn't gone into the quarters since that day. Or maybe they wanted to keep the stark reminder of his last moments in his home. It bothered me to let the marks of the scuffle remain, so I pushed the door open, righted the chair, and made the bed. I didn't really know why I had to fix it, I just did.

Chidori didn't hear me sneak up behind her in the greenhouse. 'Merry Christmas,' I whispered in her ear and tickled her waist.

She spun around. 'Oh my goodness, you startled me.'

'Sorry.' I wrapped my arms around her and pulled her close so our noses touched. 'I couldn't wait to bring by your Christmas gift.'

'Oh, Hayden, I'm so glad you're home, but I don't feel much like celebrating Christmas this year. I don't think I'll have the desire to celebrate again until the war is over.'

'Well, I do feel like celebrating.'

'Why? Did you convince the officials in Vancouver to sell the *Issei Sun* back to you?'

'No, unfortunately that didn't work out as I'd hoped. They've impounded over a thousand confiscated boats in Annieville and my request to buy it back could take months. It's a shame because they have them moored together where the low tide will damage the hulls. They'll be lucky if half of them don't end up sunk before the paper work is done. But I don't want that to ruin my favourite time of year. We deserve a positive moment during this dark time, don't you think?'

After a hesitation she reluctantly agreed. 'We should honour Christ's birthday. You're right.'

I handed her the new journal with a floral-print cover that my sister had helped me pick out when I was in Vancouver. 'It's not the *Issei Sun*, but you'll probably get more use out of a journal than you would a fishing vessel.'

'Thank you.' Chidori ran her hand over the cover. 'It's beautiful.' She reached into her pocket and placed something light and flat on the palm of my hand. A small portrait photograph of her looking over her shoulder at the camera. Her hair was pinned up with a peony tucked behind her ear. 'I didn't have a chance to buy a frame for it,' she apologized.

'I don't need a frame. I'm going to keep it right here.' I slid it into my left chest pocket and tapped it lightly. 'Close your eyes,' I whispered as I pushed her sleeve up her arm. She peeked with one eye, which made me chuckle. 'No peeking.' I wrapped the gold charm bracelet around her wrist and kissed her below her ear. 'Okay. Open your eyes.'

She beamed and held her hand up to examine the charms that sparkled against her skin. 'Oh, the tiny bird is so darling.'

'I picked that one because Chidori means one thousand birds.'

Her head tilted to the side with a surprised curiosity as her smile stretched even bigger. 'How did you remember that? I told you years ago.'

'I remember everything about you.'

She kissed me appreciatively, then examined the other charms. One was a tiny heart and one was a seal pup. 'Thank you, Hayden. This is beautiful and incredibly thoughtful. You should have saved your money, though, in case the sawmill shuts down.'

'If it brings you joy, there is nothing I'd rather spend my money on.' I rearranged some bags of seed into a seat, tugged her hand, and coaxed her to sit on my lap. 'I left blank spaces because I want to fill them with other charms over time.'

'I love that idea. I'm never going to take it off.' She sighed, wrought with worry, and her body weight sunk to rest against my chest. 'While you were gone, they issued a curfew on people of Japanese descent. Constable Stuart came by and told us we can't go out between dusk and dawn.'

'I know. When Pop and I were in Vancouver we heard that the Japanese-Canadian students at the University of British Columbia can't even be on the campus after dark, which means they can't use the library in the evening or attend football practice and things like that. There's talk that the Japanese Canadians who are supposed to graduate this spring won't be granted their degrees.'

Her eyes blinked with a profound slowness as the unfairness and the implication that her studies would be put on hold indefinitely sunk in. She exhaled and squeezed my hand. 'Hayden, we need to prepare for the inevitability that they are going to force my family into a work camp in the interior of the province. You and I are going to be separated.'

'There has to be a way to prevent it.'

'You won't be able to stop them.' She sat up with her eyebrows creased together and desperation in her voice. 'If you fight. They'll arrest you.'

'They can't send innocent people to work camps.'

'They took Uncle Massey.' She sprung to her feet and swung her arm to point angrily at the door, or maybe at the world. 'He's innocent. He has a right to a trial by jury of his peers, but how do they propose to provide that basic civil right if he committed no crime? The only thing he did wrong was to be born in Japan and arrive here when he was two years old. If he's not at one of those work camps, or in prison, then it means they sent him back to Japan, and there was absolutely nothing we could do about it.'

I stood and cradled her cheeks in my palms. I wanted to tell her everything was going to be okay and the war would be over soon, but I didn't believe it enough any more to say it. I sighed and pulled her to my chest. I didn't know what to say. The only thing that came to mind was, 'We are strong enough to survive whatever happens.'

Chapter 21

F/O Pierce Duration as POW: 119 days.

I stood in the yard today with my face tilted towards the dreary sky. Diamonds floated down gently from Heaven and dusted the ground. They might have been God's tears, but at least they were something pure and perfect. It reminded me of the day when I gave Chidori her charm bracelet and she gave me her portrait photo. If I am ever freed, I'll buy her a charm of the Eiffel Tower or Big Ben or something exquisite to add to the bracelet – reminders of what was wonderful in Europe before the war arrived and turned everything ugly. And I'll frame her photo for my nightstand.

On Christmas Eve, the guards permitted the prisoners from all the barracks to congregate together in the hall where they had deloused us. White powder residue still covered the floor and made it slick, so we all walked gingerly. Rows of benches were lined up end to end and a movie screen was set up at one side of the hall. A Christmas service and a movie was just the change in routine I needed to lift my spirits, then something even better happened.

The fellow standing near the front of the queue was probably twenty-five pounds lighter than when I last saw him in May, but I recognized him right away. 'Gordie!' Ecstatic, I jumped over rows of benches like a deer to catch up to where he was in line and butted in front of him before a guard could notice.

'Pierce!' Gordie said in an excited but hushed voice. 'Blow my wig. I can't believe you're here.'

Golly, it made my Christmas genuinely merry just to hear his voice. I had to stifle my elation as we continued to walk in single file. 'Hey, pal,' I said without looking back at him. A guard eyeballed me. 'I was worried you were killed,' I whispered.

'Good as new. When did you get here?'

'I was shot down the same day as you. I spent two months in a hospital, then a good while in jail before they brought me here in August.' Vibrating with restrained excitement, we sat next to each other on the bench and talked quietly without looking at each other so the guards wouldn't notice. 'Were you injured badly?' I asked.

'No, they brought me straight here.' He shifted his weight to nudge his shoulder against mine. 'It's aces that you're here.'

'Sorry about getting you shot down.'

He rested his elbows on his knees and stared down at the floor so nobody could see his mouth moving. 'What are you blabbing about? It wasn't your fault. We were outnumbered.'

'I didn't see you bail out.'

'I didn't. The damn canopy wouldn't release. I pancaked a belly-landing and kicked the shield off before the flames got too big. I was only banged up and gashed in a few places, so I ran, but the Nazis picked me up before I had a chance to hide in the forest.'

I smiled and my face felt strange because it was so unaccustomed to doing it. 'It's really great to see you.'

'You too, pal. You too.' He lowered his voice until I almost couldn't hear him. 'Do you have any Jewish fellows in your barrack?'

'A few, I think.'

'Make sure they don't mention it around that goon there with the white hair and the crooked nose.' Gordie angled his gaze to the corner at the front of the room where a couple of guards were laughing. His nose was more than crooked. It was ruddy, swollen and pocked like a sea sponge. Gordie waited for a different guard to walk down the aisle, then continued, 'Last week Old Ugly Nose shot dead a Jewish chap in our barrack for no reason. He told him to turn around against the fence. Shot him in the back and claimed he was trying to escape. So, don't turn your back near the fence either.'

I'd heard the rifle shot that day, but it never occurred to me it could have been from them murdering a prisoner. I had assumed the guards were trying to bag a rabbit or something. Killing a prisoner violated Red Cross conventions, but it maybe shouldn't have surprised me since half of what our captors were required to do wasn't consistently being done. 'I'll let my bunkmates know.'

Gordie glanced over both shoulders and leaned closely to

me. 'One of the guards slipped us a radio. We've been getting reports from Britain on how the war is going. The Russians are making a push. If they don't let us all have yard time together soon, I'll leave you notes. There's a crack outside the latrine wall to the left of the door.'

Hot damn. That news was the best Christmas gift ever. I had a million questions, but our conversation was interrupted by the priest who led us in a prayer and Christmas carols. I sang my lungs out because the songs and the service reminded me of home. After the carols, a guard prepared a projector to play a film. *The Wizard of Oz* – either an ironic or fitting screening to play to a bunch of prisoners who wanted nothing more than to go home. I couldn't decide.

'We'll be home soon,' Gordie whispered. 'Guaranteed.'

I slid Chidori's picture out of my pocket and stared at it as the movie rolled. Part of me was hopeful he was right, but part of me didn't want to be hopeful about anything. When the film was over, I hugged Gordie and wished him a Merry Christmas before we were ordered back to our barracks.

That night I dreamt I was home on Mayne Island. Chidori and a little blond Japanese boy trimmed the Christmas tree in our house. She called me to help them place the angel on top and I lifted the boy so he could reach. He grinned as he leaned forward and balanced the angel on the tallest branch. But my leg knocked the table and a candle toppled over. The Parisian silk curtains started on fire before I could douse the flames. The floors and walls ignited immediately, and we were all engulfed in a bright orange glow. Chidori and the boy melted until they resembled the ghoulishly beautiful ceramic doll that had won first prize in the art category at the fall fair. I beat the licking flames frantically with my coat, trying to extinguish the fire.

'Chidori!' I screamed.

'Hayden.'

'Chidori!' I pounded the flames, but the fire only got bigger and I couldn't see them any more. I screamed and started to cry. 'Don't worry, son. Papa's going to save you.'

'Pierce. Wake up, pal. You're having another nightmare. Ow. Goddamn it. Wake up, Hayden!'

I woke up on my knees, chest heaving, and with a tear-streaked face.

My hands throbbed from pounding them against the floor in an attempt to squash the imaginary flames. Everyone sat up in their bunks gawking at me. Chuck stretched his arm around my shoulders and escorted me back to my bunk.

'You were dreaming. There's no fire.'

Chuck's nose was bleeding. 'Did I hit you?'

'It's okay, pal. Somebody get him some water, will ya?'

9 February 1942

Dear Diary,

We have finally received official word in the post about Uncle Massey. He had been initially detained in jail in Vancouver but then in January he was given the choice to either be deported to Japan or sent to a prison road camp one province over in Jasper, Alberta. He chose the labour camp so he could at least stay in the country. The govern-

ment seized all of his real-estate assets in Vancouver. They took everything he owned with no compensation. Tosh was particularly incensed by that injustice and he has busied himself researching the law, the War Measures Act, the Geneva Agreement, and anything else that he hopes might help. Tosh and my father travelled to Vancouver to plead our case in defence of Massey and his property, but unfortunately, they hit bureaucratic brick walls.

Much to Kenji's dismay nobody has heard what happened to Michiko and her family. The prevailing assumption is that they would have been sent back to Japan since they had only been in Canada for six years. Kenji was abruptly discharged from his job with the accountant. No cause was given, but I can assure you it had nothing to do with his work performance. Even by the standards of his 'only worry if and when it happens' philosophy, he must admit the time to worry has arrived.

I am very disheartened that Tosh won't be able to attend Law School. What if the war rages on for five or ten more years? I should have gone to classes when I had the chance. I'll be too old to go to university by the time the war is over. What am I supposed to do if I have children, drag them around to class with me? I won't be able to do both.

I read through all of the history and politics books on Tosh's bookshelf while he was in Vancouver. I discovered that the Canadian government can't intern Canadian citizens who have been convicted of no crime. It violates the Geneva Convention and is illegal for a country's government to do so. But then I noticed that the newspaper *articles have carefully not used the word internment. They call it an evacuation or detainment, presumably to skirt the Geneva Convention.*

Constable Stuart knows we are not spies! And what I sincerely do not understand is – if expats are allegedly all spies, why did he not confiscate cameras and short-wave radios from the Bauers or the Tagliettis, or threaten to imprison them in internment camps years ago when we declared war with Germany and Italy? Why has the frenzy only become irrational now?

The Sakai family heard from a relative that two Japanese-Canadian milkmen were arrested in Vancouver for being out before dawn. Do you know what they were doing out before dawn? They were delivering milk. For goodness' sake, is that not the most ridiculous thing you've ever heard? Has the entire world truly gone mad?

My greatest fears, now that they are coming to fruition, have left me feeling strangely numb. It must be shock.

Chi

Chapter 22

In the third week of February, on a Tuesday, I was in town to pick up grocery rations for my mother and noticed something was wrong. The Japanese-Canadian families were especially tense and purposeful. They were behaving oddly. Mrs Kadonaga loaded her chickens into a crate and stacked them onto the back of Mr Aitken's truck to give them away. Mr Teremura gave Mrs Jones a wagon full of her family's dishes and linens. The Sumi family had nailed boards over the windows.

Something was definitely wrong, so I ran the rest of the way to the house and burst open the front door. My father sat, hunched at the kitchen table, staring down into a cup of tea with the radio on in the background. Patch sat in the corner with his ears pressed to his head as if he could sense the gravity of the mood. 'What's happened?' I asked my father.

'The evacuation orders were published by the government today. All of the Japanese Canadians need to leave the coastal areas on April twenty-first.'

'To where?'

'Somewhere outside the one-hundred-mile protection zone.' He shook his head apologetically. 'Sorry, son, that's all I know.'

Distraught, I sprinted all the way to Chidori's house. A thin plume of smoke rose from the chimneys and the Cadillac was parked next to the truck. Kenji was next to the greenhouses, digging a hole for a large brown trunk that had fine china and crystal packed in it. Tosh stood in front of a huge bonfire, throwing books into it and watching the flames flare up. He was eerily expressionless.

I leapt onto the porch and pounded on the door. Chidori's grandmother answered and bowed. 'Hayden-san. Come.' She turned, walked down the hall, and pointed up the staircase. 'Chidori. Go.' She bowed again and walked away.

It seemed like she wanted me to go upstairs, but if Chidori's father found out, I would get my hide tanned.

Her grandmother poked her head back into the hall and gestured with her frail hand towards the stairs. 'Go, go. Hayden-san.'

I climbed the stairs, trying not to make them creak. The first room on the right was Kenji's. His Asahi baseball cap hung on the hook. The room on the left was nearly empty, except for the bed and a desk. Presumably Tosh's, since he was burning all his belongings out back. Chidori's door was closed. I inhaled and knocked softly. Nobody answered. I knocked again, then placed my hand around the clear glass knob and opened the door a crack to tilt my head in.

Lace curtains floated in the breeze with a faint hint of lavender. A floral quilt with neatly folded corners covered the bed. The pillows were cased in white cotton and decorated with pink satin ribbons. The diary I had given her for Christmas was open on the bedside table next to a silver-handled brush and hand mirror. On the wall above the bed hung framed watercolours of ballerinas, and the ones hung above the dressing table were of birds.

I opened the door wider. Chidori lay on the far side of the room, curled up on the wood floor next to the bed, hugging her knees into her chest as if she had been beaten.

'Chi,' I whispered.

The sound of my voice caused her eyes to clench shut. She covered her face with her hands, ashamed to be seen in a broken-down state.

I eased across the room and crouched down to lift her off the floor. She was light, like a bird, and barely made a dent as I placed her on the bed. 'It's going to be okay. I'll figure something out.' I slid down onto the mattress next to her and wrapped my arms around her trembling body.

She buried her face against my chest and her breath sounded as if she wanted to cry, but no tears came out.

'It's okay to cry,' I whispered and stroked her hair.

'No. They win if they know they hurt me.'

'They only win if they break you. Don't ever let them break you.'

Her fingers clutched the fabric of my shirt as if they couldn't bear the thought of letting go. 'I don't know how to do that. I'm already cracking.'

'As long as we always love each other, they can never break either of us. Always remember our love is stronger than anything they can put us through. Okay?'

She lifted her chin and stared into my eyes. 'What if I never see you again?'

My throat jammed with a ball of emotion that felt impossible-to-swallow. I held her tighter and rested my cheek on top of her head. I didn't know how I was going to prevent that from happening but what I did know was I would die trying. There was no point to anything if it wasn't for her.

We remained in an embrace until it grew dark and she eventually fell asleep. The sound of her breathing was peaceful, and if I hadn't seen her distressed face earlier, I would have assumed she was serenely dreaming. I wanted to stay, but it was getting late and improper for me to be in her bedroom. I carefully slid off the bed, placed a blanket over her, and tiptoed back downstairs.

Mr Setoguchi was reading in his chair in the living room. Our eyes met. My breath stopped moving in and out as he stared at me. When he finally focused back down at the book in his hand, without any comment about my presence, I made my exit.

Chapter 23

'Pierce, pass the gravy boat, will ya?' Philip joked. The other lads in the barrack laughed as I handed an imaginary gravy boat across the table and he pretended to elegantly pour it over his empty plate. 'Mmm. Just like home,' he said with a big grin, then stuffed his mouth with a make-believe feast. His pantomime made my stomach growl and my mouth water. The good mood the Christmas festivities had put me in was gone, faded away. Back in the doldrums.

F/O Pierce Duration as POW: 215 days.

They gave us all shots in our arms for Lord knows what. It made everyone queasy and it caused a handful of us to become violently ill. Marlon, Lenny and I vomited and suffered from diarrhoea so severely that the guards threw us into the latrine and locked the door. We had to sleep on the floor for two nights and the smell was worse than rotting fish carcasses in August. Eventually, a doctor was brought in to examine us. He gave us some sort of fluid that made Lenny and me feel better. Marlon didn't recover.

He died two days later.

F/O Pierce Duration as POW: 251 days.

I have been too lethargic to write in my log because nothing different really happens around this stagnant place. Except, there was a rifle shot yesterday. If a guard ever asks me to turn around, I won't. He'll just have to do what he's going to do in my chest, then explain to the International Red Cross how I was trying to escape by running backwards. Maybe they were hunting and plan to serve rabbit stew for dinner. Ha. Comical.

'Put that damn journal down, Hayden. Let's throw the football around,' Arnold said.

I sighed and closed my notebook. 'I don't feel up to it. It's too cold outside.'

'Get up. I ain't gonna let you just give up and die from the blues. You're the only one in this gloomy, Godforsaken ice tundra who can throw a proper spiral.'

I rolled off my bunk and dragged my feet to follow him outside into the snow-covered yard. We played catch for a while before I noticed a piece of paper sticking out of the crack in the latrine wall. I acted as if I had dropped the ball, then wandered over casually. Gordie had written that the Russians were gaining ground. A sliver of hope. I handed it to Arnold and then went long to catch his next pass.

F/O Pierce Duration as POW: 252 days.

The bucket of drinking water froze. Indoors! And we have to ration what's left of the coal, so we only light the stove at night. If I ever get to leave this frozen hell, and if Chidori and I have kids, I'm going to teach them how to throw a proper spiral – even if they're girls … scratch that. *When Chidori and I have kids, not* if. *When I return home, not* if.

19 March 1942

Dear Diary,

We have been notified that we will only be permitted to evacuate with one-hundred-and-fifty pounds of belongings. I desperately wish I could take each of my diaries with me, but given that I have a stack of nearly thirty journals collected through the years, I must admit it is not a practical use of limited space. I will travel with the new journal Hayden gave me for Christmas and leave the others in my closet with the rest of my belongings that I cannot carry with me.

Obaasan asked me to accompany her on a walk to view the cherry blossoms before we leave. There is a Japanese tradition celebrated for two weeks every spring when the cherry blossoms bloom. It is called Hanami. It is a reminder of our mortality and the importance of seizing the present moment because life, like the blossoms, is ultimately fleeting. I will have to ask her how the philosophy applies if the present moment is not something I want to hold onto.

I accept the past is gone now. I can only pray that the

future is more promising than the present. I dread saying my goodbyes. It will feel too final when I do. And Hayden, what will I do when the time comes? I cannot even fathom that heartbreaking pain right now.

What else is there to say at a time like this? I must have faith that the war will end soon and we will be permitted to return home quickly. I do remind myself every day, as Hayden suggested, that we are strong enough to survive whatever happens. We must never give up and never break. I have faith that I can do that, especially if the ultimate goal is to see Hayden again one day.

Farewell Diary, my old friend. I pray we meet again soon. Shikata ga nai.

Chi

Chapter 24

I was blindly determined to protect Chidori from being taken away from Mayne Island. I thought of every possible way to convince the officials to let her stay with me. I even considered hiding her, but I was personally informed with an official hand-delivered letter that anyone found assisting the Japanese would be arrested and jailed. I came to the conclusion that being officially married might be our only chance. I didn't know for sure if they would let the bride of a non-Japanese Canadian stay with her husband, but it was worth a try. The day before the officials were supposed to meet the ship at Miner's Bay, I went to the Setoguchis' in desperation to speak with her father again.

He was busy in the greenhouse when I found him, getting everything in order so the employees could manage things while he was gone. I followed him as he walked down the rows because he didn't have time to stop working. 'Mr Setoguchi, I'd like to ask your permission to marry Chidori.' I paused to let him respond, but he didn't say anything. 'I think if we are married, she won't have to be evacuated. She and I could stay here and take care of the greenhouses until you get back.'

'The last time I checked, the war was still raging, Hayden. Even if the authorities allow Chidori to remain here as your spouse, if you are called to service, she'll be left here all alone during a very dangerous time. It's safer for her to stay with her family. Together.'

I sighed and stared out the glass panes at the blue sky. My stomach clenched painfully because he was right. 'I'll come with you. They can throw me in the prisoner camp too. At least she and I will be together.'

He continued to check each plant. After a long while, he said, 'No point in you being detained. If overseas conscription isn't instated, you're better off staying here and earning a living while we're gone. Say your goodbyes, Hayden.'

I stopped following him and stood in the middle of the greenhouse like a deflated tyre. With no further arguments I eventually left.

Chidori was on the back porch of their house with her mother and grandmother. They were sewing cash money into the linings of clothing. When I reached the bottom step, she rested the clandestine coat on her lap.

'Come on, let's go for a walk.' My voice sounded identical to the time my father had to tell me my first dog had died. I hadn't meant for it to, that's just how it came out.

Chidori glanced at her mother before she met me at the stairs. Her palm rested on my cheek and she closed her eyes as if she was trying to memorize how it felt. I wanted to kiss her, but her grandmother and mother were both watching.

Instead, I laced my fingers around hers and escorted her to the path that led to Bennett Bay.

'How is your mother holding up?' I asked as we strolled.

'She was very upset about not being able to bring all of the possessions that are precious to her. She was torn between family mementoes with sentimental value and her collection of treasures with actual monetary value. She was adamant about packing things like dinner placemats that prove we are a dignified family, which seems so silly to me, but she insisted that dignity is one thing that must be held on to. Grandmother told her it was best to leave all of the belongings behind so nobody can take them from her later. Ever since then, Mother has been repeating *Shikata ga nai* like a prayer.'

'What does that mean?'

'Nothing can be done about it.'

'Like giving up?'

'No. Flowing with the current, accepting what cannot be changed and making the most of whatever is left afterwards.'

I nodded, but I wasn't ever going to accept losing her. We walked in heavy silence along the road towards Bennett Bay. Once we reached the pebbly beach, I guided her to sit on a log. 'There is one precious family memento I would very much wish for you to take with you, if you don't mind.' I kneeled on one knee, removed my cap, and pulled a box out of my pocket.

'Hayden.' She smiled hesitantly. 'What's this?'

'You'll have to open it to find out.'

She tipped the lid open and gasped. 'Oh, my goodness.'

I clasped her hand in mine. 'It's safer for you to stay with your family for now, but I am going to marry you as soon as this is all over if you'll let me. Will you?'

Her mouth gaped open as she stared down at the engagement ring. 'It is stunning.'

'It was my grandmother's.'

She slid the ring onto her finger and held her hand up to the light to admire the sparkle.

'So, what's your response?'

'Yes. Of course. Yes.' She threw her arms around my neck and squeezed tightly.

Chapter 25

I wished our barrack was able to mingle with Gordie's. I longed for someone different to talk to, especially since all the fellows in my barrack talked endlessly about their sweethearts. Talking about Chidori only made me more downhearted, so I preferred to keep my thoughts about her private. I often wondered if she still wore her charm bracelet and her engagement ring. If I were to get out alive and make it all the way back home only to find out Chidori was sweet on some other bloke, it would literally kill me.

'An extra slice of black bread for whoever guesses closest to the time that Pierce wakes up from his nightmare shrieking,' Matt hollered.

I lowered my book and watched as they placed their bets. 'I want quarter past one,' I said.

'You can't bet on yourself.'

'Why not? It's not as if I can control it.'

Matt contemplated for a second, then nodded to agree. 'All right. Quarter past one for Hayden.'

'Couldn't we wager something better than a slice of black bread that tastes like sawdust?'

'We would if we had anything better.'

Chapter 26

On 20 April 1942, Chidori and I spent her last day before the evacuation together. We ate lunch at the Springwater Lodge and then spent the afternoon exploring the entire island, all of our favourite childhood haunts – tidal pools of starfish, beaches of sea glass and meadows of wild flowers. The last thing we did was hike the highest peak in the middle of the island to take in the view of the surrounding islands. I carved our initials in the flesh of an arbutus tree. She etched a heart around our initials and then picked up two small pebbles.

'Here.' She handed me one of the pebbles. 'You take one and I'll take one so I'll always have a little piece of Mayne Island with me wherever I end up.'

I tucked the pebble into my pocket and gave her a kiss, but unfortunately because of the government-imposed curfew we had to leave so she would be home before dusk. We walked as slowly as possible to delay the inevitable, then as the sun set, I stood on her porch and rested my forehead on hers. She wrapped her hands around mine and we just breathed.

'Today has been a perfect day,' I finally said.

She nodded to agree but also sighed.

'I already miss you.'

She tilted her head back and held my face. 'Promise you will be here when I come back home.'

'I promise.' I had to gulp back the emotion that crept up my throat.

'And promise you won't get tired of waiting and marry someone else.'

I laughed. 'I'm not going to marry anyone other than you, even if I have to wait until I'm one hundred years old.'

Pleased with that answer she grinned. 'Well, I hope the war ends quickly so I don't have to marry an old man.' As quickly as it had glimmered, the brightness in her eyes faded again. 'In all seriousness, please wait for me.'

'You don't even need to ask me to do that.'

She leaned in and kissed my cheek. 'Will you be at the dock to see us off tomorrow morning?'

'Of course.'

She nodded and let my hands drop as she turned away, but I tugged her arm and spun her around to kiss her one more time.

'I love you as much as God does,' she whispered before rushing into the house. She blew me a kiss and then closed the door.

My heart sunk into my belly with a thud and the contents of my stomach churned as I walked home in the dark.

There were chores to be done, so I finished my work by the light of a lantern. I had missed dinner but wasn't much in the mood to eat anyway. Dreading the following morning, I built up the fire in the living room instead of going upstairs to turn in for the night. A letter addressed to me from Rosalyn was set at my place at the table, so I sat down and opened it.

Dear Haydie,

I worry how you are coping during these last days before saying goodbye to Chidori. As your big sister, I have watched your love for each other grow from the innocent joy shared between childhood friends into the adorable flirtations of puppy love and finally into the unbreakable bond of true love. To find a soul you can share all of yourself with is such a beautiful thing. It is heart-wrenching to have that person taken from you and I am truly sorry you have to feel the pain that comes from being uncertain whether you will ever see her again.

I'm saddened to report that all of the Japanese-Canadian nurses I work with were relieved of their positions at the hospital. As a result, we are very short-staffed and I have been assigned to do a special rotation at the Hastings Park facility where they are holding the Japanese Canadians before they are relocated to the internment camps. There has been an outbreak of lice at Hastings Park due to the uncomfortably close living conditions. Extra nurses are needed to make sure it is brought under control. I hope Chidori and her family will not be there long. I will write you after my shift to let you know the conditions inside the facility. Then you can inform Chidori's family so they will know what to expect and what to pack to come prepared.

*If I could give you one word of advice, it would be to
not let one moment of your time with Chidori be wasted.
Put aside disagreements, feel the touch of her hand in yours
frequently, and speak the words from your heart freely. We
only have the present moment, so treasure it before it
becomes the past.*

I love you,
Rose

I dropped the letter on the table and shot up. My parents
were asleep, so I snuck out and carefully clicked the front
door shut behind me, then ran all the way to Chidori's house.
I jumped to grab the roof of the porch and pulled myself up
the same way I had pulled myself out of the *Issei Sun*'s cold
storage hundreds of times. Chidori's bedroom window was
open a crack, so I lifted the sash and stepped into the darkness. The sheets rustled as if she had been startled.

'It's me,' I whispered.

'Hi,' she whispered back, and her smile was audible. She
shifted over on the bed to make room for me.

I kicked off my boots and climbed under the cover with
her. 'I know it's improper to be here, but I received a letter
from Rosalyn that made me realize we shouldn't waste even
one minute of our time together. Is that fine with you?'

'Yes.'

I searched for her hand and when I found it, I pulled it up
to hold it against my heart. Her fingers intertwined with mine
and she squeezed them tightly. I inhaled to smell her hair and

pressed my cheek against hers to commit to memory the smoothness of her skin. My lips searched for hers and she kissed me back with an intensity that I had never felt before. Being that close to her was the best feeling in the world. But I knew it was going to be followed with the worst the following day.

Chapter 27

F/O Pierce Duration as POW: 254 days.

In my nightmare last night, I got sucked right through the earth into hell and was consumed by flames. I woke up screaming at twenty minutes after two.

  Virgil won the bet.

  I'm quite certain there is something wrong with my mind.

F/O Pierce Duration as POW: 260 days.

Today, I dropped the rock from Mayne Island that Chidori gave me before she left. It mixed in with the other stones in the yard and I couldn't tell which one it was. I searched on my hands and knees, but all the rocks look the same. It's lost here. Forever.

F/O Pierce Duration as POW: 270 days.

I have a craving for chocolate, which is strange since I never much cared for chocolate before. A mouse ran across the floor the other day in search of food. It didn't find anything, obviously. It squeezed back out through a crack in the floorboards and I bitterly envied it because it could just leave and find some food outside the gate. If I used a tin can like a shovel, I could probably dig a tunnel under the fence. I wonder how long it would take.

If that mouse ever comes back, I'm going to catch it and cook it up.

The lack of sleep must be muddling my thoughts. The melancholy that runs on my mother's side of the family probably doesn't help. The content of the letter in my pocket that I pretend to know nothing about doesn't help either.

The only thing keeping me sane enough to survive this miserable place is Chidori.

F/O Pierce Duration as POW: I lost count recently.

A rainbow arced over Chez Stalag Luft. It disappeared after only a few seconds, though. Who could blame it? It took a look around and realized it had no business being in a place like this.

'Give to me,' the guard with the white hair and nasty nose that Gordie had warned me about pointed at the picture of Chidori I was holding.

I slid the photo back into my pocket and stared at the ground.

The butt end of his rifle smashed between my shoulder blades and knocked me to my hands and knees. His long gnarly fingers rummaged through my pocket and he snatched the photo. I seized his arm and tried to stop him, but he kicked me in the stomach. Doubled over and gasping, I grabbed his ankle and yanked. My arms were too weak to pull him to the ground, but he stumbled briefly. Once he regained his footing, he kicked me in the ribs until I was lying on my back and then he held the gun to my head. His boot landed on my chest and he shifted his weight to apply more than enough pressure to prevent me from being able to sit up.

He studied the picture of Chidori and grabbed his crotch. 'Jap prostitute. I sex her for you.'

My jaw muscles locked up as I resisted the urge to tell him to go to hell. The barrel of the gun pressed harder against my forehead. He glared at me right in the eye and waited for me to react. My chest heaved, attempting to breathe under the weight of his boot. A crowd of other inmates circled around us, but so did a bunch of nervous guards.

The goon's heel slid up higher until it crushed my throat. With the gun tucked under his armpit to free both hands, he held up the picture of Chidori, then sneered as he tore the photo into pieces and sprinkled the scraps down on my face.

My arms wrapped around his leg and my rage fuelled enough strength to knock him off balance. Without his foot on my throat I was able to get my feet under me and yank him to his knees. He swung the gun around and caught me across the cheek, which sent me flying back. I landed on my backside.

A gun fired in the air and everyone froze in a startled position, including my assailant. The shot had come from the rifle of his commanding officer. One glare from the skinny mous-tached officer made the white-haired guard stand down. Maybe the body count had been getting too high to justify to the authorities, or maybe the CO actually had some respect for international law, I didn't know. But my life was spared and two other guards grabbed my arms to drag me to lock-up.

I was thankful that the CO had stepped in, but that veil of protection ended when he left the compound in the evening. The white-haired guard ordered the guard on duty outside the cell to leave. Once we were alone he bound my arms and legs with rough twine. With his boot toe he slid a sloshing full steel bucket of urine across the floor and hoisted me by the armpits to force me to kneel. His palm thrust my head into the bucket and held me down as I struggled helplessly without the use of my arms. My lungs contracted in protest, pleading with me to inhale. He crushed all of his weight down on my shoulders, knowing my instinct would cause me to gulp back the urine if he held me down long enough. Instead of pulling my head up as he expected, I lurched my torso sideways and knocked the bucket over. Livid, he punted the empty bucket across the room and it ricocheted off the bars of the cell. Then he booted my ribs until I blacked out.

Admittedly, it would have served me right if the goon murdered me. Chidori would become so cross if she found out I had gotten myself killed over a photograph. And all for nothing since the photo was already torn into confetti.

I should have learned my lesson the first time I almost died from my own stubbornness. Chidori and I were about eight years old. We were swimming in Bennett Bay and got caught in a rip current that pulled us out into deeper water. I feverishly tried to swim back against the flow into shallow water but made no progress and exhausted myself in the process. She had calmly floated and let the current take her out until it weakened and then she swam perpendicular to the rip into calmer waters. She called to me to do the same but for some pig-headed reason I believed if I struggled hard enough I could out-power the current. I was wrong. A teenager who had been at the beach that day swam out to me, held me as he let the current take us both out further, then at the spot where the outflow lost its strength he cut across at an angle to free us from the drag, just as Chidori had done. I never did figure out why I had been too stubborn and stupid to surrender.

Why hadn't I learned anything? I was stuck in a rip again. Chidori was calling to me. I needed to stop acting stubborn and stupid.

When the guard returned, I didn't fight back. Surprisingly, the beating didn't hurt any worse. It didn't hurt any less either. But my pacifism did seem to take some of the fun out of the abuse for the guard. And the following day, the minister from the International Red Cross arrived at the camp. Thankfully, someone had reported that I had been sent to solitary confinement after a scuffle in the yard. He inquired about my well-being and I was released. Whether my rescue was a coincidence or a result of my conscientious surrender, I didn't know. I did know what Chidori would have believed the reason to be. And she would have been proud.

F/O Pierce Duration as POW: No idea.

Surrendering to my fate in solitary confinement might have saved my life but my body has not recovered from the shame of being brutally victimized. My hands have developed a tremor that doesn't stop all day or night. The water spills out over the edge of my cup if I don't hold it with two hands. And I can barely read my own writing because the pencil bounces around on the sheet like a telegraph tapping out Morse.

I pray Chidori and her family are not being horribly mistreated by guards or forced to live in squalor. I have had to coerce myself to believe she is safe and well, otherwise I would die of guilt for not rescuing her.

In my nightmare I was strapped, like an ox, to a huge wood cart and struggling to pull it up a steep hill. The cart was filled with the mangled bodies of all the pilots I have killed, along with all my squadron mates who were shot down. The British fellow from the train was also piled on top, clutching a broken doll coated in ceramic and barnacles. The mother seal from Mayne Island and Rose were in the cart, too, along with a load of other tragedies I didn't want to remember. The cart grew heavier, and if I slowed down, it became more difficult to keep the forward momentum of the wheels. I stopped to take a break and the cart lurched backwards. It hurtled down the hill, drag-

ging me with it. My skin burned off from the friction and my exposed bones snapped against the rocks. I fought to free myself from the harness, but I was trapped.

I woke up wrestling Nigel in the bunk next to me. It took three other fellows to pull me off him. It was eighteen minutes after three.

Lloyd won the bet. And I was officially considered a danger to myself and others.

Chapter 28

Tuesday 21 April 1942 arrived. Fifty Japanese-Canadian men, women and children were to make their way to the dock at Miner's Bay and wait for the *Princess Mary* to take them away from Mayne Island – the only home most of them had ever known.

Early in the morning, I had slipped out of Chidori's bedroom window and was standing on their porch when she and her family stepped out their front door with the 150 pounds of belongings they were permitted to take. I leaned against the post nonchalantly, as if I had just strolled up and was waiting on them. When our eyes met, Chidori blushed from our secret. Before anyone else could notice she reached over and fixed my hair, which was mussed from sleeping in her bed all night.

While everyone was busy with the luggage, she kissed me and whispered, 'Please don't kiss me at the dock. I don't want to cry in front of everyone.'

I nodded to promise and lifted her bags to carry them to her father's truck for her. Chidori's grandmother and mother sat in the cab with her father. She, her brothers and I climbed onto the flatbed with the luggage. Tosh and Kenji both sat on trunks and rested their elbows on their knees, staring down at their shoes. Chidori and I sat next to each other on the floor of the flatbed with our backs rested against the cab of the truck. Her expression became layered with sorrow as we pulled away from the house and left it behind.

Once we were at the dock, Mr Setoguchi handed me the keys to the truck. 'Would you please drive it back to the house for us?' His voice didn't reveal any emotion, but his sadness was evident in his demeanour as he passed the responsibility over to me. 'Park it in the barn.'

'Yes, sir.'

Chidori heaved her own luggage off the truck without waiting for my help and avoided looking at me as she dutifully fell into place in line. Torn between wanting to stay by her side and respecting her wishes to let her go without making a scene, I wandered over to stand next to Joey, Donna Mae and my father. They had arrived with nearly every other resident of Mayne Island to say goodbye to their friends, classmates, employers and neighbours.

The Setoguchis reached the front of the line, faster than I'm sure any of them wanted to. When Chidori's grandmother tried to board the ship ramp, she stumbled slightly. Kenji stepped out of line to steady her arm. The naval officer who had checked their names off on his list shouted at Kenji to step back in line. He didn't because their grandmother was very unstable. He assisted her all the way onto the ship, then walked back down the plank to return to his place in line. The officer shoved Kenji's shoulder, which made him trip over a piece of luggage and fall to the ground. I lunged forward to help, but my father grabbed my arm and held me back.

Kenji stood up with a scowl for the officer, but he didn't retaliate. Tosh did. Tosh stepped out of line with a defiant stare-down for the officer, and ignored both the command to return to line and the threat of arrest. The crowd released a collective gasp as two other officers pounced on Tosh and handcuffed him. I struggled to free myself from my father's grip.

Joey jumped in front of me and clamped his hands on my shoulders. 'No point in all of us getting arrested.'

I squirmed, but neither Joey nor my father was going to let me get involved. Chidori's frightened gaze met mine. She dropped her satchel and rushed towards me. I broke loose and lunged forward to embrace her. She pressed her lips to mine then whispered, 'Please don't lose your temper. There's no point. Promise?'

After a deep breath to settle myself I said, 'I promise. I love you.'

'I love you too, Hayden. So much.' She burst into tears as they escorted her away and ushered her up the ramp.

I didn't want to upset her further, so I stuffed down my anger and dismay to keep my vow and maintain my composure.

Once the *Princess Mary* was completely loaded, it left the dock. All of the passengers stood on the deck to wave goodbye. Chidori blew me a kiss and we maintained eye contact with each other until she was too far away to see. Just like that. It was all over. They were gone.

My father asked, 'Are you ready to head home, son?'

I wiped the cuff of my sleeve across my cheeks and sat on the edge of the dock. 'No, sir.'

He nodded, patted my back and then left. I pulled the photo of Chidori out of my front shirt pocket and let my feet dangle over the edge. Before I had left her bedroom in the morning, she had written on the back: *Hayden, they will never break us. Love, Chi.*

I desperately hoped it was true that they couldn't break us, but in that moment I felt so beaten. Every muscle in my body ached with grief over the injustice, I couldn't see straight, and bile rose to my throat. It made me sick that once the crowd dispersed they went about the rest of the daily business in town normally, as if nothing had changed.

I was alone on the dock, except for the company of one haggard-looking seagull. He stared at me and bobbed his beak up and down as if nodding and saying, 'I know how you feel, pal.'

Footsteps approached up the dock behind me, but I wasn't in the mood to socialize, so I didn't turn. 'A letter came for you.' It was the postmaster Mr Hogarth. 'I saw you sitting down here looking glum and thought it might be something to cheer you up a little.' He held the envelope out.

His footsteps were long faded before I finally worked up the energy to look at the letter. It was from Rosalyn. Since she had promised to notify me of the conditions at the Hastings Park facility, I tore it open.

Dearest Hayden,

Please be seated to read this. I regret that what I have to share with you is not pleasant. I hope you receive this in time to warn Chidori and her family before they leave Mayne Island. If it doesn't arrive in time, please accept my apology and my condolences.

The Hastings Park facility is very unsuitable. The women and children are being held in a building where the livestock is normally stored, with barbed fencing around the yard. There are no toilets, just a trough of sorts with only recently installed makeshift modesty partitions. The stench is dreadful and illness has been spreading through the facility. There are no bathing facilities and very few showers, which are to be shared amongst thousands of people. The families are issued army blankets, but there are no sheets unless they brought their own from home with them. The families have hung clothes across the openings of the cattle stalls in an attempt to create privacy, but it is crude.

I try not to feel pity for them because I'm sure they already feel such shame to be forced to live in these conditions. Mrs Setoguchi is so dignified and I fear she will be terribly offended to be subjected to living conditions that are so beneath her.

The men are separated from the family and their bunks are simply straw mattresses thrown on frames crammed together in rows. From Hastings Park, the younger men are sent to labour camps while the women and children are interned with the older men in tent cities somewhere in the interior of the province. I don't know all of the details of how they plan to move twenty-three thousand people. I wish I could be of more assistance, but the guards will not allow me to talk to anyone. I have only been able to ask quick questions here and there, and many of them don't answer – perhaps because they are afraid of the guards overhearing us, or perhaps they don't trust me. Either way, I understand their reluctance.

Some families have self-financed their own voluntary evacuation by train east of the Rocky Mountains. Please advise all of our dear friends from Mayne Island that if they can find a town outside the protected coastal zone willing to welcome them in, they might be able to avoid the camps by financing the train tickets themselves and renting property in Alberta or farther east – if it is not too late to make such arrangements.

Unfortunately, I have more ghastly news that I cannot bring myself to tell Mother and Father. I haven't told anyone yet because if I say it aloud, it will make it true. It makes me cry to even think about it. I received word that Earl was shot down and is now missing. Oh, dear Hayden, I am beside myself with worry. His commanding officer wrote to tell me that his airplane was hit. He was forced to parachute out. The rest of his squadron saw him land safely and watched as he ran through a field towards the protection of a grove of trees. They said he was shot and fell, then got back up and disappeared into the trees. They hope he was taken in and is being hidden by a sympathetic family in the French countryside, but he may have also been captured by the Germans. If he is alive, they will go back in for him, so please hold him in your prayers.

Also, please show this to Father. I cannot bring myself to write it again. All of our greatest fears may be coming true. Please hug Mother for me.

Love,
Rosalyn

I read the letter over again, leaned back flat on the dock, and stared up at the sky. When I was a kid, I wondered why I couldn't see God up in the clouds. I asked my Sunday school teacher once and she told me, 'God is actually in each and every one of us at all times. We can't see Him, but we can feel His presence.' She placed her palm on my chest over my heart and asked, 'Do you feel Him, Haydie?' I thought I did when I was a kid, but as I lay on the dock, I wasn't so sure.

When it turned to dusk, I drove the Setoguchi truck back to their empty property and then – in complete disillusion-ment – dragged myself home. My parents were in the family room on the couch, hugging.

'How are you holding up, Hayden?' my father asked.

'Not well.' I dropped Rosalyn's letter on the table in front of them and headed up the stairs to my room.

Chapter 29

Jack passed behind me in the yard and whispered with urgency, 'Hayden, what the hell are you doing?'

'Looking.'

'Goon up,' he said to warn me of an approaching guard. 'Get away from the fence. They're going to shoot you.' He stopped a distance away to give the appearance he had nothing to do with me.

'How far do you think it is to the border?' I asked with my face upturned to the one sliver of sunlight.

'Too far. Have you completely lost your senses?' He paced around, torn between wanting to rip me from the fence and wanting to walk away to save himself. 'Step back before you take one in the back.'

My fingers clenched the wire, touching the freedom on the other side. 'Would that be so terrible?'

'Hayden, your girl is waiting on you at home. She's dreaming about living with you in that house I drew for you. You just need to be patient. We'll be going home before you know it. You'll see her in no time.'

'She's not there.'

He paused, attempting to sort out what I was talking about. He must have realized that he was running out of time to change my mind and that what he said next was crucial, so chose his words wisely. 'You'll be reunited with her as soon as the war is over. Don't do anything foolish to ruin that.'

Jack was a good chap, but I wasn't sure I believed him. I closed my eyes and inhaled the air on the other side of the fence as I contemplated. A breeze picked up through the trees and Chidori's voice whispered in my ear, 'Don't let them break you. Come home to me, Hayden.'

My fingers released the fence.

F/O Pierce Duration as POW: Don't care.

I hate it here. I hate it here. I hate it here. I hate it here. How does everyone else carry on as if it's not insufferable? I made a grave error. Why did I come here? What was I thinking? I should have found Chidori and stayed with her. I didn't make anything better by fighting in the war. Everything is worse.

I need to get out of here, or die.

Chidori and I walked in the grass next to a creek, holding hands and making each other laugh. We didn't know we had a worry in the world. But then thunder cracked and two trench-coated Gestapo agents jumped out from the trees and pointed pistols at us. They forced us to march in the rain to an internment camp filled with piles of dead bodies layered on top of each other in grotesque mounds of flesh.

At the gate, Chidori grasped for my hand frantically, but an officer separated us and ripped her away by the waist. She kicked and screamed, trying to free herself from his hold but he threw her to the ground and climbed on top, pawing at her blouse. Enraged, I launched my body and knocked him off her. We rolled in the dirt, struggling. I grabbed his neck with one hand and covered his evil mouth with my other hand. The full force of my weight pressed down to suffocate him.

'Get off,' the Gestapo garbage cried out from under the pressure. I dug my fingers tighter into his throat to cut off his breathing. He coughed and clawed at my face. 'Stop!' he choked out.

'You should have kept your filthy mitts off her,' I growled.

I was tackled from behind and woke up fully when I hit the ground. Matt straddled across my waist. He'd had enough of the nightly assaults and grabbed me roughly by the shoulders, then slammed me repeatedly against the floorboards until I stopped flailing. His knees braced my arms down and his forearm angled across my throat. His face was inches from mine and he was breathing heavily. He stared me down 'Are you awake now?'

I nodded. Billy, whom I'd mistaken for the Nazi police officer, was still gasping to recover from being strangled. 'Sorry.'

They had all grown justifiably intolerant of my mental deterioration. Patience with me had worn thin.

Chapter 30

After Chidori was taken away from Mayne Island I didn't leave my bedroom for five days, except to use the outhouse. I had no reason to. I wasn't hungry. And there was no work at the mill. Patch alternated between sleeping on my floor and snuggled right up on my mattress next to me, but my mother eventually banished him as a disincentive to my despondence. After Patch was not allowed to comfort me, my mood became very dark. Then after a few nights of not sleeping, my thoughts became strange. Since Ma had witnessed the impact of the disease of insanity in other relatives, she grew rightly concerned and sent for Joey to come over in an attempt to cheer me up.

'Hey, pal,' Joey said as he entered my bedroom. 'Want to go outside and toss the baseball around?'

'No thanks. I don't feel up to it.' I rolled over on my mattress so my back faced him.

'Come on. Some fresh air and,' he chuckled, 'a bath would definitely do you some good.'

'I just want to be alone. Thanks anyway, Joe.'

The casters on my desk chair squeaked as Joey sat down.

'Snap out of it, Hayden. What good does moping around and acting as if you're dying do? You might as well get back to living your life. Lying around in bed for weeks or months ain't going to stop a war or bring Chidori home.'

Holy smokes. That was it. He was right. I abruptly sat up and shot out of bed to slap him on the shoulder. 'Thanks for the idea.'

'What?' Joey's face angled with perplexed amusement.

Wholly inspired, I left my room and rushed downstairs with him following behind. My mother was pleased to see me awake and full of energy, and she thanked Joey profusely for changing my mood so quickly. But my father's expression fell stern, as if he knew that my overly sudden change in disposition was not a good sign.

'I've decided to volunteer to go overseas.'

'Pardon me?' Ma scowled at Joey as if he'd advised me to come up with the impulsive idea. 'No. You absolutely will not do such a foolish thing.'

'I have to volunteer. What they're doing to the Japanese Canadians is wrong. I need to do something to fix it.'

Ma moved to stand in front of me. 'Getting yourself killed overseas is not going to change anything. It certainly won't bring Chidori home. Have you lost your ever-loving mind?'

'Chidori will be allowed to come home once the war is over. It's my duty to make sure the war gets over sooner rather than later.'

'Don't be reckless. You can't win a war all by yourself. You'll be killed.' Her hands flew to her mouth to muffle her sobs. 'John, talk some sense into him. He's thinking rashly.'

My decision was made. I hadn't put much thought into it, but I didn't need to. It was the right thing to do. 'Someone has to fight for what's just. Besides, overseas conscription is probably going to start soon and I'll be sent anyway.'

Patch whimpered as if to protest. I crouched and pressed my forehead to his. 'Sorry, pal. But this is something I need to do. You be a good boy while I'm gone.'

My farewell to the dog made my mother bawl and she rushed out of the room.

Pop nodded at me as if he understood but wished he didn't.

Chapter 31

F/O Pierce Duration as POW: Springtime, maybe. Each day is an eternity, so you'll have to do the math.

My tremor is getting worse and sometimes my entire body shudders in time with my hands. Everything is brown and dull – the buildings, the ground, our clothes, our food, the dust that blows in through the cracks, the rodents and bugs. Even things that should have colour, like the sky or a fellow's eyes, are all hazy brown. I wonder if there are still colours where Chidori is. I miss pink the most. I want to see the colour pink that her lips turn after she kisses me. I love that colour.

I know what happened to Rosalyn. Everything must have turned brown in her life.

F/O Pierce Duration as POW: Definitely spring. There's no snow, just mud.

My mother makes the most delicious zucchini loaf, and sometimes I think I can taste it on my tongue, but then I swallow and my mouth tastes rancid again. The white-haired, nasty-nosed goon smirked in a smug way today when I saw him out in the yard. I laughed because if he knew what I was planning he wouldn't be smug.

'What are you thinking about, pal?' Arnold asked me. 'I was thinking about how badly I crave an apple. I would kill for an apple from my farm back home. Bright red-green on the outside. Sweet juicy white on the inside. I would literally snap someone's Goddamn neck for a McIntosh apple.'

Arnold gaped wide-eyed at me for a second, then glanced cautiously at a couple of the other fellows.

I was unravelling. I knew that.

F/O Pierce Duration as POW: Does it matter?

Forcing myself to stay awake prevents nightmares, but the lack of sleep is driving me insane – more insane. In the last twenty-four hours, I've thought about suffocating Malcolm because he snores, hitting Barney over the back of the head with a frying pan because he slurps his soup, and stabbing Edward with a shard of glass because he is always in such a damn jolly mood. Truly, how can someone be that happy in these conditions? It's unnatural. Instead of killing every one of my bunkmates, it would be easier to kill myself. I have decided how I would kill myself. I would stand on a brown chair and wrap my brown belt around the brown rafter to make a brown noose. All I would have to do is kick the chair out from beneath me.

F/O Pierce Duration as POW: Long enough to detest the colour brown for the rest of my life, which might not be much longer now.

I heard Chidori's voice again while I was in the yard. She reminded me that I was strong enough to survive this. She might be wrong, but in the event that she is right I decided to keep suffering for a little longer. If the sun ever came out, I think I would be cheerier. The weather alternates between heavy greyish-brown clouds and pouring rain. That's it. No other weather. Even the rain seems brown because it makes rivers of brown mud run through the camp and splashes the mud up to coat the outside of the buildings. If I ever return home, I'm never going to wear brown again. I'm never going to eat soup again either.

F/O Pierce Duration as POW: Days turn to weeks turn to months turn to years.

I wonder what would happen if I set the entire camp on fire. At least flames licking up the sides of the buildings would be colourful. I can't write more because my hands shake too much.

F/O Pierce Duration as POW: Long enough for Chidori to already be married to someone else and have a baby.

F/O Pierce Duration as POW: Too bloody long.

Please God make it end.

F/O Pierce Duration as POW: An estimated 7,300 hours.

I really don't care about anything but Chidori any more.

F/O Pierce Duration as POW: Approximately 438,000 torturously monotonous minutes.

Chidori, can you feel me? If you can, I'm sorry. I don't think I can do it any more.

Chapter 32

The night before I shipped off from Vancouver to Basic Training in Vernon, my parents came into town and met Rosalyn and me at a restaurant. The last time I had seen my sister was only a couple months earlier, but when I picked her up at the nurses' dormitory where she lived, she was almost unrecognizable because of the shocking amount of weight she had lost from the worry over Earl. She had applied bright lipstick to brighten her face, but there was no hiding how gaunt she had become. I didn't say anything about her dreadful appearance because I didn't want her to think she looked unattractive, but I did ask how she was feeling. She lied.

Pop had already convinced Ma to stop hounding me to change my mind about volunteering for the Armed Forces – in the hopes that if they didn't pressure me I would quit rebelling and come to my senses on my own. I was too defiant and determined for that strategy to work, but I did appreciate that they were at least outwardly being less oppositional to my goal. And once they saw the poorly state Rose was in, their full parental concern shifted to her.

Ma pressed her with questions about Earl and her duties at the hospital, then lectured her on the importance of eating three square meals a day without skipping. Eventually, Rosalyn's face grew even paler and her hands trembled so terribly that she spilled her tea all over the tablecloth. She looked about to faint.

'Rose, are you sure you're feeling all right?' I asked and supported her elbow so she wouldn't slide off the chair.

She forced a pleasant smile and placed her weak hand on top of mine. 'Fine, Haydie. Just fine. A little tired maybe.'

'Earl's going to come home,' I said quietly and squeezed her fingers to reassure her.

'I know.' She blinked slowly, her eyes glazed over, and she drifted off into her tortured thoughts again. I tried to tell a light-hearted story about Joey and Donna Mae, but Rose wasn't paying attention, and halfway through, she interrupted to say to Ma and Pop, 'You mustn't believe everything you read in the newspapers. Simply because it is written in a newspaper doesn't make it true.'

'What do you mean?' Ma asked before shooting a worried glance at Pop.

Rose reached into her handbag, pulled out a folded newspaper, and placed it on the table. 'One afternoon, one of my nursing friends and I were leaving the teashop and got to talking with the Takeuchi boys on Powell Street. Do you remember them? They lived on Mayne Island when I was in grade school, then moved to Vancouver?'

'Yes, of course. They were fine boys. How are they?' Ma said cheerfully.

'Not good, Ma.' Rose shook her head at our mother's obtuseness and then poked her index finger repeatedly against the newspaper column. 'They were taken away like Chidori's family. And before that happened, the newspaper reporter lied about something that happened. He slandered their good names.'

'What lies?' Pop asked. 'Was your name printed in the story as well?'

'No, nobody cared to mention that I defended the boys. They ignored my side of the story completely.'

'What happened?' I asked.

'As the boys and I chatted on the sidewalk, a more recently immigrated Japanese woman and her young child were stopped by two RCMP officers who asked to see her papers. She didn't understand what they were asking her in English. The woman bowed repeatedly to the officers and glanced over at the Takeuchi boys in hopes they could assist her. The boys explained to her in Japanese that she was being asked to show her papers.'

'I'm confused,' Ma said. 'How could a reporter cast two boys helping to translate in a negative light?'

'The RCMP officers took offence to what they assumed was the boys giving the woman instructions. The officers claimed that the boys were directing her to disobey. More likely, the officers preferred not to admit that they needed help.'

Pop nodded as if it didn't surprise him.

'Wait, it gets worse,' Rose continued. 'The officers took one look at my friend Louise and me and assumed that the boys had been harassing us. In their mind it was implausible that I would have been willingly conversing with two Japanese boys. Suddenly more interested in us, they let the woman go without checking her papers and walked over to ask the boys what they thought they were doing pestering us. The boys were nothing but polite but without waiting for them to explain how we all knew each other, the officers pushed both of the boys against a shop window to wrench their arms behind their backs. The window broke from their weight and a shard of glass cut one of the officers.'

'Oh goodness, nothing good will come from injuring an officer,' Mother said, missing the point.

'The officer cut himself, Ma. When he smashed two inno-cent boys into a window.' Rose sighed from the effort of telling the story, then focused more on Pop and me as she shared the rest. 'A crowd of folks gathered around and some fellow from the newspaper took a photograph of the boys being arrested.' She unfolded the newspaper to the photo to show us.

The photo showed the officer's face bleeding and the broken shop window in the background. The caption read: *Two Japs Arrested. Harassed White Girls. Assaulted Officers*.

'The article reports that the boys smashed the window and cut the officer, which is absolutely not true. I just wanted to warn you not to believe everything that you read in the news-paper. They can make the truth look any way they choose, and they can also print thumping lies. The average reader is none the wiser. It is a shame. A horrible shame. The boys spent two nights in jail and had to pay for the broken window before they were then forced to evacuate to Hastings Park.'

'Oh, dear, that is a shame,' Ma said. While we were all pondering the injustice in heavy silence, she took over the conversation to tell her own story about how one of our relatives had been treated unfairly during the Easter Rising.

'Ma, what does a religious protest in 1916 have to do with Rose's story about the Takeuchi boys?' I asked, trying to contain my frustration.

'They were both a shame.'

I shook my head in exasperation. Thankfully Pop changed the subject to something completely unrelated and distracted Ma. I slid my arm across my sister's shoulders and gave her a squeeze so she would know that at least I understood. 'I'm going to do whatever I can to end the injustice.'

Her eyes met mine, but all I saw was intense sadness.

After dinner, we walked Rose back to her dormitory. She hugged me for an extra-long time and whispered, 'Make sure you return home, darling brother.'

'I will. I promise.'

She chuckled softly without smiling. 'That's what Earl said.' Then she turned and disappeared into the lobby of her building.

As my parents and I strolled back to the hotel, Ma chatted about pretty much everything we saw – the rose-beige colour of a Model A Coupé, the size of the lettering on a porcelain store sign, and the closeness of an iron bench to the sidewalk. She always talked about nothing when she was trying to keep her mind off something that made her uncomfortable. So she was talking about a whole lot of nothing.

'I'm worried about Rose,' I said to my father after my mother had gone into the hotel lobby. I stood outside with him while he finished his cigarette.

He shrugged and took a drag before answering. 'Her fiancé is missing in action, she's witnessed some unsettling deaths at the hospital, and her kid brother is shipping off. She's heavy with concern. We all are.'

'I don't want to add to her burden. I'll be in the country until I finish training. The war might be over by the time I get my wings, or I might wash out.'

'I doubt you'll wash out. You're going to be a fine pilot.' Pop butted out his cigarette, then turned to lean his back against the wall. He watched the folks pass on the sidewalk for a long spell. 'Your mother means well.'

'I know.' I shoved my hands in my pocket, feeling guilty that I'd been annoyed by her guilelessness. 'I'd rather she actually understood, though.'

He nodded.

I kicked the toe of my boot against the sidewalk with conflicted emotions. 'I'm going to miss you, Pop.'

He nodded again before reaching forward to pull me in tightly against his chest. 'I love you, son. You make sure you come on home.' He patted my back, then released me from the embrace and turned to go into the hotel.

It was the first time since I had made up my mind to volunteer for service that I felt a shred of second-guessing. But then I thought about Chidori imprisoned for no reason and the shred was replaced with sheer determination.

Two streets over from the hotel was called Hastings Street

and it made me wonder if maybe Hastings Park was nearby. I jogged over to a fellow who was opening the door to his pick-up truck. 'Excuse me, is Hastings Park far from here?'

'The place where they're keeping the Japs?'

'Japanese Canadians. Yes.'

'Just under five kilometres. I'm heading past that way if you want a lift.'

I nodded, grateful, and opened the passenger door to get in.

'There ain't much else out that way.' We pulled out onto the road. 'Do you have a reason to be there?'

I nodded again, not particularly inclined to discuss my personal life with a stranger.

He glanced over at me and quickly realized I wasn't going to be a real chatty chap. He thankfully didn't ask any more questions.

I hopped out when he stopped, thanked him through the open window, and crossed the street towards the barbwire fence. Dusk had fallen, but the silhouetted outlines of the buildings were visible. Thousands of cars that had been confiscated from the Japanese Canadians were lined up in the field. The only people around the facility were guards. I hooked my fingers through the chain link for a good while, just staring, until one of the guards wandered over to me.

'You can't be here.'

'My fiancée is inside. I'm leaving for service tomorrow. Would you ask her to come outside so I can say goodbye?'

'That's not permitted.'

'They must be able to have visitors. Even prisoners in jail are allowed to have visitors.'

'Not at this time of night and not without a pass. Besides, they're enemy aliens, not prisoners. They've been stripped of their rights.'

'She's not an enemy alien. She was born in Canada and did nothing wrong. Please just ask her to come out into the yard. I won't take long.' I pulled her picture out of my pocket and showed it to him. 'This is what she looks like.'

He shone his torch at the photo and shook his head. 'Even if I tried, there are hundreds of women her age in there. I'd never be able to find her.' He leaned his back against the fence and cupped his hands over a match to light a cigarette. 'Why are you marrying a Jap?'

My jaw tensed and I had to speak through clenched teeth. 'Because I love her. Why did you marry your wife?'

He chuckled. 'Because she was the only one who said yes. I tell you what, kid, write her a note and I'll see what I can do about getting it to her.'

'Thank you.' I fished around in my pockets and found my ship ticket to write on the back.

Chidori Setoguchi: I came by Hastings Park to see you, but couldn't get in. I leave for Basic Training tomorrow. Please contact my parents once you know your new address. I miss you and I love you. Hayden Pierce.

I curled the ticket to pass it through the fence to the guard.

'When did she get here?' he asked as he tucked the ticket into his pocket.

'April twenty-first.'

252

'She's more than likely already gone by now.'

'Gone where?'

'An internment camp in the interior, or maybe to work on a sugar-beet farm in Alberta. I'll get it to her if she's still here.' He turned and walked away.

I sighed and stared at the buildings until it got too dark to make out the outlines. The hopelessness in my gut tried to rear up, but I pushed it back down by focusing on the fact that I was boarding a train the next morning to do something about it.

Chapter 33

F/O Pierce Duration as POW: 26,000,000 seconds and counting.

Chidori appeared in the water as I drowned. She swam next to me and her black hair swirled around her face. She reached her arm out and said with the calmest voice, 'They can't break you. Our love is too strong.' When I extended my reach to touch her she faded. I popped my head out of the ocean into the middle of a war zone. Everything – submarines, ships, airplanes, men – fired ammunition at me. Explosions went off all around, so I dipped back down into the water and let myself sink deeper into the darkness to get away from it all. I floated into the depths for a long while before a hand clamped around my arm and pulled me all the way across the ocean and back to Canada. When we surfaced, my saviour wasn't even breathless. It was Gordie. I was about to thank him but then he sank. I dove down repeatedly to save him, but I couldn't find him.

I woke up screaming at three forty-seven.

Harold won the bet, which was fair since he also gained a black eye when he tried to wake me up.

To the son I will never have,

Sorry I couldn't be your Papa. I wanted to be your father more than anything in the world, but it looks as if someone else is going to need to do that for me. I haven't actually lived that long myself, but I have learned a few things about being a man that I can share with you.

First, ladies fancy fellows who know how to dance, so make sure you learn how to dance. On second thought, maybe it doesn't matter whether you know how to dance, since I never did have a proper dance with your mother, and she learned to love me anyway. You need to be polite to a woman – no cursing, no spitting, always open the door for her, carry heavy items for her, ask her opinion about topics, tell her she looks pretty, give her your coat if it's chilly, stand when she enters or leaves a room, and ask permission before you kiss her. If you happen to be a fellow who doesn't fancy women, I suppose my advice still applies. Be kind. Be yourself. And never let anyone tell you who you should or shouldn't love.

Second, read as much as you can. Books teach you things about people and the world that you would never know otherwise.

Third, learn how to swim even if you don't ever live near water. It might save someone's life one day. And it will ensure that you don't lose your own life in a way that could have been prevented. If you can convince your great uncle Massey to learn how to swim while you're at it, I would be much obliged. I never thought it was right for a man who made his living on the water to not know how to swim. And if you get caught in a rip don't fight it; go with the flow.

Fourth, make sure you own a sharp suit that fits you well, even if you don't need it for your everyday work. Ask your father to show you how to tie a necktie. Ask him to also teach you how to fix an engine, because chances are you'll own a car or a tractor or a boat and you don't want to be stranded.

Fifth, have a firm handshake and look folks in the eyes when you meet them. Be honest and generous like your mother. Judge people on their merit, not on the colour of their skin or the God they believe in. Better yet, try not to judge people at all if you can. There are going to be people you don't respect much, but still treat them cordially. Solve problems with words whenever possible, but you can sock a fellow in the mouth if he disrespects or hurts someone you love. Come to think of it, one fortunate thing about me not being able to be your father is you won't inherit my temper. It only ever made things worse, so you're better off without that.

If you're born a girl, that would be dandy too. I would have taught you all the same things I taught a son, including how to throw a proper spiral and hit a curve ball. You can learn everything else you need to know from your mother. She's better at managing a rowboat, fishing, and everything to do with school than I am anyway. You're lucky to have her as a mama. You take good care of her.

Even though I will never meet you, I love you. I love you as much as God loves you.

Sincerely,
The man who desperately wishes he could have been your papa, Hayden Pierce

I tore the pages of the letter out of my journal and folded them to place in my pocket next to the letter Pop had sent me before I was shot down. Even though I had tried to forget about it, every word was still etched in my memory. I didn't even need to unfold it to read it again.

The next day, when I was out in the yard, I noticed a slip of paper in the crack of the latrine wall. Gordie had left me a note to let me know it was Easter.

God will judge the world in righteousness. On this day, He gave us living hope through the resurrection of Jesus Christ from the dead. Hold on, Hayden, freedom's crowning hour awaits. The Americans have an ace up their sleeve. Wait for it.

Folded up in the note, to my astonishment, was my photo of Chidori that the guard had torn into confetti. Gordie had somehow glued it back together with some sort of resin. So moved by the thoughtful gesture, I dropped to my knees and wept. There was no favour in the world that I could return to him that would even come close to what getting the photo of Chidori back meant to me. I would be eternally grateful and indebted to him.

As I stared at her, a songbird chirped from its perch on the barbed wire.

Chapter 34

In May 1945, shouting echoed from the prison yard. I climbed up on an upper bunk and peered out the brown film on the window. A bunch of fellows were jumping up and down.

'Hey, come look at this,' I hollered to my bunkmates.

We all huddled around the windows to watch the unusual sight of giddy prisoners.

'What do you think's going on?' Luke asked.

Before any of us had a chance to come up with a theory, the door to our barrack flung open. Gordie stood grinning at us with his arms stretched wide. 'The Russians have arrived! We're liberated!'

'What?'

'Mussolini and Hitler are both history. We're free, you sons of bitches, we're free.'

I knew I wasn't dreaming because nothing good ever happened in my dreams. I jumped down from the bunk, stuffed my journal into my back pocket, and ran to the door. Ecstatic that the suffering of incarceration was over, I leapt up onto Gordie's back and he piggybacked me out onto the yard where we hooted and hollered. To my absolute delight, the Russians really were there. Huge beastly men with heavy beards and mounted on gigantic black horses. The German goons had all dropped their guns on the ground and were lined up along the fence with their hands laced behind their heads. It was intensely satisfying to walk past them as they stood impotently in surrender.

I spotted the white-haired nasty-nosed guard. It would be my only opportunity for retribution. I hopped off Gordie's back and picked up one of their Karabiners, but I wasn't the best shot with a rifle, so I walked up closely and lifted it to aim at his forehead. He pleaded in German, presumably asking for me not to kill him. My finger twitched, itching to squeeze the trigger. The decent thing to do was offer forgiveness and let God take care of his punishment. The problem was, God had likely witnessed too many wicked deeds to keep a tally of every one.

As the images of my time in solitary confinement flashed through my mind, the guard clasped his hands together, begging me to show mercy. He knew he deserved to die after what he had done to me and the others who came before and after me. But I was the better man. I was free. He had to live with the guilt for the rest of his life. He didn't break me. I clenched my eyes shut, dropped the gun to the dirt, and walked away.

The Russians handed out vodka, so I grabbed a bottle as Gordie caught up with me. I swigged some, then handed it over to him. He drank a mouthful, and winced as it burned his insides.

'Let's go get something to eat,' I said.

Gordie glanced back over his shoulder at the liberated camp and waved a dismissive good riddance, then followed me out the open gate to freedom.

We didn't have any money, so I wasn't sure how we were going to get anything to eat. I didn't care, though, because I was prepared to steal if I had to. We walked in a flurry of excitement along with hundreds of other POWs and Russian soldiers to the nearest town, which was only four kilometres from the camp compound.

Most of the townsfolk locked their doors and shutters when they saw the flood of boisterous men. After four rejections, Gordie and I were ushered by a little old Polish lady into a house that had half its roof bombed out. She nodded a lot, but didn't speak as she served us a small portion of lamb and potatoes with red wine. It took over the number one spot on my list of all-time favourite meals.

She pointed at a photo of a young man in uniform on her fireplace mantel, then with tears in her eyes she touched her heart and pointed at the meal. I didn't know exactly what she meant by her pantomime, but it felt like maybe she was serving us the welcome home dinner that she had planned for someone else. Maybe someone who would never be returning home. Whatever her reason, I was eternally grateful for her generosity. Gordie and I barely talked because we were too occupied with eating. The wine in combination with the earlier vodka went straight to my head, probably because I only weighed about one hundred and twenty pounds. The woman broke off a chocolate square to share for dessert from a secret stash she had hidden behind a wallboard. I stood to wash the dishes for her but then drunkenly started laughing at nothing and accidentally knocked over a vase. Gordie caught it before it hit the ground and pulled me by the shoulders.

'Okay, lightweight, we better get you out of here before you do more damage than the bombs.' He pushed me towards the door,

'Thank you,' I said as I stumbled outside. Darkness fell but people strolled unrushed up and down the cobblestone street.

Gordie thanked the woman repeatedly for treating us the way that she had perhaps hoped a stranger would have treated her son, then he said goodbye. He tucked something into his pocket and stood next to me on the sidewalk, surveying the scene. After a deep breath he said, 'Ah, do you smell that?'

I sniffed. 'Sewage?'

'Freedom. That is the smell of freedom, buddy boy.'

'Oh.' I bent over and vomited the entire contents of my stomach.

'Dang.' Gordie grimaced at the revolting sight, then teased, 'I guess your delicate stomach isn't used to having real food in it.'

I retched a few more times until nothing more came out. When I lifted my head, Gordie wasn't beside me. He was across the yard, bent over a low stone wall, heaving his dinner too. I crawled on my hands and knees over to where he was. 'What was that you said about having a delicate stomach?'

'Shut it,' he groaned, and doubled over in another wave of nausea.

I laughed and we both sat against the wall until our stomachs stopped cramping. It was late in the evening by the time we got up and wandered around the streets to soak up the festivities. The townspeople celebrated the end of the war with the POWs, and it got rowdy. Two young women walked towards us, whispering. They shared a bottle of wine between them. I grinned idiotically, mesmerized by the colours of their clothes. Both had very dark wavy hair. One wore a knit snood net with ringlets popping out to frame her face. The other covered the top of her head with a scarf that tied under her chin, but the length of her hair hung freely down her back. The taller gal wore a blue dress with tiny multicoloured butter-flies all over the fabric. It was so pretty I reached out and ran my fingertip across it. She giggled, maybe a little tipsy herself, then introduced herself and her friend, or maybe it was her sister. I wasn't really in any condition to remember what they said their names were, so I stared at the soft pink fabric of the other young lady's dress. She also wore a light yellow sweater and looked delicious, like strawberry and banana taffy candy.

Gordie made cordial pidgin-English conversation with them, but I had to use all my concentration just to walk straight. One of them wrapped her arm around my waist and helped me along. Eventually, we arrived at a jolly town square with a stone water fountain in the centre of the plaza. The aroma of different foods and alcohol mixed together with the pots of vibrant flowers and intoxicated me even more. About to fall down, I sat on one of the benches along the path and leaned my head back to gaze at the brilliant stars.

Fiddle music erupted out of a pub nearby, and Gordie danced on the grass with the woman while I rested my cheek on the arm of the bench. At some point, one of the ladies pulled my hand to make me stand up. I stumbled forward and she had to steady me as we swayed to the music. Her soft warmth reminded me of bread when it first comes out of the oven. I didn't have the sense to understand why a gal who smelled that wonderful would want to be dancing up against a fellow who likely reeked worse than a wet dog.

'What's your name?' I whispered in her ear.

'Anastasia.'

I lifted my head up and scanned the plaza. 'Where is my friend?'

'With Raina. We go there?'

Her bright red lips and pink cheeks captivated me. 'Yes. We go there.'

I stretched my arm across her shoulder and leaned my weight on her as she led me to a stone building with a narrow blue wooden door. She unlocked the latch and helped me up two flights of rickety stairs to an apartment. The interior was visually as lively as an art gallery. The walls were painted orange, the drapes were gold and silver stripes, and the rugs were a radiant pattern of greens and blues and reds.

Gordie was seated on a purple velvet couch, watching the other girl dance seductively across the living room. Big band music played on a radio as she took off one item of clothing at a time, throwing them at Gordie.

'Hey, Pierce. Have a seat and enjoy the show.'

I sat down. Anastasia served a plate of biscuits. I devoured them all. When I lifted my head again, Raina was standing in only her high heels and silky white undergarments.

'Whoa,' I said, which made Gordie laugh. 'I need to leave.' I tried to stand but lost my balance and ended up on the floor. With the little muscle control I had left, I rolled onto my back and stared at Raina as she continued to dance around above me. 'Gordie. Help me up. I need to leave,' I slurred.

'In a minute,' he said, without looking at me. He was fixated by Raina as she played with the straps of her brassiere.

Anastasia slid off the couch and knelt on the rug beside me. Her hand ran along my leg as she inched closer to me.

'You remind me of cotton candy,' I said to her, which made her frown and then laugh.

'You enjoy candy?'

'Yes. Very much.'

She unzipped the back of her pink dress and pushed it down over her shoulders. I sat up and tried to get to my feet, but she quickly slid her dress off over her legs, pulled me back down, and straddled my thighs. Her chest squished against mine and she kissed my neck. Her lips moved along my jaw and face until they found my mouth. The alcohol made my mind swirl. Her lips made my blood rush. I closed my eyes to make it stop. That was the last thing I remembered.

Chapter 35

I woke up sprawled on the purple velvet couch in Anastasia and Raina's apartment. Sunshine angled through the window and the glowing orange of the walls made my hungover brain throb. Anastasia was in the kitchen setting a kettle on the stove. She shot me a sympathetic smile when she noticed I was awake.

'Good morning. Sleep good?'

'Actually, yes. That was the first night in a long time I didn't have a nightmare.' At least, as far as I remembered. The entire night was foggy.

After the kettle boiled, she wandered out of the kitchen and into the living room with a cup of tea for me. She had changed into a short buttercup yellow housecoat, which showed her underpants when she bent over to set the teacup on the side table. The china was the same floral pattern my grandmother used to have.

'You need shower?'

'Yes. If you don't mind.'

She plopped down on the couch and propped her feet up on an ottoman as she lit a hand-rolled cigarette. 'Help to yourself.'

Not looking forward to the answer, but hating the dread of not knowing, I asked, 'Did you and I, uh, you know? I can't remember.'

Her lips pouted and she shook her head. 'No. Your friend say you dizzy for dame. Whatever this is meaning.'

Relieved, but still confused, I asked, 'Where is my friend?'

She nodded towards a closed door that must have been a bedroom. Then she pointed at an open door. 'Shower. I make food.'

I stood and crossed the living room to the bathroom. The soap smelled like a sanitary apothecary, which is exactly how I wanted to smell. The warm water from the shower was so welcome it damn near made me cry. The only reason I got out was because the aroma of eggs frying enticed me to hurry.

So much time had gone by since I'd seen my reflection in a proper mirror, I barely recognized the burn-scarred face looking back at me. Dark circles shadowed under my eyes, and I was so thin my bones poked out in sharp angles. My hands still had the tremor as I scrubbed my shirt in the sink with soap, then wrung it out.

I carried my shirt back into the living room to hang it in the sunshine on the fire escape, next to a small chicken coop. Anastasia piled a plate high with eggs, toast and fried potatoes as I sat down at the small green café table in the kitchen. 'This looks delicious. Thank you very much.'

Gordie and Raina emerged from the bedroom. Raina's red silk housecoat was untied and flapping open to reveal her nude body underneath. She didn't seem to care. Gordie handed her money from a stash he had stuffed in his pocket. Then he slapped my back and sat down to eat. Raina stuffed the money into a tin can in the cupboard before she sat on the kitchen counter and bit into a piece of toast. She stared at the scars on my body.

'Where'd you get the money from?' I whispered to Gordie.

'Don't worry about it.' He leaned back and stretched his arms above his head, then chuckled and shoved my shoulder. 'How are you feeling after that nosedive into the alley?'

'What?'

'You jumped out the window and fell off the fire escape into the alley. Yelling about how you needed to get home to Chidori. Don't you remember?'

I surveyed my body. The only thing that hurt was my elbow. 'No.'

'Good thing you were liquored up and landed on those empty crates.'

'How did I get back upstairs?'

'I carried you. You weigh less than a sack of potatoes. Anastasia could have carried you.'

They all laughed at my expense and I smiled a little.

Raina stretched her leg over and poked my thigh with her toe. 'What is it that is wrong with you? A man jumps out window away from woman who makes sex with him. I have not ever seen this.'

'I'm engaged.'

Raina snorted and she and Gordie teased me some more as we ate. Anastasia showed a little more compassion and restraint, as if she felt sorry for me, but even I had to admit the good-natured jokes were amusing. I didn't mind taking a little ribbing as a free man since it was infinitely better than being trapped in the POW camp with nothing to laugh about.

When breakfast was over, I washed the dishes in the sink, then walked over and climbed out the window to sit on the fire escape next to the chicken coop. As the sun rose higher in the sky, the world felt different, as if peace had dawned on the crowds of POWs and Russian soldiers who wandered along the street at the end of the alley.

Gordie stepped out onto the fire escape and sat next to me. 'You okay?'

I sighed as I realized I wasn't entirely. 'Did you steal that money from the old lady who fed us dinner?'

Without looking me in the eye he shook his head slowly. 'She gave it to me. Said something about her son and using it for food.'

I studied his demeanour and couldn't work out if he was telling the truth about stealing it or not, and I wasn't sure if I cared. But I did care what he spent it on. 'Do you think Chidori's been messing around with other fellows while I've been away?'

'No,' he replied without taking any time to think about it.

'How can you be so sure?'

He shrugged, maybe not so sure.

'Do you think your wife has been messing around on you?'

'No, she's a good girl.'

I didn't want to judge him, but I was honestly surprised and disappointed that he fell to the temptation of a woman who wasn't his wife. 'Don't you love your wife?'

'I love her more than anything in the world. What I was doing last night had nothing to do with love.'

I glanced over at him, trying to sort it all out. It was impossible for me to imagine ever wanting to be intimate with anyone other than Chidori. The idea that she might not have waited for me literally nauseated me. 'I just want to go home,' I said finally.

'I hear ya, pal.'

We sat in silence for a long while before I said, 'Thanks for gluing the picture of Chidori back together after the goon tore it to pieces. It really meant a lot to me. More than you can know.'

He nodded to accept my gratitude.

'How did you get the glue?'

'We scraped the dried resin from the spindles of the chair and melted it until it was glue again. We fixed all sorts of things once we figured that trick out.' He leaned his forearms on the railing and watched the people on the street below. The scars from the airplane wreck were emblazoned across his back and reminded me of mine. We were permanently marred by the war, both inside and out. And although there was nothing I wanted more than to be home, the possibility I was too changed terrified me.

I touched the smooth scar tissue that stretched up my neck and across my jaw. 'What if Chidori takes one look at me and is repulsed?'

He laughed. 'Don't worry about that. You weren't all that good looking to start with.'

'Ha. Now I know you're lying for sure.' I smiled and ran

my hand through my hair. It was scruffy and the texture of straw.

Someone whistled from the end of the alley, catching our attention. Jack waved at us frantically. 'Get your arses over to the railroad station on the east side of town. The Brits are sending a Flying Fortress to Barth to evacuate us out from there.'

I glanced at Gordie and beamed. 'Hot diggity. Let's go home.'

'Hell yeah.'

Chapter 36

F/O Pierce 05.03.45 Freedom Duration: 2 days.

The train out of Poland could only take us halfway to Barth, Germany, because the tracks had been blown up. The plan, which we came up with by majority consensus rather than direct orders, is to start walking in the morning. We're bunked with no gear in dark, boggy conditions under a grove of trees. The rain has turned into a continuous downpour. So far, freedom is physically less comfortable than being a Kriegie but, despite the cold and damp, there is a calmness about my fate that I haven't felt in years.

F/O Pierce 05.04.45 Freedom Duration: 3 days.

Walking cross-country towards the river through the flooded fields took much longer than it should have. The first bridge we came to was washed out, so we continued fourteen kilometres out of our way to cross on a flimsy pedestrian rope bridge. After some conflicted debate and disagreement, half of us decided to occupy a barn and several outbuildings for the night. Even though we are sheltered from the weather now, my clothes are still soaked through. We haven't eaten since we left Anastasia and Raina's apartment. Some of the other fellows are becoming irritable with the conditions and the disorganized leadership. Not me. I see the light at the end of the tunnel. I am unrestricted and at liberty to make my way home, which is all the motivation I need to continue to endure hardships.

F/O Pierce 05.05.45 Freedom Duration: 4 days.

We abandoned the original plan to follow the railroad tracks and instead kept to the roads, which made travelling faster, but now I have worn through what remained of the sole of my boots. We've split into groups since not everyone can walk at the same speed. Gordie and I are in a mid-paced group because my legs are weak and I can't keep up. He could have joined the faster-moving group, but he chose to stay with me. I don't know why. I'd be running if I had the strength he has. I ate some flowers I found at the side of the road. Hopefully they're not poisonous or anything.

F/O Pierce 05.07.45 Freedom Duration: 6 days.

I spent twenty minutes climbing a steep hill only to stumble near the top and roll halfway back down. My arms and face are raw from the scrapes. My legs are shaking from *both the fatigue of the effort and the lack of sustenance. Goddamn, if it weren't for Chidori I'd prefer to stay here and wait for death. But enough moaning. Gordie is sitting at the top waiting for me, so off I go to try again.*

F/O Pierce 05.09.45 Freedom Duration: 8 days.

We have finally reached the railroad tracks that lead into Barth! Waiting eagerly for a freight train to hop.

The train whistled as it entered the corner. Twenty of us hid in the bushes and waited for it to slow down. I stuffed my journal into my waistband and stood next to Gordie. He shoved me to make me go first. It took every ounce of energy I had to run and grab the handle of the freight door. I hoisted myself up and kicked my leg into the car. Gordie ran alongside the train, waiting until I was safely inside. He grabbed the handle and swung his leg up, but missed. His legs dropped back down and dragged on the ground dangerously close to the wheel.

'Give me your hand,' I shouted and reached for him.

The train sped up and his grip on the door handle loosened.

'Come on, Gordie. Reach!'

He flung his free arm again, and I leaned out of the car to clasp his hand. His grip tightened around my fingers, but the momentum of the train pulled his weight away. We clung to each other for probably close to a quarter-mile but his grip began to slip. His eyes locked with mine in an apologetic way before he let go. He hit the ground and rolled several times before lying motionless on his back.

'Shit.' The terrain passed increasingly quickly below me. 'Shit. Shit. Shit.' Without pausing to think of the consequences, I closed my eyes and jumped off the train, then flipped with a painful thud into the ditch.

It took a good while and wore holes in the knees of my trousers, but I eventually crawled back to where Gordie still lay on his back. He stirred and groaned when I shook him. 'What the hell, Pierce?'

'Sorry. I wasn't strong enough to haul you in.'

He sat up and rubbed the back of his head. 'No. What the hell? Why did you jump off the train?'

'I wasn't going to leave you behind.'

He grumbled and shook his head incredulously at how idiotic that was. 'Well, great. Now we're both stranded.'

Gordie and I knew there was no point trying to jump another moving train, so we made our way along the tracks to the next town. The locals mumbled things that sounded at best unwelcoming and at worst downright hostile as we passed them. When I noticed we were being followed, we picked up the pace and ducked into an abandoned shop. We hid until it got dark, then slipped through the streets and crawled under the train station platform to wait for the morning train to arrive.

Gordie snuck out at dawn when the first sound of passengers creaked above us. He stole clothes from unattended luggage and tickets from an elderly couple who had left them on the bench. I felt a pang of remorse about stealing from old folks who likely had little money themselves, but they'd have a better chance of talking their way onto the train than we would. And it certainly wasn't the worst thing I had done over the course of the war.

We boarded and sat in the passenger compartment as if we belonged. A few people gave us dirty looks, but since we didn't speak English in front of them, they left us alone the entire way to Barth.

F/O Pierce 05.12.45 Freedom Duration: 11 days.

Evacuated 11:00 hours. B-17 Flying Fortress.

Although battles in the Pacific and Asia are still being fought against Japan, the war in Europe is officially over. We won. Germany signed the surrender and we are officially going home. The American airmen were flown to France to board a ship from there. The Brits and anyone who had been in a POW camp since '41 were the first to be flown out to London. Gordie and I spent two nights sleeping on the ground at the Barth airfield, waiting for our turn. We've arrived in London now and we're bunked up together in tent barracks again. I don't think I'll actually believe anything has actually changed until I'm home on Mayne Island and holding Chidori in my arms.

Gordie wrote letters to his parents and his wife to let them know he's back on friendly ground and will be home soon. I'm afraid to write in case I jinx something, but I did finally drop a letter in the post for my parents. I asked them to inform Chidori when she returns. Once the government releases her from the internment camp, she will surely beat me home.

The government gave us a pamphlet titled 'Canada in the Last Five Years'. I'm reluctant to read it, but I suppose it's better to know what I've missed.

F/O Pierce 05.20.45 Freedom Duration: 19 days.

I can't sleep, but this time it's not from nightmares or the feeling that something terrible is about to happen. It's from the anticipation. It's possibly mixed with the frustration of having to wait around. Gordie and I have done some sightseeing in London to expend our unused leave, but the only sight I want to see is home. Mercifully, we board the cross-Atlantic ship tomorrow.

F/O Pierce 06.17.45 Freedom Duration: 46 days.

The ship finally arrived in Halifax last week. It feels a relief to be on Canadian soil, but I've been informed that it will be another week or so before we get sorted onto trains to take those of us from BC across the country. Gordie's assigned to a train that leaves for Winnipeg later today. He's been talking about his planned reunion with his wife non-stop for three days. It is torture to be this close to Chidori and still not be able to slide my fingers over the silky smoothness of her skin. If she has fallen in love with someone else, this might be the last time I ever write.

'All right, Pierce.' Gordie raised his glass for our farewell toast at the pub. 'I can't say it's been a blast. But I can say there ain't no other fella I would have rather gone through hell with. I'll still always have your back; all you need to do is ring me up. Pals.'

'Pals for life.' I clinked my pint to his and took a sip of ale. I was too choked up to say more, so I set my glass down and gave him a hug.

He swatted my back. 'Don't forget to invite me to your wedding.'

I nodded and swallowed the emotion.

'Well, I need to get over to the train station. I guess this is goodbye for now. Safe travels home.' He stood and shook my hand.

'I'll walk you to the station.'

He agreed and we left the pub. I was terribly uneasy at the thought of not having Gordie around, but I was glad for him that he was getting to go home.

When the train pulled into the station, we embraced once more and he picked up his kit. As he walked away, I shouted over the sound of the engine, 'Gordie. I owe my life to you several times over. Thank you for everything.'

He grinned and saluted.

'I'm going to miss you.'

He stepped up onto the train and hung out the door, holding the bar. 'Save the mushy stuff for Chidori. I'll write you.' He waved and disappeared inside.

F/O Pierce 08.06.45. Home.

Chapter 37

During the week-long cross-country train ride to Vancouver, I rehearsed the reunion with Chidori in my mind a thousand times. Sometimes I imagined that, although she didn't know exactly when I was supposed to arrive, she'd by chance be waiting at the dock in Miner's Bay when the ship pulled in. Other times, I surprised her at her house with picked flowers from the garden while she played violin in the solarium. Once, I envisioned showing up only to find that Chidori was married to someone else and expecting a baby. That scenario made me so depressed I decided it would be better if I didn't visualize the reunion any more. And as it turned out, none of it mattered anyway.

From the train station in Vancouver, I had to run to catch the sailing to Mayne Island. The crew had already prepared for departure but held the ramp for me because I was in the fresh uniform I'd been issued in Barth.

The vessel seemed smaller, and the passenger cabin smelled mustier than I remembered. I had to step out on deck to escape the stuffiness. The wind tore through my hair as we crossed the strait, and the salt from the spray coated my lips as I hung over the edge of the railing. I was so close.

The strangest sensation washed over me at the thought of being only minutes from the moment that had kept my hope alive for more than three years. A dream, only it was about to come true. My elation could not have been stronger as we finally passed the Georgina Point lighthouse and entered Active Pass. I could barely contain the urge to jump off the ship and swim the rest of the way. The first buildings visible on the island when we rounded the corner into Miner's Bay were the doctor's office and the Springwater Lodge. Just as when I left.

Before the vessel was even secured, I hopped over the ramp railing with my kit and crouched down to touch the wood of the dock with my palm. The old, familiar planks, warm from the sun, reminded me of all the time I had spent as a kid sitting on the dock while my father and Massey sold fish from the *Issei Sun*. Before the other passengers disembarked, I jogged up the dock and ducked into the general store to buy a bouquet of flowers for Chidori. A young man who I didn't recognize worked behind the counter.

'Hi Hayden. Did you just get home?'

'Yes.' I handed him money from my stash of military back-pay, trying to place his face.

He must have noticed my wheels turning because he said, 'Gavin.'

'Oh, Donna Mae's kid brother. You've shot up since I saw you last. How's that sister of yours?'

'Fine. She's expecting a baby.'

'Really? Did she and Joey get married?'

'Yup. They live over in Victoria now.'

'That's swell.' I opened the door to leave and added, 'Tell them I'm home, will ya?'

'Sure thing.' He waved and then helped the next customer.

A black dairy delivery truck rolled up and parked out front as I exited the store. The driver was heavier than when I had last seen him, and he sported a moustache, but he was unmistakably Rory. His eyes met mine as he stepped out of the open sliding driver's side door. When he recognized me he tipped his cap back. 'Hayden.' He extended his arm to shake my hand. 'Good to see you. Welcome home, pal.'

I shook his hand but frowned as I attempted to sort out why he was being so friendly. I still considered him the schoolboy bully that he had been before I left. But he'd evidently outgrown that. I wasn't sure how to respond to his new level of maturity, so I ended up sounding like my mother and made a completely redundant comment. 'You work for a dairy now.'

'I own it.' He slapped his palm on the hood of the truck with pride. 'I started it after the evacuation.'

'And Fitz? What's he up to these days?'

'He's a bank manager over in Victoria. Engaged to be married.' Rory slid his hands into leather gloves.

'Wow. Manager? Impressive.'

'Yup, he's a bigwig now.' Rory reached into the open sliding door and lifted a crate of milk bottles from the floor of the truck.

To be perfectly frank, it annoyed me that they shirked their duty and hadn't served. Or, maybe I simply resented that – since they hadn't been conscripted – they had ultimately made the more prudent choice by not volunteering. It didn't matter. What was done was done.

'Are the flowers for your ma?' he asked.

'No. They're for Chidori.'

He paused briefly to check my expression, as if he worried I was not quite right in the head, then placed the crate on the ground in front of the store. 'Chidori's not here.' He pushed his cap back on his head and then rested his hands on his hips, undecided whether he wanted to be the one to break the hard truth to me or not. 'They never came back.'

'Why? Because the war in the Pacific isn't over yet?'

'Actually, I heard on the radio the Americans dropped a new type of bomb on Japan that was so massive they wiped out an entire city.'

I frowned as Michiko and her family crossed my mind. 'Which city?'

He shrugged. 'I don't know, but that battle's essentially over. Japan will have no choice but to surrender now. Regardless, I doubt any of the Japanese-Canadian families will ever return to Mayne Island.'

All of the organs inside my body contracted at the same time and sucked the air out of my lungs. 'Why?'

'The government auctioned off all of their properties and belongings. There's nothing left for them to come home to.'

It felt as if I'd been hit with that American bomb that was

big enough to level an entire city. 'Is the auction how you ended up owning the dairy truck?'

'You bet. And thank my blessed horseshoes I got it for less than the appraised value, so I was able to keep my operation profitable through the war. Lucky, huh?'

My knees weakened and my mind spun with hundreds of questions about who had bought everything and if anyone had tried to stop it from happening, but the most important question was, 'Where are they all now?'

He shrugged apologetically, then hauled another crate of bottles.

I stood in the middle of the parking lot, numb with disappointment as he unloaded the rest of the milk, cheese and eggs. Once he was finished he glanced at me. 'You okay?'

I shook my head, not able to produce a more elaborate response.

'You want a lift home?'

I nodded, climbed into the passenger seat, and placed the bouquet on my lap. We didn't speak as we crossed the island, but when he stopped on the road in front of my parents' property I said, 'She'll come home as soon as I let her know that I'm back.'

He half-smiled, as if he felt pity for me. 'I'm sure she will. Say hi to her and your folks for me.'

Still not accustomed to his friendly, grown-up demeanour, I stepped out of the truck. He waved and drove away in a cloud of dust.

My father was in the front yard, working on the truck engine. When I walked up the driveway, still holding the flowers, he stood upright. Relief washed over his face as he wiped the grease off his hands onto a rag. 'Eleanor!' he shouted. 'Eleanor! Get out here.'

Ma opened the front door and stepped out onto the porch, squinting against the sun. She focused on Pop initially, wondering what he was hollering for, but then she followed his gaze until she saw me. Her hands flew to her mouth as she gasped and rushed down the steps to meet me. As soon as her arms were wrapped around me, I started to cry, which made her sob.

Father's arms circled both of us and he cupped my neck. 'Welcome home, son.'

'Oh, Hayden.' Mother squeezed me for a long while before leaning back to get a good look at my face. 'Why didn't you ring us? We are so glad to see you. Are you okay?'

I nodded and wiped my eyes with my sleeve. I handed her the bouquet.

Pop hugged me again and slapped my back. 'Damn, it's good to see you.'

Ma studied my scarred face with concern before she pinched my cheeks lightly. 'You're too skinny still. I'll make us a nice welcome home dinner.'

'No soup.'

Her eyebrows angled sharply into a frown in response to my abruptness.

'I mean thank you, but I can't eat soup any more.'

After a hesitation, she said, 'All right.' Her worry deepened across her forehead, but she managed to bolster a smile. 'I wish you would have rung on the telephone to say when you would be arriving. We would have met you at the dock and I could have prepared something special.'

'Sorry. I wanted to surprise you.'

'It's okay, darling. It is the best surprise. Truly. The very best surprise. Our prayers have finally been answered.'

I nodded and hugged her again before we made our way towards the house. 'Patch!' I hollered and then whistled. 'Come here, boy.'

Both my parents stopped in their tracks and exchanged an unsettling look with each other. A young docile golden retriever wandered out from behind the barn to check out who had been calling. I waited for a flash of black and white from a spunky Border collie to tear around the corner.

'Patch died,' Ma said.

The news hit me as sharply as the time my Spitfire under-carriage wouldn't drop and I had to smash down a hard belly-landing on the tarmac.

'This is Lacey.' She patted the golden retriever and looked up at me. 'Doesn't she have a lovely temperament?'

My father studied my reaction and seemed to sense what my mother was oblivious to.

When I didn't make any overture towards the new dog, Ma shrugged, baffled by the awkwardness, before she headed into the house to get the meal started. Pop gave my shoulder a compassionate squeeze. 'Sorry about Patch. Your mother thought it best at the time not to dishearten you with the news.'

I nodded and swallowed hard to hold back the thwarted sting, then shifted my focus. 'I need to let Chidori know I'm home.'

His eyelids dropped in a longer than normal blink as he prepared to deliver the next round of rotten news. 'The Setoguchis didn't come back.'

I climbed the porch steps. 'I know. That's why I need to contact her. She'll come home once she knows I'm here. Where did you store the letters she wrote?'

'I'm sorry, son.' He paused and rubbed the tension out of the back of his neck. He squinted at me through the sun and then reluctantly delivered the blow. 'Chidori never wrote.'

And that struck like the butt of a rifle to the temple. 'That's impossible. She promised she would send a letter here to let me know where she ended up.'

He shook his head apologetically. 'While your sister was sick, and we were staying in Vancouver, Mr Hogarth held our mail for us. Your mother picked it all up when we returned. There wasn't anything from Chidori or the Setoguchis.'

'Their letters must have been intercepted by the government. She'll be able to write now,' I theorized the most logical possibility to reassure myself.

Pop rested his hand on my shoulder, maybe because he could tell I would literally need the support when he burst my bubble. 'The government censored parts of the letters but didn't block correspondence. People here on Mayne received letters from other Japanese-Canadian families over the years.'

'Well, there must be some other reason,' I said, clinging desperately to the unravelling threads of hope. 'I'll write to Massey. He'll know where they are. You have his address at the work camp, right?'

'I did, but I don't know where he is any more. In his last

letter, he said he had been released from the work camp in Jasper and hoped to reunite with the family if he could find them. But he wasn't sure yet where he was going to settle. We haven't received another letter with his new address yet.'

Not willing to wait that long, I said, 'I'll write letters to every Japanese-Canadian family I can contact. One of them must know where the Setoguchis ended up.'

'Years have passed, son. Have you prepared yourself for the possibility that Chidori has a new life?'

If he'd stabbed me with the pitchfork, it would have hurt less than the puncture of those words. It took every thread of will I had to suck in enough air to speak. 'I'm going to find her. I have to find her as soon as I can.' I stumbled back across the porch and down the steps to the yard.

'You can't find her right now. Where are you going?'

Not enough pressure was left in my lungs to respond, so I staggered down the driveway towards the road. It genuinely felt as if I'd been impaled and my insides were leaking out. My fingers searched my chest, and I fully expected to find the bloody, gaping holes. There was no physical wound, but I would be begging for a real pitchfork to the heart if I found out she had moved on with her life without me.

Chapter 38

It took much longer than it should have to hike the trail to the peak where Chidori and I had carved our initials in the arbutus tree. The carving was faded, but still faintly scarred the flesh. Thinking about that last day we had spent together filled me with joy, until I noticed the pebbles on the ground and remembered where mine was – lost forever. I sat down and rested my back against the trunk. The view over the other Gulf Islands was exactly the same as it had always been. To look at it, no one would have known how much time had passed or how much had changed in the world.

'Chidori, if you can hear me,' I said to the air. 'I'm home. I'm going to try to find out where you are, but if I can't, please know that I'm here waiting for you.' I picked up a new stone and dropped it in my pocket. The wind swept up in a gust and the birds simultaneously fell silent. 'Chi, I really hope you didn't break your promise. I fought and then surrendered with a strength I didn't know I possessed, all to get here. And I won't have any reason to live if we aren't reunited.'

A million different questions about what I could have done differently – which all started with *what if* and ended with

293

unsatisfying answers – rambled through my mind. Whether my choices were mistakes or failures or necessary evils, I would maybe never know, but undeniably my life would never be the same again. Change, I could handle. What terrified me was the uncertainty of whether my life after the change would ever be good again. The wind died down and at least one thousand birds began chirping in the distance. I hoped it was a sign.

I hiked back down the trail and followed the road to the Setoguchis' old farm. When I reached the entrance to their driveway, I paused. The yard was overgrown. The house desperately needed painting and the porch steps sagged to one side. Massey's cabin had been converted into a chicken coop. The greenhouses were gone and only a stone foundation remained where the structures once stood. One of the windows in the barn was cracked and the roof must have taken a beating in a storm. Mr Setoguchi would have never let that type of disrepair linger.

I inched closer and peered through the bushes at Chidori's bedroom window, half-hoping to see her waving at me. With my eyes closed I tried to imagine her there. It worked until I opened my eyes again and she wasn't. Two boys and a girl appeared from behind the house, chasing a ball around in the grass. One boy was about fifteen, one was about thirteen, and the girl was about ten years old. She spotted me and headed my way, so I turned and carried on.

A minute later, the bushes rustled and she popped out in front of me. She had curly brown hair, large dark eyes and she wore a white dress more suited for Sunday school than playing in the yard. 'Hey, mister. Why were you poking around my house?'

'No reason. Pardon me.' I walked faster.

'Where are you off to in such a hurry?'

'Nowhere.'

'Your legs are moving. You're going somewhere.'

I glanced over sideways at her, wondering why she wasn't at all cautious of a peeper who had been hiding in the bushes. 'Didn't your ma ever teach you not to talk to strangers?'

'You don't look like a stranger. Besides, I don't have a mother any more.'

I was taken back, surprised she had said it so matter-of-factly.

'I don't have a father any more either,' she added, and skipped to catch up to me.

'Who do you live with in that house then?'

She clutched the needle tips of a low-hanging cedar branch, as if she were holding hands with it, then released it after she passed by to let it spring back behind her. 'The Maiers. Our foster parents. Our real parents were killed in the war.'

She had an accent I had heard before but couldn't quite place. 'Which country?'

'I was born in Hungary but my family fled to London when I was young because Jews from our town were being forced to go to camps.'

I studied her expression for a few strides to determine whether she was aware of what had truly occurred in the camps. If she did know the truth, it didn't show. It was best if she didn't. 'Your parents were killed in London?'

'Yes. The night before we were supposed to leave on the ship my uncle's flat was bombed in an air raid. He and my parents died.'

'I'm sorry to hear that.'

We both walked in silence towards Bennett Bay as the gravity of our combined grief lingered in the air between us.

Eventually I asked, 'How did you end up on Mayne Island?'

'My brothers and I came to Canada on an ocean liner with other war orphans. We boarded a train in Halifax and another ship in Vancouver to finally arrive here. It took a lifetime. The Maiers clambered to pick us up as if we were free puppies.' She looked over her shoulder back in the direction of the house. 'I didn't think I was going to enjoy living here, but I have the most enchanting room. On the wall are lovely pictures of ballerinas and birds. I even have my own dressing table that makes me feel like a princess.'

The memory of Chidori's room panged in my heart. 'I know the girl who used to live in that room. Those are her old belongings.'

'Oh. She had fine taste. I reckon it's the best room I've ever had the pleasure of resting my head in.'

'You make sure you keep good care of those things.'

'Yes, sir. I will.' She stretched the length of her stride to match my pace as if she wanted to appear to be on a stroll together.

'I don't suppose you know where that family is now.'

'No, sir.' She hopped fallen logs to keep up with me. 'May I tag along with you?'

'No. You should head on home now.' I cut through the

bushes where the short-cut trail to the beach used to be. The girl followed me. I had to push aside prickle bushes and stomp down some fern leaves, but the old path was still partially visible.

'What's your name?' she asked.

I didn't answer.

'My name is Marguerite. Call me Margie. Everyone does.'

'Why don't you go play with your brothers, Marguerite? I want to be alone.'

She tugged at leaves as she half-walked and half-skipped down the trail. 'All I ever do is play with my brothers. Why do you want to be left to yourself? Is it because you're sad?'

I glanced at her briefly, then cut through the bushes.

'Did you fancy the girl who lived in my room before me?'

'Yes.'

She nodded as if she had already figured as much. 'Do you still fancy her?'

'Yes.'

'Why aren't you together?'

'We were separated by the war.'

'The war's over now. You should go search for her.'

'I don't know where she is. She's supposed to meet me here.' When we stepped out onto the sand of Bennett Bay, the sight of Chidori's rowboat, weathered from being left abandoned out for three winters, made me stop in my tracks. After a moment to recover, I crouched next to it and pushed the grass aside. The lettering was faded and chipped off in spots, but *Chi Chi* was still visible. I closed my eyes and remembered all the times we'd gone fishing, the night she went missing, and how I had asked her to marry me on the log next to that boat. My heart jumped around inside my chest thinking about all that, but when I opened my eyes, all I saw was a beat-up old rowboat.

Staggered by grief, I sat on the log and stared out over the water.

Marguerite sat next to me. 'Is her name Chidori? I believe that's the name of the girl who used to live in my room.'

'Yes, how do you know that?'

'Some of her personal belongings were left in the room.'

I nodded, but didn't say anything because it upset me to know that all of the possessions they couldn't carry with them had been sold to strangers.

She looked at my uniform. 'You just returned from fighting in the war?'

'Yes.'

'Did you kill anyone?'

'Yes.'

She pointed her fingers and made sound effects to pretend to shoot. 'I wish I could have killed those dirty Nazis who locked up all the Jews and bombed my parents.'

'No. You don't want to kill anyone.' I placed my hands on hers to lower her finger guns. 'If you're going to wish for anything, you should wish there is never another war and that no other children will lose their parents. You understand?'

She nodded, not entirely in agreement.

I stood. 'I need to get going. Ask your foster parents if they have an address for the family who used to live in the house, will ya?'

As I walked away she shouted, 'Are you Hayden?'

I turned to face her. 'How do you know that?'

'Chidori's journals.'

'Those things in her room don't belong to you. You shouldn't be snooping through them, you understand?'

'Yes, sir. But why did she leave them behind?'

I swallowed hard because the reality stung. 'They thought they were coming back.' I picked up my pace and ducked into the forest. I honestly wanted to hop a ship that instant and search the province for Chidori, but I didn't even know where to start.

Chapter 39

The sky outside my childhood bedroom window lightened with the dawn and created geometric shapes of sunlight on the ceiling that were the same as when I was a child. It felt both familiar and odd to wake up in my own star-quilt-covered bed. *On the Origin of Species* was still on the bookshelf, my saxophone was still in the corner, and my baseball glove was still hanging from the bedpost. The room smelled like leather and linseed oil, exactly as I remembered, but something intangible felt different. Smaller.

I dressed, then without glancing in the direction of my sister's old bedroom, I headed downstairs for breakfast. My parents weren't around, but there was an unopened envelope from Rosalyn on the kitchen table in front of my old chair. I sat, took several deep breaths, and opened it. When I unfolded the sheet of paper, a charm fell out onto the table. A tiny gold rose.

Dear Haydie,

If I could give you one piece of advice, it would be to cut yourself free from the past before it drags you down. I know you'll understand. Don't ever give up. I'm sorry I wasn't as strong as you are.

Forever in your heart,
Rose

My first instinct was to take the charm over to the Setoguchis' farm to give it to Chidori for her bracelet, but then remembered I couldn't. Choked up by both reminders of my sister and Chidori, I reached into my pocket and pulled out my hankie. The charms of the Eiffel Tower, Big Ben, and a snowflake that I had bought in London rolled to the centre of the fabric. I dropped the rose onto the handkerchief next to the others and carefully folded the corners in before putting it back in my pocket. The tremor in my hands returned.

'Good morning.' Mother stepped in from outside with a basket of fresh eggs from the coop and leaned over to kiss my cheek. 'Oh.' She paused and took Rose's letter from me. 'Your father must have absentmindedly left this out. There's no need to bring up those memories.' She stuffed the letter away into the pocket of her apron. 'Did you sleep well?'

I didn't bother telling her about the nightmare of drowning in an ocean of blood that left me dripping in sweat and gasping for air in the middle of the night. Instead, I said, 'I need to use the outhouse.'

Her face angled into a frown of motherly concern, but she had no choice but to let me go.

Marguerite was perched on the woodpile when I walked back through the yard from the outhouse. A stack of journals was piled on her lap. Without acknowledging her, I leaned over the edge of the well and dropped the bucket down to scoop some water to wash my face.

'Morning,' she said as she scrambled down from the wood-pile and joined me at the well. She was wearing overalls that were two sizes too big and needed to be rolled several times at the cuff so she wouldn't trip. 'I brought some of Chidori's journals over. I thought you might want them but I couldn't carry all of them.'

I glanced at her, then splashed my face. The water straight from the bucket tasted so pure. My body yearned to drink up enough to replace every drop of tainted water that resided in me. Marguerite kneeled on the grass and opened one of the journals to show me. I had to look away because the sight of Chidori's handwriting scrolled across the pages made my heart ache.

'This is you, isn't it?' She held up a yellowed photo of Chidori and me when we were twelve.

'You shouldn't have read those. They don't belong to you.'

'I apologize. How was I to know I was ever going to meet the people in the stories?' She tucked the photo back into the journal. 'Chidori loves you more than anything in the whole wide world. You should hear all the nice things she has written about you. *Hayden walked me home from school today and carried my books for me. He has the bluest eyes I have ever seen, and he gets the most adorable dimple when he smiles. My heart spins cartwheels whenever he is near. I wonder if he thinks about me when we are not together. I hope he asks me to marry him one—*'

303

'Those are someone else's private thoughts. You shouldn't be reading them.'

'I already read all of them. I can't unread them.' She leaned on the edge of the well next to me. 'I'll help you search for her.'

'She's somewhere far away. You won't be able to help.'

'I could pray for you. God owes us.'

'God doesn't owe us anything. We're alive. That's more than thousands of other innocent people got.'

'He owes me.'

I pointed to scold her. 'He spared you and brought you to a place where you would be safe. You need to be thankful for what you have, not resentful for the things you've lost.'

She shook her head to disagree. 'You aren't at liberty to tell me how to feel. It's not like I'm whining about losing my favourite doll or my brand-new flute.' She pointed to scold me right back. 'He took my flesh and blood. My parents. That wasn't fair and I am permitted to feel resentful over that. He owes me.'

I ran my hand through my hair and gazed out over the wheat field where Pop was just coming in on the tractor with the golden retriever plodding placidly behind. 'God doesn't owe me nothing. If God owes you something, you should save his indebtedness for yourself. My ma's waiting on me for breakfast. You should go on home.' I walked four strides and she caught up to me.

'I know your kind of sad. The one that haunts you.'

I stopped near the steps to the porch and looked down at her.

'I was there too.' She bent over to stack the journals on the porch. 'I'm going to help you find Chidori because once you're together again, your nightmares will go away.'

'How do you know about the nightmares?'

'I told you. I know your sad.' She reached over and touched my hand. 'I'll see you later, Hayden.' She waved as she skipped through the grass to the road.

After spending the morning with my family, I visited a couple of neighbours' houses to ask if they'd heard anything about where the Setoguchis were. Two of them hadn't kept in contact with any of the Japanese families, and the one who had only knew where the Nagatas were. She gave me the Nagatas' address so I could contact them. Before heading to the next house, I decided instead of going door-to-door all over the entire island, it would probably be easier to hang out in front of the general store to catch everyone while they were in town.

By late afternoon, I had collected three more addresses, but nobody knew off-hand where the Setoguchis were. I sat on the bench to write a letter to each family I had an address for and sealed the envelopes just as Mr Hogarth stepped out of the post office.

I checked my pocket watch and rushed over as he slid the key to lock the door. 'Mr Hogarth! Wait up. I have some letters I need to post.'

He stopped and squinted over his glasses. 'I'm closed. Drop them through the door slot or bring them by tomorrow before the morning ship.'

I lunged forward and dropped the envelopes through the door slot.

He slid his cap back and pushed his glasses up his nose. 'You live on the island?'

'I'm Hayden Pierce. John and Eleanor's son. Don't you remember me?'

He nodded, but didn't actually seem to recall. His hair had turned completely white since I had last seen him, and he stood more stooped over.

'I wanted to ask you if you remember getting any letters for me while I was away fighting in the war.'

'What did you say your name is?'

'Hayden. Hayden Pierce. The letter would have been sent to my parents' address some time in the last three and a half years.'

'I can't remember every piece of mail. Sorry.' He adjusted his hat and shuffled down the street.

I kept stride with him. 'The letters would have come from Chidori Setoguchi. Do you remember any letters coming from the Setoguchis to anyone on the island?'

He shook his head. 'Sorry, son. If they were sent to you, your parents would have gotten them. If they were sent to someone else, I don't recall.'

It seemed futile to pick his brain, so I stopped walking and let him carry on his way.

The church was up the hill from where I stood. I had no inclination to visit the gravesite, but something outside of myself compelled me to wander over. A reverend, who was new since I last attended a service, crouched in the front yard tending to some flowers. He looked up and nodded pleasantly, then went back to his gardening. I hopped the split-rail fence and meandered around the small cemetery. It didn't take much searching to find the headstone with my sister's name engraved on it. A fresh flower braid had been draped around the base of the granite.

Rosalyn Grace Pierce
4 October 1921–12 March 1944
A beautiful light extinguished too soon.

I ran my finger over the letters, then sat in the grass and leaned up against the stone to unfold the letter I had received from my father before I was shot down.

Dear Son,

I write to inform you of very grave news. Your sister has died. She took too many of the pills the doctor prescribed. Apologies for having to tell you in a letter. The funeral has been arranged at Saint Mary Magdalene Church for next week. Your name is up on the bulletin for the congregation to pray for you.

Love, Pop

It was a wonder that so few words could deliver the impact of being run over by a tank. I closed my eyes and folded it back up. After a long while of letting the sun warm my face, I whispered, 'I know why you did it.'

I half-expected her to respond or appear, but I waited and it didn't feel like she was with me in any form.

'Earl couldn't keep his promise to come home, but I did. I wish you would have held on a little longer and let me prove that to you.' I pulled my air force wings out of my pocket and placed them on the base with the letter. 'Sorry it took me so long. I love you, Rose.'

I left the cemetery and made my way back to the general store. Donna Mae's brother was working the cash register again. His eyebrows angled when I placed two bottles of vodka down on the counter and handed him the money. 'Having a celebration?'

'Not exactly.' I opened the first bottle as I left the store and started drinking as I walked down to the wharf. The least I could do while I waited for news was drink away my nightmares.

Nothing in town had changed, even though everything had. I sat on the bench next to the Springwater Lodge drinking for longer than I intended, then staggered up the road to the Agricultural Hall. The hall was all locked up and the fairgrounds were abandoned, but my mind filled with images from the last fall fair as if it had happened only the day before – the boys playing soldiers, the schoolgirls braiding flowers into each other's hair, the Setoguchis selling their vegetables, and Rose dancing on the grass in front of the amphitheatre. For a second, the scent of warm cinnamon buns and the melody of Chidori's laughter floated across the breeze, but then the images faded away. Lost forever.

I took a few more swigs of alcohol that burned. Once the pain was numbed, I stumbled home.

For a couple of days, maybe almost a week, I only left my room to use the outhouse. Since my body was accustomed to the POW camp, I didn't even need to do that very often. I ran out of vodka on the third day, so I stole a couple jugs of my father's home-brewed ale from the barn and took them to my room. Everything became blurry in my mind and the hours passed in a haze, which was what I wanted – at least until I heard back with the Setoguchis' new address.

One evening, there was a knock on my bedroom door. It wasn't my parents checking on me. I knew that because they'd stopped bothering to knock once they realized I was being unresponsive.

'Go away,' I mumbled and rolled over.

Joey popped his head in and said, 'Howdy.' The cheeriness on his face was forced, as if he had been warned beforehand to prepare himself for the foul state I was in, but was nevertheless still shocked to witness it.

I heaved my weight out of bed and stood to greet him with a hug.

Joey slapped my bony back and shook me by the shoulders. 'Goddamn, you're scrawny now. And you smell awful.'

I chuckled, sardonically. 'You think this is bad? You should have seen me three months ago.'

He shoved my chest. 'It's good to see you, pal.'

'Yeah, you too.'

'I'm only home until tomorrow to visit my folks, but Donna

309

Mae asked me to invite you to come stay in Victoria with us for a visit. I'll apologize in advance because she's not a very good cook.' He sat on the foot of the bed and slid his hand into my old baseball mitt. 'Don't tell her I said that.'

One of my parents had likely called him and asked him to come over on the ferry to cheer me up. Although it was friendly of him to make the trip, I wasn't going to feel truly better until I heard from Chidori. I sat on my desk chair. 'I hear you're going to be a father. Congratulations.'

'Thanks. It's terrifying, but what can I do about it now?'

I laughed and studied his face. He looked the same, only older. 'What have you been doing for work?'

'I'm the chief operations manager at the shipyard.'

'Wow. You moved up the ladder quickly.' My tone had more disapproval to it than I intended.

'Yeah, well,' he removed his fedora and combed his fingers through his hair. 'With so many men overseas—' He interrupted himself to change the subject, 'My pop says you can start back at the sawmill whenever you're ready to start working. He's holding a position for you.'

I nodded, appreciative of the offer. 'Thank you. I'll need some money to buy the lumber for Chidori's and my house.'

'Chidori?'

'Yes. I'm just waiting to find out where she's living so I can contact her to let her know she can come back home now.'

'She can't come back here.' His hands rested in his lap, wringing the brim of his hat as he studied my shaken expression, then he glanced down. 'Didn't you know that?'

'No.' I stood. 'What do you mean she can't?'

'The government hasn't lifted the travel restrictions on Japanese Canadians. They probably won't be able to enter the restricted zone until all the servicemen get back and have a chance to buy land and get set up with employment. That won't happen for several more years from now.'

'I don't understand.' I paced the length of my room and back. 'The war is over. She's a Canadian. She never should have been sent away in the first place. They can't prevent her from coming home.'

He held his hands up defensively. 'Don't get mad at me. It's the government who refused to lift the restrictions when the war ended, not me.'

'Sorry. I'm not blaming you. I'm just frustrated.' I opened the window to calm myself with fresh air. 'They'll have to let her come home if we're married, won't they?'

'I don't know. When was the last time you spoke with her?'

'The day she was taken away.'

His laugh was shockingly loud. 'Oh. You aren't kidding? You haven't talked to her in over three years?'

I closed my eyes for a long blink, realizing how crushingly far-fetched my dreams sounded.

'Jesus, Hayden. She's probably married and has two kids by now.'

Although I knew that was probable, I didn't want to believe it. 'She promised she would wait.'

He shook his head, heavy with pity. 'I don't want to rain on your parade when you are already so glum, but that was a different time. You can't expect you'll just be able to pick up where you left off.'

'She promised,' I said with enough conviction to anchor my own faith.

He leaned forward to rest his elbows on his knees. 'Let me give you a little advice. Take the mill job my father has offered you, build your new house, and settle down with some other nice Mayne Island girl. Save yourself the heartache.'

Furious, I stormed out on him.

Chapter 40

After leaving Joey behind in my room by himself, I rummaged through the barn for more of my father's ale. He must have wisely hidden it somewhere else or dumped it. The only thing I could find was an old bottle of cooking wine. I took that, waited for Joey to leave, and headed back to the house. The porch creaked when I stepped up onto it, and just before I turned the doorknob, I heard another creak behind me. I spun around prepared to fight. 'Marguerite! Jesus. You scared me half to death. What are you doing sneaking around here?'

'I want to see the inside of your home.' She walked past me, pushed the door open, and stepped into the house. 'I feel like I already know it from Chidori's descriptions.'

'Whoa there. Nobody invited you in. It's getting dark. You need to get on home.'

'It's a full moon. Besides, it's Mayne Island. Nothing bad ever happens here.' She wandered through the living room wearing what I could only guess was a traditional Hungarian folk dress of some sort. The skirt was a wild floral pattern over a white petticoat, with a white apron, a bright green lace-up vest, a puffy sleeved blouse, and an embroidered hair band with silk flowers attached above each ear.

'Were you just at some kind of dance performance or something?'

'No. This is just what I felt like wearing today.' She admired everything in the living room with great attention, then headed into the kitchen. I followed her and opened the cupboard to see if Pop's bottle of rye was still hidden behind the flour. It wasn't. 'Are you intending to get sloshed?'

'Yeah, so skedaddle,' I said as I took the cap off the bottle of cooking wine.

The golden retriever pressed its nose against the back screen door to check out who was inside the house. 'Where are your folks?' Marguerite asked.

I shook my head, unconcerned.

'Then I reckon I'll stay until they return. What's the dog's name?'

'No idea.'

'Have you had supper?' Not waiting for my answer Marguerite searched through the cupboards and pulled out a sack of rice.

'I'm not hungry, and you're not staying.' I left her there and climbed the stairs back to my room. The cooking wine made me feel dizzy in a nauseated way. I fell onto my bed and stared at the ceiling.

When I lifted my head, Marguerite stood in the doorway with one of Rosalyn's hair clips in her hand.

I shot up and shouted like a bear, 'Put that back where you found it and get the hell out of here!'

Her body flinched from the roar of my voice, she blinked hard, then spun around. The floor in Rose's room squeaked as she put the clip back. Her footsteps clambered down the stairs, then the front door slammed. I stood and watched out the window as she ran across the yard in a flash of colourful Hungarian folk dress and disappeared into the darkness.

The next morning there was a very soft knock at my bedroom door. I knew it was Marguerite before she even poked her head in. Although I was filled with regret for snapping at her, I grumbled, 'Go away.' The door creaked open and she crept in. 'The Maiers wouldn't be thrilled to know you're sneaking around in a strange man's bedroom.'

'Sorry for touching your sister's hair clip without asking.'

'It's fine. Just don't do it again.' I pulled the cover over my shoulder and face to block out the light.

'Did your sister really kill herself?'

Jesus. Were all kids so forward? I sat up. 'Who told you that?'

'Nobody. I overheard folks talking about her.' She stepped inside my room and stood in the corner with her hands clasped together, as if she had promised herself not to touch anything. Her hair was braided into pigtails with blue ribbons tied at the ends. She wore a more traditional girl's blue dress that had a black collar and black buttons along with a matching blue tam, maybe the outfit she wore on the orphan ship.

'You shouldn't be eavesdropping, especially not on gossip.'

'Is your sister dying like that why you have nightmares, or is it because of the war?'

315

I swung my legs over the edge of the mattress and rested my elbows on my knees. 'Don't you have someone else you could pester?'

She shook her head. 'No.' She studied me seriously as she sat on my desk chair and rested her elbows on her knees to mimic my posture. 'If your sister would have held on, things would have gotten better. You know that, right?'

'What would you know about that?'

'Plenty.' She reached over and was about to lift my saxophone from its stand. She paused. 'Is it fine if I look at this?'

'No. Please leave me alone.' Exhausted, I lay back down and stared at the ceiling.

'Will you teach me how to play it?'

'No.'

All out of ways to engage me in conversation, she stood at the foot of my bed and watched me for a good while before eventually leaving.

The following week I received correspondence. The eldest son in the Teramura family sent me a letter informing me that their father had been initially taken away to Petawawa, which was essentially a POW work camp on Canadian soil. And although the rest of the Teramuras had been at Hastings Park with Chidori's family, his family was sent to Lemon Creek Internment camp, which was a shanty-town of cabins built in the Slocan Valley to house them. Chidori's family didn't go to Lemon Creek, and he hadn't heard where they ended up. There were other internment camps in British Columbia – Greenwood, Sandon, Kaslo, New Denver Tashme, and more.

He also wondered if maybe they had decided, like the Koyama family, to move east of the protected area on their own dime to become a self-supporting family. If the Setoguchis had done that, they could be in any number of communities – Minto, Bridge River, Lillooet, Christina Lake, Chase, Taylor Lake or Salmon Arm. Or anywhere east of the Rockies, realistically. It would be nearly impossible to track them down if they hadn't sent word to anyone. And that was the part I simply couldn't comprehend. Why hadn't they sent word? Even if something tragic had befallen Chidori, her parents or brothers would have attempted to notify me ... wouldn't they?

My mother was in the living room, crying to Pop about how watching me suffer was too much and how she couldn't survive losing both her children to suicide. After almost an hour of her sobbing about what she had done wrong to raise two morose children, I got up, went downstairs, and told them I was going for a walk so she wouldn't worry. Or maybe so I didn't have to listen to her any more. I didn't actually go for a walk. I sat with my back up against the barn, drinking from a bottle of vodka that I had picked up when I was in town collecting the post. The golden retriever moseyed over and flopped down next to me. The sun had started to set when little footsteps approached. I hid the bottle behind my back as Marguerite walked towards me wearing a grey wool pleated jumper and blazer that was embroidered with *London Junior Collegiate Preparatory*. And yellow rubber boots, even though the dirt was dry as stone.

'Hi,' she said quietly, and sat down beside the dog to stroke her palm across the fluffy fur.

'When are you going to take the hint that I don't want you coming around here?'

Ignoring my question, she asked, 'How long do you think it will take before you hear where Chidori lives?'

'I don't know, why?'

Her eyebrows rose in an adult-type concern. 'I'm just wondering if you'll die before that happens.'

I chuckled, lifted the bottle that I'd been hiding behind my back, and tilted it in a gesture of cheers before I took a swig. 'You and my ma both.'

She sighed and was quiet for a spell. 'You can talk to me about your sad if you want.'

'What's there to talk about? I want Chidori to come home and, even in the unlikely event that she also wants that, she can't.'

'Not that sad.'

Taken back by her forwardness once again, I swallowed back more alcohol. 'I don't want to talk about the other sad.'

'It might help if you aren't carrying the burden of all that rubbish by yourself.'

'It's horrible enough that my mind has to know what it knows. Sharing it with you would only spread the evil to both our minds.'

She braided strands of long grass together. 'My foster parents sent me to a doctor who helps folks who are haunted by the horrible things they witnessed in the war.'

'A doctor can't fix what's in my mind. I just need to make better memories to replace the bad ones.'

Her gaze met mine and she peered right into my thoughts. 'Promise you aren't going to give up on Chidori.'

I blinked hard and braced myself for what was about to come out of my mouth. 'It's been three and a half years. Chances are she's moved on.' I winced and reached over to rest my hand on the dog's shoulder. 'Maybe I should too.'

'No. You can't. She's your one true love.'

I shook my head and forced back the tears that threatened to surface. 'She didn't even write.'

'The Chidori from the journals would have written if she could have, and the Hayden from the journals would have never given up until he found her.'

'Yeah, well, neither one of us are those people any more. And one thing I learned in the war is that sometimes the only way to win is to give in.'

'More often you have to fight to win. You came this far. You can't quit now.' Marguerite bit at her lower lip and gazed off into the fields for a short while before standing. 'Let me know when the Hayden from the journals gets home from the war.' She turned and walked away.

My head throbbed and the drink did nothing to numb the pain. The dog moved to rest her head on my thigh and fell asleep. I slept right there in the dirt too.

Chapter 41

Ma was seated at the kitchen table, staring at her teacup as Lacey and I stumbled in from sleeping outside. I always knew the dog's name, but I hadn't wanted to get too fond of her. After she spent the entire night at my side, I had to admit she had at least earned the right to be called by her name. There were tears in Ma's eyes when she glanced at me. 'Hayden, what are you doing to yourself?'

'Nothing. I'm fine.' I clutched the back of the chair to steady my balance.

'You won't be able to work at the mill for Joey's father if you keep yourself in this state.'

'I'll be fine. No need to worry.'

She fidgeted with the needlepoint tablecloth, visibly troubled. 'I saw that peculiar mute girl sitting with you last night. She isn't bothering you, is she?'

'Mute?' I chuckled at the irony.

'The little Jewish orphan the Maiers are fostering. Margie or something. Wasn't that her?'

I nodded, confused. 'Mute?'

'She hasn't spoken since she witnessed her parents being

killed during a bomb raid in London.' Ma's face contorted into an odd expression. 'You were sitting with her for nearly an hour. Did you not notice that the poor child does not speak?'

I laughed and shook my head. 'No. I have definitely not noticed that the poor child does not speak.'

'Hayden, I can't bear to watch you do the same thing to yourself that Rosalyn did. There is a church social Friday night. You can see some of your old friends and maybe meet some new ones.'

'I'm not in the mood for socializing.'

'At least start working. Joey said his father won't be able to hold the position for you at the mill for much longer.'

'I'll think about it.'

She wrung her hankie into a tight coil. 'If you knew for sure that Chidori has moved on with her life, would you leave the past in the past and start fresh?'

Something in her tone caught my full attention, and my body went rigid from the guilt-ridden expression in her eyes. 'What do you mean, Ma?' Her face sunk with despair and it took a long time before I was able to control my emotion enough to continue. 'Do you know where she is?'

Ma avoided eye contact and stood to vigorously wash her teacup at the sink.

'Chidori wrote, didn't she?'

Ma dropped the cup in the soapy water and clenched the edge of the sink to brace herself. 'I'm sorry, Hayden. She stopped writing eventually and I was trying to protect you from a broken heart. I didn't realize you would take it so hard to believe she hadn't written at all.'

'I want to see the letters. Show them to me.'

She tucked a loose strand of hair behind her ear. 'What if reading them makes you feel even worse?'

A wave of tingling apprehension rolled up from my feet and flooded into my torso with the weight of a keg barrel. 'Where are they?' My voice rose with urgency.

She didn't respond, so I scrambled around the house and searched every hiding spot I could think of – the desk, the hutch, my sister's wardrobe, behind the loose brick in the fireplace. I tore the place apart, but didn't find anything.

When I stepped back into the kitchen, frenzied, Ma's neck turned red. 'It's been almost four years, Hayden. Don't you think she's settled down with someone else by now?'

'Give them to me. Now!'

She flinched from the force in my voice and clutched at the fabric of her apron. 'It's best to leave the past in the past.'

'You have no right to keep them from me. They belong to me. Where are they?'

'Hayden, don't you think too much time has gone by to hold onto the way things used to be?'

'She said she would wait.'

'That was a lifetime ago. You were so young. I don't want you to get hurt when you find out she has a new life with someone else.'

'If that is the case, it's her news to tell me. Give me the letters.'

'Don't speak to me in that tone.' Ma's lip quivered and her eyes blinked repeatedly. 'I just want what's best for you.'

'What's best for me is knowing where Chidori is. Do you want me to end up like Rose?'

Ma gasped and pressed her palm to her mouth, then let it drop away in defeat. 'They're in the cupboard behind the canning jars. In a box labelled recipes.'

I swung the cupboard door open. There were at least fifty jars stacked two on top of each other. I slid them to the side and pulled out the box. Inside was a pile of letters tied together with a red string. When I read the address in Lethbridge, Alberta, and saw the familiar curve of how she wrote the 'n' in my name, I dropped to my knees, tore open the first envelope, and read the first letter.

12 May 1942

Dearest Hayden,

I hope this letter finds you well. My apologies it took so long to write to you. We spent two weeks locked up in Hastings Park. It was unpleasant to be housed there. Obaasan became quite frail. She developed a cough likely caught from the woman in the cubicle next to us. I am concerned because we were crowded together with people who might have tuberculosis. Mother has also weakened in health, not so much by the physical conditions, but by the shame of being branded disloyal to Canada.

I cannot get the unpleasant smell of the livestock stalls out of my nostrils. Why would they house human beings in animal quarters? I have inhaled floral and cedar fragrances, trying to erase the stench, but I fear it has been etched into my brain forever. Father and Kenji were housed in the men's quarters, but luckily we are together again now. We are on a train headed for the Alberta border as I write this. Father arranged for us to work on a farm outside of the restricted area so we can stay together as a family. The other option was for Father and Kenji to work at a road camp while the rest of us went to an internment camp in British Columbia. He didn't want that because he heard the internment camps were nothing more than tents or shoddy cabins in a field that had to be shared with other families. He felt that would be unsuitable, especially if we are forced to stay away into the winter months. Although Father had to pay handsomely for the transportation, and will have to pay rent once we are in Alberta, he was determined we not be separated. Hopefully farming in Alberta won't be much different than what we are used to at home. Sadly, I don't know what has become of Tosh. He was arrested for the altercation that occurred on the dock at Mayne Island before we left on the ship. We assume he is being detained in Vancouver somewhere with other prisoners. I hope he is safe.

It comforts me to know you are safe on Mayne Island. A group of men stood in uniform on the train platform as we left Vancouver. My eyes played a little trick on me as our train passed by. I thought I saw a young soldier who resembled you, but I blinked, and when I looked again I couldn't pick him out of the crowd of green coats. I fear for those young men who are shipping off to war.

I cannot wait until the war is over so I can go back home, forget about everything that has happened in the last while, and start our future together.

Love, Chidori

I was incredibly relieved that she had not been incarcerated under guard control for the entire time, but I still worried about how uprooting and relocating had impacted her. And how her new life would inevitably change her. After reading two more letters in the kitchen as Ma watched me, I stood and headed out the back door to sit on the porch. Lacey flopped down at my feet as I opened the next envelope. The paper smelled of blossoms. I held it to my cheek for a moment before continuing to read.

9 *July 1942*

Dear Hayden,

I wonder if you have not received my letters yet. Perhaps your replies have been intercepted by the government because I am Japanese-Canadian. Please write as soon as you are able. I miss you terribly. We are very busy working on the sugar-beet farm just outside of Lethbridge, Alberta. As I suspected, the farming is nothing we are not accustomed to. In fact, we have helped the owner, Warren Blake, improve his productivity. Mr Blake is too elderly to do the work by himself, and the war left him very short-handed for labourers. We toil long hours, but he pays us a fair wage. And he is kind like your father.

The wood cabin we rent from Mr Blake was initially in dismal need of repair. The inside walls were covered in mould and the shake roof had gaps so big you could see the sky through them. Kenji repaired all the holes. Father wired the electrical hook-up to give us power for lights and cooking. Mother, Obaasan and I cleaned and insulated with old newspapers over the timber wall joists. We also wrapped rags around the old pipes to keep them from freezing in the winter. Alberta winters can apparently be brutally frigid, especially in comparison to the mild temperatures of Mayne Island. We will do more improvements once we save money. Mother doesn't approve that the kitchen only has open shelves rather than cupboards, or that the bathroom is an outhouse, but she is reluctantly making do. The cabin has two bedrooms divided with two-by-fours and sheets. Obaasan and I sleep together and Kenji sleeps on a cot next to the stove. That is going to change, though. We need to expand because Tosh joined us today!!!! Isn't that wonderful news?

He was released from a work camp where he had built roads. They reviewed his case and determined he was not a criminal threat and there was no reason to keep him detained in a work camp. He was not allowed to go back to the coast, so his choices were to go to an internment camp in the interior of British Columbia, relocate farther east and start a new life by himself, or find us here in

Alberta. I don't know how he did it, but he asked around until he found out where we had gone from the friends of a family who travelled to Alberta on the train with us. He just showed up today, walking up the dirt road with a big grin on his face. I hugged him so tightly it likely took his breath away. A little sparkle has returned to Mother's eye since Tosh's return.

I love you and look forward to the day when I may hug you tightly enough to take your breath away. Please write soon.

Chi

                                    23 February 1943

Dear Hayden,

How is everyone on Mayne Island? Are Donna Mae and Joey still going steady? I sent a letter to her too, with no reply yet. Perhaps she moved away. I hope you are all okay. We were notified in writing that in accordance with Order in Council PC 469 our house and most of our possessions left on Mayne Island, including the vehicles and farm equipment, were auctioned by the Custodian and Soldiers' Settlement Board for a fraction of the worth. We were not notified in advance of the January sale and did not consent. Apparently, the government kept most of the proceeds to pay for so-called administration fees related to the evacuation, to subsidize our time spent at Hastings Park, and to fund the internment camps that were built.

If I knew we were financing our own incarceration I would have insisted on better accommodations than a livestock facility.

The Prime Minister obviously lied to the House of Commons when he stated that Japanese Canadians would be treated justly. Does he not realize that incarcerating law-abiding citizens as aliens based on racial grounds violates all charters and laws and rights? And selling off the hard-earned property of a family who has been in Canada for two generations is certainly not just.

Father was saddened most about losing his Cadillac. He saved for a long time to be able to afford it. Were you aware they confiscated and sold our belongings? Perhaps you were able to go to the auction. Although I didn't have anything of much value, many of my journals were still in my room. If you had the opportunity to save some of them, I would be eternally grateful. I hope the reason you have not written back is not because you have changed your mind about how you feel about me. I will never change my mind about how I feel about you. I fear the reason is because you have gone off to war, which is utterly devastating for me to admit.

I miss you so much my soul aches.

Chi

I stood and paced on the porch, troubled to think how much pain and sorrow she must have felt when I didn't write back. If I had been home when the government sold their home and belongings, I would have bought all that I could afford. If my mother had promptly given me her address in Alberta, I would have written her every day that I was overseas – even while I was imprisoned – in hopes that the letter would reach her. Frustrated by all the missed opportunities, I tore open the next envelope and sat on the railing to continue to read, letter after letter.

19 August 1943

Dearest Hayden,

As the months pass here on the Blake farm, the routine of our life has become very familiar. Mother has decorated the cabin in her impeccable style, although obviously not as grand as our previous house. For a spell, she seemed very sorrowful, and only left her bed for short periods of time. To cheer her up, I recreated the rock garden she had built at home on Mayne Island. It is an almost perfect replica that took me two weeks to complete. To my delight, she now spends time walking along the path every day. The boys attend dances and watch movies at the theatre in town. I read and play my violin. I also have four music students now. We all go about our farming chores and spend time together as a family, much as we always did. But despite those glimpses of normalcy, it is still not the same as being home with you. What have you been up to? I am going to pretend you have not gone overseas, even though my soul feels the dread of you fighting. The thought that you might be injured or worse is simply too much for me to fathom. So, I will fool myself into believing you are safe and happy on Mayne Island. Do you still go to the movie theatre in Victoria with Joey? Are you working at the mill? Are you taking classes at the university? Or, have you moved? Or, perhaps you don't want to communicate with me? I hesitate to entertain the last option nearly as much as you being in combat.

Freedom is such a relative thing. We seem free, but we really aren't. We aren't free to go home. We aren't free from discrimination. Kenji was tripped coming out of the general store last week, which caused him to spill the bag on the sidewalk. Grown men picked up the items, and instead of the decent thing, returning them to Kenji, they spat at him and walked away with the groceries. Can you believe the nerve? We still live in fear. My father asked my mother to sew a pocket on his pyjama top so he'll never be separated from his enemy alien card, even when he's sleeping. He frets about being caught without his identification in case someone comes looking for 'Japs' to deport. I hate that my father is afraid. I hate that I'm afraid. I hate that word.

My heart breaks in anguish for you, over and over again,

Chidori

Chidori's letters over the rest of 1943 became progressively more disillusioned, and her hope of ever seeing me again began to disintegrate. The post stamp on her last letter was dated for 12 June 1944. More than a year had passed since she had sent it. Only a few reasons existed for why she would have stopped writing, and none of those reasons were a truth I wanted to accept. I didn't open the last envelope because I dreaded knowing why she had stopped writing.

Instead, I slid it into my pocket and walked to her old house to be reminded of a time when she loved me. Her bedroom window was open a crack and the lace curtains fluttered in the breeze. I sat with my back against an arbutus tree, imagining her blowing me a kiss from the window.

After a while, Marguerite quietly crouched down on her knees beside me. Her dress was actually a perfectly typical yellow little girl's dress with ruffles. Her straw hat was something else entirely, though. She had woven an entire garden of roses, peonies and daisies around the brim. And a fake bird made of real feathers was perched on top, stuck with a hat pin.

'That's quite the hat.'

'Thank you. I made it myself. Here, I brought you some of my foster mother's homemade soup to make you feel better.' She placed a Mason jar on the ground next to me.

I pushed it away without looking at it. 'I don't eat soup.'

'It's jolly delicious, really. You should at least try it.'

'I can't eat soup any more. Take it away. Please.'

Marguerite stared down at the jar for a moment before placing it behind her. 'Is that because you were a prisoner in the war?'

I nodded. She straightened out the fabric of her skirt to

tug it over her knees. Then she reached down and let a ladybug crawl up onto her finger. It scampered around on the back of her hand for a brief while before it flew away.

'What's this I hear about you not talking to anyone?' I asked.

She shrugged and her cheeks turned pink.

'People think you're mute.'

'Sometimes I have nothing to say, is all.'

I laughed. 'How come those sometimes never occur when you're with me?'

Her mouth turned up in a sheepish grin. 'Don't you enjoy talking to me?'

'I didn't say that. I'm just having a hard time imagining what it would be like if you weren't chattering constantly. Do you at least talk to your brothers?'

'Not any more. You're the only person I've talked to since my parents died.'

Her disclosure was both heartbreaking and strangely comforting. 'Why?'

'I told you, I have nothing to say.'

'I meant why me?'

She tugged at the grass. 'I have nightmares about the bombings. I see my parents' dead faces every time I close my eyes. You are the only person who really knows my sad.'

I studied her for a spell, then nodded because I did know. We were a strange and unlikely pair.

She caught and released another ladybug, then asked, 'What did you love best about growing up on Mayne Island?'

'Chidori,' I said without even pausing to think about it.

She pointed at the envelope that half stuck out of my pocket. 'Is that from her?'

I nodded.

'Really? Oh my goodness. Why didn't you say so earlier?' She sat up excitedly and pressed her fists to her lips in excitement. 'What does it say?'

I sucked in air and choked out, 'I don't know. I can't bring myself to read it.'

She stood and spun around. 'Why in the world not?'

I closed my eyes and exhaled to steady my erratic pulse. 'Too much time has passed since she wrote it.'

'Just read it and get it done with.' She stomped her foot on the grass and gestured wildly with her arms. 'The suspense is killing me.'

I sucked back a few steeling breaths and handed the envelope to her. 'I can't. You read it.'

She tore open the envelope and unfolded the paper. Then, as if she were public speaking in school, she straightened her posture. '*My Dearest Hayden.*' She looked over and raised her eyebrows in encouragement. 'That's a splendid start.'

Not sure it was, I waved for her to keep going so I could get the torture over with.

'*I hope this letter finds you well. My greatest wish is that you are safe and happy wherever you are. You may not be aware that I wrote numerous letters after we were first separated years ago. So many things have changed since then, including us, surely. Our life together on Mayne Island seems only a distant dream now. It was such a wonderful dream, and it still brings delight to my heart whenever I think about that peaceful time. Sadly, it is gone now. We were young and naïve about the world when we promised to wait for each other—'*

'Okay, stop reading. I don't want to hear the rest.' I stood abruptly and rubbed my palms on my trousers.

Marguerite paused and her eyebrows creased together. 'Why? You don't know what she's going to say.'

'Yes, I do.'

'No you don't. Shush.' She focused back on the letter and tracked the page with her finger until she found the spot where she had left off. I headed for the forest but she followed and read as she ran to catch up to me. *'You have certainly gone off to war and I pray the reason you haven't written is not tragic. I prefer to convince myself that you have built a nice life for yourself on Mayne Island. There was a time when I wanted nothing more than to return to Mayne Island to be with you, but with regret, that is not how things worked out for me. I have had to rethink my future and come to the difficult acceptance that it will not include Mayne Island. Or you.'*

'Stop reading, Marguerite.' I walked faster and rubbed my eyes with my sleeve. The crushing in my airway was worse than when the white-haired, nasty-nosed guard had dug his heel into my throat. Marguerite chased after me, and in her attempt to read and keep up, she tripped on a log and landed on her face without putting her arms out to break her fall. Her fantastic garden hat fell to the ground and the flower braid broke apart. After a shocked delay, she started to cry and flung her hands up to cover her cheek. I rushed back and scooped her up, then sat on a stump with her seated next to me. 'Let me see.' I gently pulled her wrist to check the injury. A superficial scrape covered a large portion of the left side of her face.

She inhaled to compose herself, wiped her tears, and brushed her knees, which were also scraped.

'Do you want me to give you a piggyback home?' I asked as I picked up her hat and reassembled the flower arrangement.

She shook her head. 'No. We have to finish reading the rest of the letter.'

'It's fine. I'll read it after I take you home.'

'No.' She pushed off the stump and bent over to pick up the letter from the ground. I didn't have the heart to argue with her when she was hurt, so I closed my eyes and braced for impact as she reread the line she was on before she tripped, '*I have had to rethink my future and come to the difficult acceptance that it will not include Mayne Island. Or you. I wish that were not the case because I have never stopped loving you.*'

Marguerite's head snapped up to grin at me. 'Did you hear that? She never stopped loving you.'

I nodded, cautiously optimistic.

She kept reading, '*I think about you with every breath I take.*' Marguerite's eyes popped open with thrilled anticipation. '*If you want to stay on Mayne Island and live out the dream you started before the war, I completely understand, but please know that I will never stop loving you. You probably think I'm foolish to have kept our promise to wait for each other for all these years, but you once told me our love is too strong to be broken. I believed you. I honestly do not want to ever be with anyone else, so the promise has not been difficult to keep. There is a part of me that hopes you feel the same way. There is also a part of me that reluctantly accepts it may not be true for you any more. And even more dreadfully, I have to accept that perhaps you are not alive to receive this. I believe I would have felt the loss in my soul if that were true, but I fear that possibility.*

Although I have changed in so many ways both from age and circumstance, it is perhaps more remarkable that there are traits about me that have remained exactly the same despite the adversity. I recently read this passage by a French philosopher and writer named Albert Camus that helped restore my faith that good will prevail:

In the midst of winter, I found there was, within me, an invincible summer. And that makes me happy. For it says that no matter how hard the world pushes against me, within me, there's something stronger – something better, pushing right back.

I pray you have also discovered the summer inside you and are pushing back against the winter. I will never forget the life we had before. You were, and will always be, my one true love. I forgive you if you do not feel the same in return. I also forgive you if you are gone. I don't want to make a nuisance of myself, so this will be the last letter I write to you. I wish you nothing but the very best. Love Chi.'

Marguerite clutched the letter to her chest with sheer joy. 'Golly. You need to go there as soon as humanly possible.'

I nodded and then shook my head, overwhelmed by the intensity of my adoration for Chidori and my distress at the probability that I had already lost her forever. 'What if it's too late? She wrote that over a year ago.'

'You must go and find out for sure.'

'What if she has a husband? I can't just show up.'

'Ring her up.'

I exhaled, not sure what to do, then took the pages from Marguerite to devour the letter again.

Chapter 42

The telephone earpiece tremored against my cheek as I waited in my parents' kitchen for the line to connect to the Blake residence in Alberta. My voice was primed to fail me the way it had at my third-grade spelling bee competition. The word I had been given was 'sanguine'. I knew it, but I froze when I made the mistake of looking at the audience, which consisted of pretty near every resident of Mayne Island. Chidori sat in the front row, and when my eyes met hers, she nodded encouragement to remind me I knew it. I took a deep breath, squeezed my legs together so I wouldn't wet my pants, and spelled the word.

I needed her to nod at me to get through the telephone call.

'Hello.' It was an older gentleman's voice.

I cleared my throat. 'Uh, hello, sir.'

There was a long silence. 'How may I help you?'

'Um.' I wiped the sweat from my brow with my sleeve and switched the receiver to the other ear. 'I'm calling to speak to Chidori Setoguchi, if that is possible. I'm not sure if I have the correct number.'

339

'It is the correct number. She's not here right now.'

'Oh, okay.' I paced a few steps in each direction, then leaned on the edge of the sink to support my weight.

'She's in town picking up some items for the wedding. If you're calling to respond to the invitation, I can pass the message along.'

'Wedding?' My knees gave out, and I had to reach for the stool to prevent myself from falling to the floor. 'No. No. I'm not calling about ... wedding? No.'

'Is there a message you'd wish me to pass along to her?'

'No, sir. No message. Thank you.' I hung up and stared at the wall.

A chair scraped across the wood planks behind me. Pop cleared his throat and said, 'Lethbridge is only a one-day train journey from Vancouver.'

I slowly turned on the stool until I faced him. 'She's getting married.'

He sat at the table and unfolded the newspaper. 'She's not married yet, is she?'

'You think I should stop the wedding? What if she doesn't want me to?'

'You won't ever know unless you go see her. She might rather marry you instead.'

'But she can't live here.'

He nodded, completely aware of what that meant. He slid his glasses down his nose to peer over them at me. 'Were you dreaming all those years about coming home to Mayne Island or Chidori?'

My mouth stretched into a smile as the answer settled in.

I leaned over and slapped his back. 'I guess I've got a wedding to interrupt.'

Pop chuckled.

I stood, but paused. 'Wait, what about Ma?'

'You should do whatever will make you happy,' Ma said from the living-room doorway behind me. 'Just be happy, darling.' She wiped her tears with a hankie as I crossed the room to hug her.

The steamer was scheduled to leave Mayne Island at ten o'clock. I packed, said my goodbyes to my family, and rushed so I would have time to stop by the Setoguchis' old house. Marguerite was wearing knicker trousers, a newsboy cap, and an argyle sweater vest that matched her argyle socks. She spun around wildly on a swing she'd twisted into a tight corkscrew. When she came to a rest, she took in my dress clothes, clean-shaven face, and fedora. She flashed me a toothy smile. 'The Hayden from the journals is back.'

I nodded. 'I'm back. That's why I'm leaving. I came over to pick up the rest of the journals and to say goodbye to you.'

'Hold on.' She leapt off the swing and sprinted to the house. While she was gone, an entire tree full of songbirds simultaneously lifted into flight, singing as they rose. Marguerite returned with the stack of Chidori's journals, a silver locket that held a picture of Chidori's grandparents, and a silk Japanese fan. 'These are the most beautiful things she left behind. I'm sure she'll want them back.' She tucked them into my canvas bag for me and hugged me around the waist. 'I'll miss you, but I think it's the bees-knees that you're going to see her.'

'Here.' I placed Rose's hair clip in her palm. 'I want you to have this.'

'Oh my goodness.' She removed the newsboy cap and reached behind her head to loop her hair up with the clip. 'Thank you.'

'No, thank you. Even though I acted as if I didn't want to hear what you had to say, I'm glad you said it. All of it. Your words helped me a lot, and I think maybe there are some more folks who'd also be glad to hear what you have to say.'

Her shoulders dropped and she stared at her feet. 'I can't talk to anyone but you.'

'Hey.' I lifted her chin with my finger so she'd look at me. 'Maybe it's time for both of us to be more like the people we used to be before all the wicked things happened. That's how we win. All right?'

She nodded with tears in her eyes and a smile on her face.

'I have to get going or I'll miss the ship. But I'll send you a postcard and let you know how it goes.'

She flung her arms around my waist to give me another hug, then stepped back and pointed in a cautionary manner. 'Chidori is going to write about your homecoming in her journal, so make it brilliant.'

I chuckled. 'I'll try. See ya, Margie.'

Chapter 43

The train to Lethbridge hit something and stopped abruptly enough to throw most of the passengers out of their seats. Children and luggage ended up sprawled in heaps all over the cabin. I assisted a few women as I climbed over the chaos to reach the door and then leaned out to see what we had hit. The engineer stood near the front of the train and scratched his head.

'Cows,' a man who had stuck his head out the window on the other side said. 'We're going to be here a long while yet.'

I sighed and looked out over the barley fields. 'How far do you figure we are from Lethbridge?' I asked.

'Another ten kilometres.'

I couldn't wait any longer. The anticipation, and not knowing whether my arrival would be received well or not, made me vibrate worse than a grenade about to explode. I grabbed my kit, hopped off the train, and jogged through the hot and dry midday weather. I was tragically out of shape. But I kept going.

When I finally arrived at the train station in Lethbridge, out of breath and parched, I asked the ticket master directions to the Blake farm. He didn't know, so I wandered down the street and entered a general store. The clerk sold me a lemonade and pointed me down the dirt road heading east. Before I left town, I bought a bouquet of garden roses for Chidori from an elderly woman who had a stand set up on the boardwalk in front of her house.

'Are you just returning home from the war?' she asked.

My initial reaction was to say no, but when I considered it with more thought, I realized I was. 'Yes, ma'am.'

She smiled with a reassuring warmth. 'Welcome home.'

The flowers started to feel foolish when I imagined myself walking up to the house to find Chidori's fiancé there to greet me with my sweat soaked through my shirt and the dust stuck to the wet patches. I stopped at the fork in the road and glanced back to where I'd just travelled from. Chidori was probably happy. Seeing me would only remind her of all the things we had lost and make her melancholy. The right side of my body wanted to confidently sprint the rest of the way and see her, even if it would only end in rejection. The left side of my body wanted to slink back to the train station like a broken-down coward and find a place to start over, a place that wouldn't remind me of her in any way.

My body was still stuck in a tug-of-war when a truck surrounded by a cloud of prairie dirt rolled up the road. The driver slowed to a stop and rolled down the window. He was Japanese and about fifty years old. 'Where are you headed, son?'

I glanced in the direction of the Blake farm, then in the direction of town. 'I, um, I'm looking for the Blake farm.'

'Are you in town for the Setoguchi wedding?'

The question hit like the truck had lurched out of gear and rammed into my gut. I sucked in a breath, cleared my throat, and croaked out, 'Yes.'

'Hop in. It's on my way.'

I nodded and considered retreating back to town once more before sliding in the passenger side. I had read Chidori's last letter so many times that I had committed to memory the Albert Camus quote: *In the midst of winter, I found there was, within me, an invincible summer. And that makes me happy. For it says that no matter how hard the world pushes against me, within me, there's something stronger – something better, pushing right back.* I believed it to be true for both of us, and I reassured myself that even if we could be nothing more than friends, I would still value the opportunity to simply be a part of her life again.

The driver and I made pleasant small talk as the truck bounced another kilometre down the road. Once a farmhouse appeared on the horizon of the prairie, I became distracted from the conversation. At the end of the driveway, the truck brakes squeaked and the wheels slowed to a stop.

'Thank you,' I said as I hopped out and then shut the door.

He waved and drove off, perhaps curious what the story was behind a stranger showing up with flowers in hand. All I could hope was that the tale was not going to end up a tragedy of Shakespearean proportion. A hummingbird felt trapped in my chest, beating its wings wildly from the uncertainty.

The main farmhouse was two storeys, painted white with

blue trim, and had a wraparound porch. A small wood cabin stood about two hundred metres down the road. An extension and a glass solarium were built out from the side, and a Japanese rock garden was intricately arranged in front of it. Just as Chidori had described. With a steeling breath I walked across the field to the cabin, swallowing repeatedly to produce enough moisture to be able to talk. It wasn't working that well. I closed my eyes, said a prayer, and knocked on the cabin door.

Nobody answered, so I knocked again. There wasn't any movement inside. I cupped my hand to peek in the window. It was tidy and simple. On the desk near the window was the journal I had given Chidori for Christmas, which raised my hopes.

The optimism was short-lived, though, as I made my way to the farmhouse and spotted a man off in the distance working in the beet field. He was too far away to make out his face. It was hopefully Tosh or Kenji but could have been Chidori's future husband.

Nausea flared up in my stomach as I realized how woefully unprepared I was to meet her new fiancé. As I stood, staring out at the field, the sound of singing rose from somewhere behind the farmhouse and reached me. My soul recognized the voice instantly. It was a voice that had been inside me the entire time. That settled it. I had to see her, no matter how fatal the result might be.

I snuck around the side to the backyard, then stopped in my tracks as sheets billowed in the breeze on the clothesline. A pair of polished black shoes turned in the grass and an arm gracefully pushed the edge of the cotton to the side. Loose pieces of her hair, like shiny raven feathers, hung down from the clip I had given her a lifetime ago. Her complexion glowed softly in the sunlight, even more stunning than I remembered.

She lifted her head when she sensed the presence of someone watching, and her eyes locked with mine. Even if it was going to be the last time I ever saw her, I would be eternally grateful I had made the trip to witness the vision of beauty in a blue dress that stood in front of me. She placed her hands on her belly as if to settle a flutter and her lips moved as if she said my name, but the sound didn't actually come out. She took a step closer and squinted. 'Am I dreaming?'

'I surely hope not, but if you are, I pray you never wake up.'

'Hayden,' she sobbed and covered her mouth with both hands.

The tears of joy running down her face washed away all my doubts and fears. My smile broke the spell that kept us locked in our stare, and she sprinted towards me. I dropped my kit and the bouquet of roses and rushed to meet her as she squealed and leapt into my arms. I spun her around so many times I got dizzy and fell to the grass with her tumbling on top of me.

Her hand slid along the side of my face and she gazed deeply into my eyes. 'Are you really here?'

I nodded. 'With apologies, I'm here to interrupt your wedding. I hope you don't mind.'

She wiped her tear-streaked cheeks with her fingertips and grinned. 'Tosh is getting married, not me.'

With immeasurable gratefulness I closed my eyes and thanked God. Maybe He had owed me one last favour.

Chidori showered my cheeks and neck with kisses and the loose tendrils of her hair tickled my skin. 'Oh, Hayden. I've been dreaming about this day for so long. I'm utterly gushing with joy.'

I was too choked up to speak but nodded to agree, then rolled both of us so she was lying on her back on the grass and I was stretched out on my side, propped on my elbow next to her. The charm bracelet on her wrist sparkled in the sunshine and it made me beyond happy to know she still wore it. I reached to find her left hand and checked to see if she also wore her engagement ring. I wasn't sure what I would have done if it wasn't there, but it was, so I kissed her hand and blinked back my relieved tears.

She gently ran her finger over the smooth pink skin of the burn scar on my neck, then whispered, 'I knew in my heart you would come for me eventually.'

'We can't be broken.'

She smiled and clutched the fabric of my shirt to draw me closer. I kissed her again, then hugged her tightly against my pounding heart. Every hardship we had endured melted away, until the only thing left to feel was love. Everlasting love, which nobody could take away from us. We won.

THE END

Author's Note

On April 1st 1949 the restriction that prevented Japanese Canadians from travelling west of the Rocky Mountains was finally lifted by the Government of Canada, four years after the war had already ended.

None of the Japanese-Canadian residents from Mayne Island ever returned home.

From 1984-1988 the National Association of Japanese Canadians (NAJC) Strategy Committee, led by Art Miki, lobbied and successfully negotiated a redress agreement with the Government of Canada for economic losses incurred by Japanese Canadians as a result of the forced relocation. In 1988, Canadian Prime Minister Brian Mulroney stood in the House of Commons and officially acknowledged the human rights violations that occurred against innocent Japanese-Canadian citizens at the hands of their own government. Redress payments of $21,000 were made to each living Japanese-Canadian who had been expelled from the coast in 1942 or who had been born before April 1st 1949. Unfortunately, this settlement occurred forty years after the fact, and many of the citizens who had lost everything had already died and never received an apology or compensation.

Seventy years have passed since the war officially ended for the Japanese Canadians. Perhaps some people might argue that the past is the past and we should forget about all the injustice that happened and move on. But for my nephews, whose great grandfather Ted Kadohama was interned in Taylor Lake, and for all future generations, if they truly understand history they will be able to acknowledge the mistakes that were made, recognize prejudice when it is being repeated, stop messages of fear and bias from spreading, and have the courage to stand up for what is right.

I grew up in Steveston, British Columbia – an historic fishing village, and one of the few communities on the coast where Japanese Canadians returned after 1949. I also have a home on Mayne Island where the novel is set. Much of my historical research began while I was writing a psychology master's paper on the intergenerational impact of the internment on Japanese Canadians. As I began to write a novel, the research expanded to include the records of my grandfather who was a WWII Spitfire pilot shot down during the battle of Dieppe, RAF pilot logs, POW journals, museum collections, Government of Canada documents, and archival information.

I have made efforts to create an historically accurate backdrop of true or conceivably feasible events from Mayne Island, the internment, and the war, but this is entirely a work of fiction and not an authoritative record of events. Any errors in historical facts are my own. Please note that, although some of the surnames mentioned in the book would have existed on Mayne Island in 1942, the names of characters and the incidents portrayed in the novel are wholly a product of my imagination and do not represent any real person or family, living or dead.

In writing this novel I respectfully acknowledge the more than twenty-two thousand Japanese Canadians from British Columbia who were forced to evacuate the coast in 1942. I also acknowledge the more than one million Canadians who served in WWII, the more than forty thousand who were killed, and the approximately nine thousand who were prisoners of war.

This project has been years in the making and I have several people to thank for helping my debut historical novel reach the readers. I am grateful for all of the students and instructors at the UBC creative writing program, where I attended alumni summer classes and workshopped a very early version of this novel. Special thanks to my fellow classmates and authors Jenny Manzer and Audrey Nolte Painter for your insights. Lisa Marks, thank you for being the first brave soul to read my novice attempts at being a writer. Thank you to my author friends Denise Jaden and Mark David Smith for your editorial suggestions. I feel very fortunate that Mark Sakamoto, author of *Forgiveness*, graciously took the time to lend his support to the project. I am also very appreciative for all my other friends and family who were kind enough to offer support or read my drafts and give feedback: Teresa Takeuchi, Justin Nomura, Allison Ishida, Greg Ng, Brian Tingle, Lana (Oseki) Cavazzi, Cory Cavazzi, Ryan Ellan from the Sunshine Valley Tashme Museum, Belinda Wagner, Erica

Ediger, Rasadi Cortes, Nicole Widdess, Pam Findlay, Veanna Reid, Amber Harvey, my brother Rob, my sister Luan, my dad Bob, and Anita Lau and her daughter Bella's book club. There are also a lot of supporters of my work who are not specifically named but quietly buy my books and tell their friends about them, which I appreciate immensely. And, as always, I owe immeasurable gratitude to Sean, my champion for life.

I would also like to make special mention of my sister-in-law Kim and her family, the Kadohamas. As well, I would like to acknowledge our very close family friends and neighbours, the Uyeyamas. Mr Uyeyama was the first person to ever explain to me what had happened to the Japanese Canadians during the war.

As always, I am eternally grateful to the Editorial Director for One More Chapter at HarperCollins UK, Charlotte Ledger, for her tireless efforts to get my books ready and out onto bookshelves. Thank you also to Penelope Isaac, Emily Ruston, Bethan Morgan, and the rest of the publishing, editorial, design, and marketing teams at One More Chapter and HarperCollins Canada.

And to my readers, thank you for always being willing to tag along on the adventure with me.